Sir Frank Lockwood's Sketch During the Wood V. Cox Case
(From the original)

FURTHER INDISCRETIONS

BY
A WOMAN OF NO
IMPORTANCE

ILLUSTRATED

NEW YORK
E. P. DUTTON & COMPANY
681 FIFTH AVENUE

CONTENTS

CHAPTER I

CHAPTER II

CHAPTER III

CHAPTER IV

vi CONTENTS

CONTENTS

viii   CONTENTS

CONTENTS

ILLUSTRATIONS

ILLUSTRATIONS

FURTHER INDISCRETIONS

CHAPTER I

Beautiful Women of the Eighties—Mrs. Langtry as a Girl—
The Dean of Jersey Fights Some Neighbours—Mr.
Abingdon Baird—At a Dinner Party—His "Damned
Lawyers"—Mrs. Langtry on the Stage—A Cruel Riddle
—The Marquess of Hastings—His Pocket Venus—Don-
ington of Yesterday and To-day—Runaway German
Prisoners—Captured—The Late Colonel North's Picture
Gallery—Durham and Chetwynd Row—Wood versus
Cox—Sir Frank Lockwood's Sketch in Court—Si
George Chetwynd—The Jubilee Plunger—Some Bets.

I HAVE made a discovery! To write a book
is in itself injudicious, but when you call it,
as I did, *Memories Discreet and Indiscreet,*
by a Woman of no Importance, it becomes a blazing
indiscretion.

My friends cavil at my *nom de guerre* and my
discretion, and in return I have tried to meet their
wishes.

It is from the unknown that the greatest surprises spring. Amongst the shoal of letters my
book has brought me there are many of kindness,
others of reproach from those who were omitted

and think they should have been included (although they do not know even who I am). Others who complain that while discretion is the better part of valour it should have no place in *Memories*. They expected apparently "confessions"—stories, that would shake the thrones of Europe—such as are left: anecdotes about celebrities via the butlers' pantry and the back-stairs.

It seems to be the general opinion that the word Discreet and what it stands for is superfluous and, in consequence, I have left it out. I have striven to compose my little concerts in the brighter keys.

Each successive generation thinks there never has been and never will be such soldiers, sailors, actors, actresses, and beautiful women again as they have seen in their day. We grew impatient with our old folk when they told us there were none to compare with the people of their time, and lo! in the autumn of our days we say exactly what they did, and no doubt we shall be ridiculed in much the same way as we ridiculed our elders and betters. History has a way of repeating itself.

For instance, I feel sure that never again will there be so many beautiful women as there were in the eighties; certainly I have seen nothing at the present time to compare with the "Professional Beauties," as they were called.

Mrs. Langtry's name was at one time on everybody's lips, and her photograph in many shop windows, on every hand we heard of her beauty, charming manners and other stories. Her golden brown hair, violet-blue eyes and classic features surmounting a perfect neck and shoulders, threw up by contrast the dark-haired, sad and pathetic brown eyed Mrs. Wheeler the more striking.

Mrs. Brown-Potter, Mrs. R. Webster, Mrs. Cornwallis West were also "professional beauties" at that time. The latter was perhaps the most discreet, as she was seldom seen without her husband, as often as not leaning on his arm.

She was immensely admired about the time I was married. Lord Rossmore writing from Ireland to a friend said he had been in a seventh heaven at a ball the night before as Mrs. Cornwallis West had condescended to dance with him. Indeed, he had been so happy that he had failed to notice the floor was empty, and not until he had collided with another couple did he become aware they were the Princess of Wales and her partner. The fact that she was dancing of course accounted for the emptiness of the floor.

Many years later, when Mrs. West's daughters had grown up and married, she drove over with them from Newlands, their place in Hampshire overlooking the Solent, to spend a Sunday afternoon at Milford-on-Sea, which Colonel West had turned into a popular resort for holiday makers by building villas. They decided to have tea at an hotel there, and while it was being prepared, Princess Henry of Pless and the Duchess of Westminster climbed down to the sea and began to paddle, calling to their mother on top of the cliff to take off her shoes and stockings and follow their example.

The hotel proprietor was much incensed at this unSabbath-like conduct, and made audible remarks about cheap-trippers being bad for the hotel until he found out who his visitors were. Then his Sabbath-like feelings underwent a change. He at once became servile and crawling.

Truly one may steal a horse and another must not look at it over the wall.

Another handsome woman of that time was Louise Duchess of Manchester. What astonishing stories there used to be flying about; but, being a personage, even the very straight-laced thought it wise to be charming to her face. The late Lady Bessborough, however, was the exception that proves the rule, and one day as she drove through Great Stanhope Street she espied the Duchess at one of her windows waving a white pocket hand-kerchief at her. Lady Bessborough kept her moral head erect, pretending she did not see, but managing to observe everything perfectly all the same.

When she alighted from her carriage she remarked in what I think was a most undignified manner to her footman, "Robert, was that—— (searching for some words severe enough) wicked Duchess waving at ME!"

But far and away more beautiful in my eyes than any of these were Georgina Countess of Dudley, the Duchess of Leinster, and Gladys Lady Lonsdale, the latter beautiful as a picture in her youth, but if possible more beautiful as Lady Ripon with her picturesque white hair.

It is not given to all of us to be beautiful in our youth, but I think it is our own faults if we are not beautiful in our old age, when time and experience have taught us to cease striving after the impossible, when we no longer kick against the pricks, but fold our hands with faces towards the setting sun, "glad we came, nor sorry to depart," waiting patiently for the Great Audit, not with hope, for that has died, nor with fear, that also has died, but with calm content, knowing we have worked out our salvation here through storm, tempest and bitter tears.

I remember Mrs. Langtry as a girl in Jersey. She was older than I and I looked up to her with some of the respect I reserved for any grown-ups or playmates bigger than myself. Her name was not Lily at all, but Emily Charlotte le Breton, daughter of the Very Reverend the Dean of Jersey, a man with a great appreciation of beauty in the fair sex.

One year when we were wintering in Jersey for my mother's health, though I was only eight years old at the time, I remember a number of people who visited my parents, the De Carterets, Pipons, le Bretons, de Saumerez, Hemerys, Knatchbulls, etc.

The Dean of Jersey was a great ladies' man. He used to come often to our church in St. Heliers and sit in our pew in order to admire and hear sing a very handsome Mrs. Knatchbull, who sat in front

of us. Her voice was beautiful and cultivated.
There was also a Mrs. de Saumerez he greatly admired, whose pew was somewhere near. The husband of this lady was a certain well-known admiral
(he may have been a lord, I have forgotten) de
Saumerez, possessed of a violent and ungovernable
temper and exceedingly jealous. It was almost as
much as a man's life was worth to look at his wife.
Colonel Knatchbull also was jealous, but did not
show it in so pronounced a manner. Neither of
these husbands accompanied their wives to church,
but came to meet them when the service was over.

One Sunday as we came out from what I considered a long and tedious service, we found the
devoted husbands waiting outside the church, and
we all proceeded down the rather narrow path to
the main road. The Dean was walking with Mrs.
Knatchbull, my father and Mr. Pipon one on each
side of Mrs. de Saumerez, all of us more or less
grouped together and the conversation fairly general. Suddenly Colonel Knatchbull struck the
Dean and told him he was something-something,
and he would not have him dancing about his wife
making eyes at her. In a minute there was a free
fight, for Admiral de Saumerez joined in, saying;
yes, it was disgraceful the way the Dean made
ladies conspicuous. He had been observing it for
some time. I was so frightened I climbed up a
wall dividing the churchyard from the highroad
from St. Heliers to St. Aubins.

From this point of vantage I observed a curious

thing happen. The row had begun by Colonel Knatchbull scolding and striking the Dean, but suddenly the cleric was left out in the cold, when the two irate husbands, for some reason I did not hear or understand, fell upon one another, the Admiral jumping up and down with passion, hitting above the belt, below the belt, and any accessible place, while in return his face was well pounded. The womenkind held on to the coat tails of the fighting men and, with the help of my father and Mr. Pipon, separated them while they continued shouting something about blood and pistols. It was only through the endeavours and influence of the Governor of the island, de Carteret by name, that a duel was averted between the Dean and Colonel Knatchbull in the first place, and the two irate husbands in the second.

When Admiral de Saumerez became angry, which was not infrequent, all in his vicinity trembled in their shoes, for there was no knowing what he would do. I remember hearing my people talking a good deal about this row and others in connection with the Admiral.

My father said he had at times seen the Admiral running along the road from sheer temper, talking loudly to himself and gesticulating as he ran.

After this row peace reigned for a while, or perhaps I should say armed neutrality was the order of the day.

When Mrs. Langtry first arrived in England she was a very quiet, unpresuming little person, but her beauty and fascinating manners turned the heads of everybody, both men and women. I have seen them standing on chairs in the Park to get a glimpse of her. Her life would be a wonderful story if it were ever written. High and low admired her, the Prince of Wales, Lord Dudley, Mr. Abingdon Baird, and heaps more.

A man of great wealth and a certain position, Mr. Baird had become mixed up with an undesirable crowd consisting of the rag-tag and bob-tail of the ring and race-course. Mrs. Langtry, Sir Frederick Johnstone, and his cousin Mr. Douglas Baird tried to wean him from his unlovely friends. This process included charming dinner parties, at which the reluctant Mr. Abingdon Baird met highborn and refined ladies, whose charms and cultured minds were calculated to lure him from his disapproved companions and perhaps turn his mind to higher thoughts. Everybody had to admit it was uphill work, as Mr. Baird was very difficult to awaken to "culture."

At one of these dinners a very high-browed dame sitting next to him tried to draw Mr. Baird into conversation. He had looked unutterably bored throughout the greater part of the dinner. She began:

"Do you like music?"

"No," grunted Mr. Baird, shaking his head and not lifting his eyes from his plate.

"Then perhaps you have not been to the opera lately?"

Mrs. Langtry

An impatient shake of the head.

"But you should really, Madame Trebelli Bertini is wonderful! Have you *never* heard her?"

"No and don't want to. Have *you* ever heard Bessie Belwood?"

Sir Frederick Johnstone sighed and said, "Hopeless!"

Poor Mr. Baird was a rough diamond, but a great admirer of the Jersey Lily, as Mrs. Langtry was called, but I do not think he liked the way she tried to keep him from prize-fighting.

In the spring of 1893 Mr. Abingdon Baird, in company with his friend Charles Mitchell, the pugilist, left this country for America. Mitchell had been matched to fight James J. Corbett, but it did not come off until January, 1894, Mitchell getting the worst of the contest. "The Squire" was, however, present at a battle between Bob Fitzsimmons and Jim Hall at New Orleans, in March, 1893, where he caught a chill and died of pneumonia in that city ten days later. Before he started his solicitors, Messrs. Lumley and Lumley, persuaded him to make a will, add a codicil or some such thing, I do not know exactly what, but as soon as his solicitors had gone he rang his bell and sent for one of his chosen friends and particular pals, who arrived to find Mr. Baird sitting at his writing-table holding his head and looking very miserable. His pal (I am not sure it was not his valet), asked, "What's up, Squire?" this being always what his intimates called him. "Oh, those damned lawyers have been here and made me sign something I know nothing about. *I* don't know what the devil it's all about." Then seizing a large silver inkstand he flung it at the head of his interrogator, saying, "To hell with the lot of you!"

The man ducked, but the inkstand hit him in the eye and continued its flight through a mirror at the end of the room. The portion of injured eye was paid for by a ten-pound note.

I saw Mrs. Langtry when she made her first appearance on the English stage, under the guidance and management of Mrs. Bancroft. This was in 1881. She took the part of Kate Hardcastle in "She Stoops to Conquer."

We were all greatly disappointed with her at first on the stage; she looked insignificant and not particularly good looking. We could not understand what had happened to her. Later we discovered the reason. She would not paint her face and make up as all are bound to do for the stage. In consequence, under the glaring and trying light on the stage she looked absolutely colourless. It is easy to understand she did not wish to spoil her beautiful skin, but she found it was a necessity to get up in the ordinary and approved fashion of theatrical people. I never thought her a great actress.

There was rather a cruel riddle in vogue in the '80's: "What is the difference between Madame Modjeska and Mrs. Langtry?—the answer being: "One is a Pole and the other a Stick!"

The most wonderful acting I ever saw was that of Sarah Bernhardt in "Fédora," in Paris. Her voice alone in the love scene as she cooed on the sofa was enough to coax the birds off the trees, and in the poison scene was painfully marvellous. I remember the theatre was very hot, and there were two or three in our box, and as I felt rather faint the door was opened, but an attendant at once came and closed it, saying the light scene through the door would be annoying to madame on the stage. The attendant was told through the closed door that there was a lady in the box who did not feel very well and wished to go out. The attendant was adamant and suggested it would be quite all right if the lady fainted on the floor, and when the scene was over they would come and fetch her! This conversation was carried on in the tiniest whispers with many "sh's," but the door was locked on the outside. Under the circumstances I refused to faint.

Not feeling very well rather spoilt the evening's pleasure for me, but I have never forgotten Sarah's acting, and I think the theatre authorities are quite right to consider the actors and actresses in every possible way. Such a little thing might throw them out of their stride, besides movements and noise are exceedingly annoying to those who are enjoying every little movement and every word on the stage.

I was at the opera in London the night Madame Adelina Patti appeared after the Nicolini episode. The house was cram full and large prices had been paid for boxes. When she appeared no doubt expecting her usual ovation, there was a silence that was oppressive. I felt the tears rising to my eyes with grief for her, but after looking in what might have been bewilderment round the house for a moment she sang as no other that I have ever heard could sing, "Home, Sweet Home."

She had touched the right chord; the house became hysterical, and the kind Prince of Wales leaned over his box and handed to her a bouquet, which she folded in her arms and laid her head amongst the flowers for a moment overcome with gratitude and emotion.

I always feel glad I did not miss that night. It was such a triumph the way she appealed to her audience and won their hearts against their wills, I might almost say, for many had gone simply to see how she would be received, and with prudish and fault-finding minds and intentions. She cast them all to the winds and brought tears to the•eyes of many.

I have wandered away again from Mrs. Langtry in a very reprehensible manner. She appeared on the stage in America in 1887, somebody told me the other day, I had not heard it before.

When first she had acquired wealth enough to begin racing, she ran her horses under the name of Mr. Jersey, and then, as now, had the same delicate turquoise and fawn hoops and turquoise cap against her name in the calendar. The best horse she ever owned was the Australian "Merman," who won her the Goodwood Cup in 1899 and Ascot Cup in 1900, three years after he had won the Caesarevitch as a birthday present for her. Of course at Newmarket she had showers of congratulations, but the Ascot triumph was the Red Letter Day of her life, although she was not present on that occasion, and strangely, the following year Mr. George Edwards brought off another stage victory with his favourite and best horse, "San Toy."

Mrs. Langtry held views of her own on the art of training. Some of them who trained for her got unmercifully chaffed about their lady employer. Pickering, for instance, was one day going to saddle a horse at one of the race meetings, and as he happened to have on a straw hat with a neat bow at the side, someone wishing to be funny, called out, "Did the missus trim your hat?"

I always admired the way Mrs. Langtry conducted her racing. She was never loud and was seldom if ever seen alone in a paddock; if she went down to see a horse saddled she always had a suitable escort.

After Mr. Langtry's death, the Jersey Lily married Sir Hugh Gerald De Bathe in 1899, and now races under that name.

In spite of Mrs. Langtry's endeavours to wean Mr. Abingdon Baird from his prize-fighting, he died as already stated in America from a chill caught after taking part in one of these entertainments. At his death his lawyers and his mother had a tremendous task in settling up his affairs. There were claims running into many thousands. One man, who had been promised £5000 for certain services rendered, eventually accepted £3000. This case and others were to have been decided in the High Court, but Mr. Baird's mother, like all good mothers, could not bear the idea of having her son's name dragged through the mud, and expressed her wish to pay everything. In consequence of this, and with the judge's permission, the court was relieved of the hearing.

It is sad that the faithful friend of man should lead so many into trouble. I do not like to remember all my old friends who have gone under through racing, not that I mean to infer it is the fault of the horses; they generally do their best to please us. It is man's own silly fault when he comes to grief. At the moment I am thinking of poor Lord Hastings, whom I never knew, as he died before my time, but whose beautiful wife I did know. They called her the "Pocket Venus," and many are the stories she told of that weak but exceedingly generous man who planned out his life for pleasure that proved so short lived. He was the fourth Marquess, born in 1842. In 1864 he married Lady Florence Paget. The marriage caused a great sensation at the time, for she was engaged to Mr. Chaplain, now Lord Chaplain, and had gone with him to do some shopping at Marshall and Snelgrove's well-known shop in Oxford Street, where women's garments and fal-lals are to

The Late Marquess of Hastings Explaining his Betting Book
to his Bride

be found in all their latest styles. While Mr. Chaplin was walking up and down outside one entrance waiting for his fiancée, she departed from another in the brougham of Lord Hastings, which was awaiting her and was married at St. George's, Hanover Square. Altogether a most romantic affair. It is, of course, an old story now, but some of the present generation may not know about it, and be interested. It was later, when the wife of Sir George Chetwynd of Grendon, that I knew her. She married him in 1870. I first met her in 1885.

If the life of Lady Chetwynd, or Lady Hastings, as she was still called by many, were written it would be thrilling. She lived through some great experiences, many of them pitiful, others exciting and occasionally triumphant, but the pitiful predominated.

Her second matrimonial venture was not entirely a success. Her husband became heavily involved financially, and found himself more than once in hot water over his racing transactions, but to that I shall refer later.

After the runaway marriage with Lord Hastings, Donnington Hall became the home of the "Pocket Venus." The picture of Lord Hastings on the sofa explaining his betting book to his newly-made wife was taken at Donnington and has never before been published as far as I know. It is a good likeness of Lady Hastings, allowing for the old-fashioned style of dress, and she considered it a most faithful likeness of her husband.

There are wonderful histories attached to Donnington Hall; of cock-fights, racing and midnight revelry in which most of the sporting people of that day took part, Pulsford Hobson, Peter Wilkinson and the Duke of Hamilton amongst others. From all I hear I doubt if the revelry in those early years of Lady Hastings' life with the gambler have ever been equalled.

One night after dinner one of Lord Hastings' (or "Harry" as his intimates called him) jockeys, named Jim Grimshaw, who was a very light weight, was, amidst much uproar, put upon the dining-table and made to dance a hornpipe.

Poor Lord Hastings' racing was meteoric, six years was the outside. He registered his colours, red and white hoops and white cap, in 1862, and died in 1868. Harry Hill and Padwick the moneylenders, were his financiers and wire-pullers. He was firmly in their grip when he married Lady Florence Paget. I am afraid her husband was very extravagant and very weak, but he was straightforward and made the mistake of believing what he was told, which naturally led to his early undoing, added to which he could not resist betting. When sitting in a railway carriage he would bet on the drops running down the window, or which fly would feast first on a lump of sugar at tea. It was altogether hopeless.

Donnington, now occupied by the German

prisoners of war, is by no means of noble structure, but a barrack-like building, its chief notable feature being the four columns or turrets standing above the entrance to the house, but its surroundings are spacious and suitable for its present purpose. I wonder what the barbed-wire cost? Thousands were I know spent on laying electric wire into the house. The questions that have been asked, judging by the Blue Book, in connection with the cost of the upkeep of that place, food provided, etc., paid for out of us poor tax-payers' pockets are many and sensational. Considering the shortage of food, how do they get the good things they are receiving? Speaking of food reminds me of the time when, after much debate and palaver, the price of potatoes was fixed at one penny half-penny ($1\frac{1}{2}$d.) per pound at a time when there were none to be bought, and also reminds me of the orders issued that all game is to be shot—no more preserving—and at the same time people are allowed no ammunition to shoot them. We shall have to sally forth with salt to put on their tails and catch them that way! It is all very strange!

Lord Hastings won some big races with his horses, including the Grand Prix de Paris, the Ascot Derby, with a horse called "The Earl," and three hours later the same afternoon the Ascot Bienniel with the same horse. The "coup" of his racing career was achieved when his good little horse "Lecturer" won the Caesarevitch in 1866. But no winning could compensate him for his losses when they were in such colossal sums as one hundred thousand pounds over the Derby of 1867, and eighty thousand pounds on the Derby the following year. He died very shortly after this, having been in bad health for some time. He had burnt his candle in too many places at once, but he was exceedingly generous, hospitable, and no man's enemy but his own. It was all very sad and no one could help feeling sorry for him. Temperament, which is bestowed upon us without our having a voice in the matter, has much to answer for.

The Meteoric Marquis was for two seasons Master of the Quorn, and the erratic conduct that characterised his term of office was rather aptly described in some verses, generally supposed to have been written by the late Lord Rosslyn, to the tune of the once popular ballad "Who can tell?"

"When will the Marquis come? Who can tell?
 Half-past twelve or half-past one? Who can tell?
 Is he sober, is he drunk? Nipping like Myneheer von
    Dunk?
 Will he ride or will he funk? Who can tell?

 Shall we have to wait again? Who can tell?
 In the wind and in the rain? Who can tell?
 While the Marquis snug and warm,
 In the hall where toadies swarm,
 Leaves us to the pelting storm? Who can tell?

 Where he'll draw by way of a lark, who can tell?
 Gartree Hill or Bradgate Park? Who can tell?
 Sport regarding as a jest, which will suit his fancy best?
 North or south or east or west? Who can tell?

Donnington Hall

Where, oh where! rings Tailby's horn? Who can tell?
Why came I with this cursed Quorn? Who can tell?
Marquis, this is not a race,
Can you look me in the face
And declare you like the chase? Who can tell?"

About the same time a clever sketch appeared in the old *Sporting Gazette.* It represented a fine old dog fox stealing away from covert with Lord Wilton and the Marquis of Hastings looking on. It was called "A Critical Moment" and the former was saying, "Now, Harry, blow away, we shall have it all to ourselves."

To which the other replies, "It's d——d fine to say blow away, but if I do I shall be sick!" Ha! ha! ha!——

It caused a great deal of amusement in the shires and the entire issue of the paper was sold out in a few hours.

The *Sporting Times* had an obituary notice on Lord Hastings under the heading of "The Spider and the Fly."

Before leaving the subject of Lord Hastings and his home, Donnington Hall, I should like to ask if anybody knows what has become of the cups he won with his more important races, the Ascot, Goodwood and Doncaster cups to wit? He died without an heir and hopelessly in debt. I should like to know what became of the objects he so greatly prized.

I also wonder if the rich German officer named interned at Donnington will take a fancy to the place and wish to buy it at the end of hostilities?

While I have been writing this book we have had some escaped German prisoners across this property (not Donnington or its neighbourhood). They have been captured a few miles from here. An officer who was riding a motorcycle spotted the two men in the last stage of exhaustion, having tramped some thirty miles if they had come as the crow flies, which naturally they had not, having to dodge about in hiding, which had taken them the best part of a week. The moment the cyclist saw the men he guessed who they were and noticed their accent as they asked their way. He allowed them to continue in the direction he had suggested to them, and seeing a car coming along the road stopped it, asking the occupant to go post haste to the next village and inform the police and ask them to come at once. It so happened that the man in the car was the head dairyman at the Home Farm here on the property where I live. He was on his way to see a soldier son at a South Coast hospital some forty miles away. He at once dashed off, the police were soon on the spot, and before many hours passed the men were captured, offering no resistance. Considering their exhausted condition I wonder the khaki-clad cyclist did not capture them, but no doubt discretion is the greater part of valour.

This place where I am writing is an ideal spot for any runaway to hide in. I have been wondering what I should do one day if in our at present (during war time) unused garages and stables I come across some German prisoners hiding. It would be my duty, I suppose, to give them up to justice, but I fear my inclinations would be to give them something to eat and drink and then ask them to "move on" policeman fashion. I should be unable to help putting myself in their place. I should so hate to be caught and think anybody who gave me away and denounced me such a sneaky skunk. Probably I should be murdered for my pains, but two skunks would not make my action any less skunkish!

Those who have seen that famous picture of Frith's entitled "The Road to Ruin," which was depicted in four scenes, will perhaps have recognised in the Ascot scene some faces amongst those figuring on the canvas, that of Lord Hastings, for instance, as the person betting over the rails with the bookmakers. The picture (the original I think) eventually found its way into the picture gallery of the late Colonel North (who was generally known as the "Nitrate King") at Eltham. It struck me it might have been an unlucky purchase, for I have heard conflicting accounts and theories of his death. Some suggested his nitrates had died out and that he was in financial difficulties? against that I am told he left by will £263,000 net and £575,000 gross, which does not sound as if he was in any embarrassment.

He was considered extravagant, but with that fortune why should he not be, especially when I know as a matter of fact that he befriended a number of people, helping them financially. Some are living now, and most ungrateful I have considered them.

He was a kind-hearted little man who knew nothing about pictures, little about racehorses, and perhaps little about nitrates.

If I remember rightly, it was to Lady Randolph Churchill he told the story of having bought a most beautiful painting in oils. When asked the subject he replied, "That I do not know, but it is twelve feet by eight." At least that is how the story goes.

At the end of his picture gallery stood an almost life-size portrait of himself in the uniform of the Eltham Yeomanry. He was exceedingly proud of this picture which had been painted by Philips, the famous portrait and animal painter. I do not think either the happiest position or dress was chosen by him, or for him. As represented in the picture, he was taken full face on horseback, the scarlet tunic combined with his rather rosy complexion was not attractive.

I believe he raced more to sell his nitrates than for any pleasure he derived from the sport, much in the same way as Sir Blundel Maple raced to assist the sale of "tables and chairs," which was his nickname amongst race-goers. There are wheels within wheels in every walk of life. Sir Blundel at one time advertised in some of the sporting papers that his shop in the Tottenham Court Road was *the* best place for jockeys and trainers to spend their earnings!

I must now return to the time when Lady Hastings had become the wife of Sir George Chetwynd, and some of the awkward experiences she passed through, the Chetwynd versus Durham row being one of them. The case will be fresh in the memory of many people; it occurred in 1889.

I have heard it stated that Lord Durham was steward of the Jockey Club at the time of the rumpus, but this is quite a mistake; he was not. I heard a good deal about this affair from Mr. Jim Lowther, who endeavoured to be impartial; also from Sir George's wife, who was less impartial. Her husband claimed £20,000 damages for what he termed a "scandalous libel," which had been uttered at York by Lord Durham following a Gimcrack dinner.

After many Jockey Club consultations and much litigation the verdict of one farthing damages was awarded to Sir George, each side paying its own costs, but Sir George was censured for the lighter charges which formed part of the alleged libel and exonerated from the graver. He resigned his membership of the Jockey Club immediately after this.

One farthing damages appears to be rather a favorite finding for wounded pride in racing disputes. I remembered another case where that sum was awarded, "Wood versus Cox," tried before Lord Chief Justice Coleridge and a great array of counsel, including Sir Charles Russell, afterwards Lord Russell of Killowen. This affair arose out of the *Licensed Victuallers' Gazette* boldly asserting in print that Wood the jockey had "pulled" a horse he had been riding in a race, the horse in question being named "Success."

I do not think Wood intended taking any notice of this, but the Jockey Club sent for him and asked him if it was true that he had pulled the horse, to which he replied, "No." Then, said the Jockey Club, you must bring an action against the paper to clear your character. Of course, there was no alternative but to go to law, which resulted in one farthing damages.

During the case, while Wood was in the witness-box, the judge coaxingly asked him, "How much do you think a jockey could earn in a year?"

"Ten thousand pounds, my Lord," came the answer, which caused the Judge slyly to pass a note to Sir Frank Lockwood, saying, "Don't you think we had better quit the bench and bar and turn jockeys?"

Sir Frank then set to work at once to sketch in his own inimitable style the judge in racing cap and jacket, mounted on the most miserable-looking caricature of the racehorse "Success."

The frivolity of judges, counsel and even magistrates, during moments of great anxiety of the parties concerned is, I think, rather painful. Truly what is one man's meat is another man's poison, the one poking fun and finding amusement in what may be and often are the most serious moments of the lives of plaintiff and defendant. In this case Wood claimed £5,000 damages.

Sir George Chetwynd on Newmarket Heath

Sir George, I know, never got over these two cases. He was not implicated in the latter, but his horses had been trained in the same stable, Sherrard's at Newmarket, where Wood was the chief jockey.

The amount of sarcasm and anecdotes flying about over this case outrivalled the Colin Campbell divorce case. Mr. Grain, brother of Corney Grain, was full of stories about it, being much interested and, if I remember rightly, had something to do with the preparing of the case.

When the Prince of Wales was returning from India Sir George Chetwynd went to Egypt to meet him, taking a horse called "Countryman" with a view to holding a race meeting in the desert. He backed the horse to win a race against a camel. I regret I did not hear, or have forgotten, which won.

In my opinion Sir George Chetwynd was impetuous, childish, and often obstinate, for which in his betting transactions he had to pay; but he was a good judge of a handicap.

Many good men and much good money passed through his hands at different times. It was towards the end of his racing career that he came in touch with Mr. Benzon, the Jubilee Plunger, whose betting was so sensational. Indeed so wild was it that Sir George determined to try and check him. The plan he devised was to get Mr. Greenwood, the then "Hotspur" of *The Daily Telegraph,* to talk to the man like a father, and point out how foolish it was to gamble in such large sums. In

Sir George's presence one day he said to Mr. Benzon, "Why can't you be content with two or three hundred at a time instead of the reckless way you bet generally?"

Mr. Benzon listened attentively, promising he would take such good advice, but characteristically could not resist a bet over it, saying he would bet Mr. Greenwood 100 to 1 that he did not have more than 200 on a horse again that meeting.

Turning away, Mr. Greenwood observed the numbers were being hoisted for the next race, and there as usual was the incorrigible Benzon at the betting rail with his book. Another pageful went the same way as the rest—lost!

After the race Mr. Greenwood asked Mr. Benzon if his advice was working all right, whereupon he replied, "Oh, by the way, Greenwood, I am very sorry but I owe you a hundred pounds," and at once offered the money, but it was not accepted.

There was a discussion one morning at breakfast at Ascot about the height of certain men, which as usual ended in a bet. One man bet Lord Lurgan was not six feet, and he bet in hats and suits of clothes. Later in the day some one was despatched to find Lord Lurgan on the course and ask him his height. The man returned to say that Lord Lurgan had replied if anybody wanted to know his exact height they were to go to the War Office as he was not quite sure of it, but that they would find he measured over six feet when he joined the Guards.

"What has that to do with it," chimed in the

man who had betted the hats and suits of clothes, "I am not betting on the height he was when he entered the Guards, but the height he is at the present time. He may have been six feet then but since that time he has dropped many inches."

For the benefit of those who never saw Sir George I had better describe him, but no, I cannot do better than give a little sketch of him taken by Finch Mason on Newmarket Heath when riding one of his New Forest ponies, his long legs nearly touching the ground. It was taken in 1878. Sir George was then rather round-backed, but stooped much more latterly.

His racing colours were like himself, a delicate shade of straw colour with light blue sleeves and cap. He was straw colour and had light blue eyes.

He lost his wife in 1907.

For some years before his death, which took place quite recently, Sir George did not race, but his colours up to the day of his death were, I believe, in the Calendar.

His eldest daughter, a handsome girl, married her cousin, the fifth Marquess of Anglesey. I well remember what a fool he made of himself soon after he married when staying at Nice during Carnival Week. I grieved for his poor young wife. Her husband behaved so badly at a ball she went to with him that she retired and left him, while a little later he was requested to leave the place where the ball was being held. I was not surprised she decided to leave him to his own devices.

CHAPTER II

I FEEL that I have sadly neglected the doctors in my last book, and I have, both fortunately and unfortunately, made the acquaintance of many. There is no profession for which I have so great an admiration; it is the calling that perhaps comes least before the limelight, yet demands great sacrifice from each member. They daily perform heroic deeds, burn the candle at both ends, in the cause of suffering humanity, and for what? Not applause, they get none, or reward, many get none from the world, not for advertisement, but because they love their work, because they feel there is no higher calling.

I am not at the moment thinking of the kind old-fashioned country family doctor who had three cures for all complaints—castor oil—poultice—or the assistance of his useful pocket-knife with which he budded roses, cleaned trout when out fishing, and operated on his patients—but of the present-day highly scientific men with investigating minds whose only reward is a nice obituary notice when they die, and a knowledge that those dear to them may be left wanting the ordinary necessities of life.

It was only in George II's reign that the Company of Barbers were forbidden from practising the art and science of surgery. This sounds like a joke but is fact, and can be verified by anyone taking the trouble to look up Statute 18, Cap. XV. That grand old sporting parson, the Rev. Hugh Palliser Costobadie, used to say "Never trust parsons, doctors or lawyers." As regards the latter I have had an experience leading me to the conclusion that perhaps his advice was sound, but the lawyer was a poor henpecked little man who had to do as he was told by his wife, so must be forgiven. As to the others, it has been my privilege to come under the shadow of some very good men amongst doctors and parsons.

Both doctors and clergymen occasionally find themselves in surprisingly tight corners and sometimes in very amusing ones, at least they appear amusing *after* the event, but are not always very funny at the time. Considering the very intimate knowledge doctors acquire of our characters, sins and mistakes, when the social mask has been removed, it speaks well for them that they ever trust anybody at all.

Good and kind Dr. Godson of Grosvenor Street was one of the most trustful of men, notwithstanding his having had from time to time some alarming eye-openers. He had a very large practice amongst the big-wigs of the land, chiefly ladies, of course, he being a ladies' doctor—one of the leading men of the day in this line. He had a decided weakness for high-sounding names, and made no bones about it, acknowledged it with charming candour, but to those who unfortunately only had more or less common or garden names, he was good to me all the same; I suppose he felt he must have a few shrimps in his net if he went fishing.

He once amused me by saying "Half the women in London come to me because they want babies, and the other half because they don't!"

The dear rosy-faced little man always looked, as Helen Mathers once described it to me, "As if he was just going to have a baby himself, or had just had one!"

During one of his visits to me I remarked that his horses were looking very sadly. He quite agreed and expressed himself as ashamed of their appearance. He could not understand it, as they had belonged to an earl, who strongly advised his buying them, saying they were just the thing he wanted.

I expressed the opinion that they were hardly strong enough for his hard work and long hours and that he had paid £100 too much for them, advising him to go to some jobmaster and hire his horses from him by the year. They would then be properly looked after, and when one lot was tired a fresh pair would be awaiting him without any thought or anxiety on his part. He was very pleased with this idea, but rather pained that he had been taken in or badly advised by his friend the earl. When the name of the peer was given to me I was not at all surprised that the horses were not satisfactory.

My friend was strangely slack in all money matters. I do not mean by this he owed anything, on the contrary always paid up everybody to the last farthing, I believe, but he was very careless with his earnings. At one time I used to collect old clothes from my friends for some poor people I was interested in. I asked Dr. Godson if he had anything he would be glad to get rid of that my maid could cut up and make do for an extremely poor clergyman with numerous children and an invalid wife. He presented me with a greatcoat and a variety of other useful things. When the first-named was being partly unpicked with a view to being made smaller for the emaciated parson I was wishing to help, from between the coat and the lining there rolled out several sovereigns, evidently fees he had shoved into his pocket and entirely forgotten. When I returned them to him he said,

"Oh, keep them for the poor parson, he probably wants them more than I do." Yet this doctor worked hard for every guinea.

I remember him once having a few words with the late Dowager Lady Lonsdale in my house. It appears that she had said something about his treatment of one of her family not being in accordance with her views of the correct thing to do. This had reached the ears of Dr. Godson, who was annoyed. One day as he was leaving my house and Lady Lonsdale was entering they met. Dr. Godson requested her to be careful what she said, and there was quite a pow-wow. I effaced myself.

When the Duchess Paul of Mecklenburg-Schwerin was so dangerously ill after being thrown out of her carriage, I recommended that Dr. Godson be sent for. I wonder if he ever was rewarded for his services. I know some people had considerable difficulty in getting what was owing to them by these German royalties.

Doctors seem to resent this sort of treatment less than most people. I remember Dr. Godson telling me as quite a good joke about his having been routed out of bed after a tiring day and told his services were required at the Hotel Metropole, a lady visiting there having been taken very ill. When he arrived, he found she was very dangerously ill, and a young and devoted husband (?) on the verge of madness with grief. He attended this beauteous lady for several days, wresting her from the jaws of death, receiving many grateful thanks from her husband. They appeared to be people of considerable means and were living in luxury. One morning when he went to pay a visit, considering his patient still too ill to get up or be left unattended, he was told they had gone from the hotel, paid their bill, but left no address! He never heard anything more of them or of their gratitude.

Dr. West, the great children's doctor, was latterly rather a foolish person I thought, and very much spoilt. He came to see a small boy of mine who was at death's door, being called in to see if he could find out what was the matter, as many doctors were puzzled. He knew no more than the rest, if as much, and after expressing it as his opinion that while there was "life there was hope," he began tituping downstairs, shaking his bunches of grey hair as he frisked, and saying, "Now I am on my way to see a most important baby, a little Rothschild." My sister, who was with me at the time, suggested perhaps my baby was as important to me as the Rothschild baby to his people. To this he replied cheerfully, "Oh, yes! Quite so, quite so," and continued tituping down the stairs.

At one time when a horse had inconsiderately rolled over me, Sir Joseph Lister (afterwards Lord Lister) came to set some broken bones. I thought him a very charming man, but he could not put a bandage on properly. I suppose he had forgotten how to do anything so elementary. I wanted to go to a bonesetter named Hutton, who was rather famous at that time, but Dr. Priestley dissuaded me.

I remember having an animated discussion with Sir Joseph as to who had really invented anæsthetics. It was a subject that interested me, because I once had the advantage of having some ancient Egyptian manuscripts translated to me by Sir Monier Williams, Professor of Sanscrit at Oxford, who had a great knowledge of dead languages. These documents referred to a "root of the earth" and certain herbs which were used in the time of the Pharaohs to deaden pain and cause people to go into a temporary sleep or trance. From the description we came to the conclusion it was an anæsthetic something after the fashion of chloroform. Sir Monier thought it quite possible some ancient warriors had been buried alive while under the influence of these ti eatments. There was also a description curiously expressed of how they stopped bleeding by the application of certain birds' nests and cobwebs. From the documents translated to me I gathered the ancient Egyptians were the inventors of anæsthetics, and not our later-day physicians, though no doubt they improved upon them.

In consequence of this conversation Sir Joseph said he would much like to meet Sir Monier, and I arranged this. I had hoped to hear much of interest, but they became so highly technical I was lost, and, as I could not interrupt them with questions, they forgot all about poor me. I came to the conclusion it is an ungrateful world!

When I was starting for India, Sir William

Sir William Jenner

Jenner, who I always thought looked like a Japanese, but who of course was nothing of the kind, came to see me and said his son was in the 9th Lancers out there and that I should be sure of seeing him. Knowing India to be a largish place I had some doubts about this. It so happened, however, that I did run across Mr. Jenner before very long, in one of the hill stations, sure rendezvous in the hot weather. Mr. Jenner was a smart, good-looking youth, very musical, and he played the piano exceedingly well. He is now the reigning baronet. He married one of Sir Donald Stewart's cheery daughters.

Sir William Jenner the doctor was a favourite at Court, having attended the Prince Consort in his last illness and the Prince of Wales at Sandringham; being made a baronet and K.C.B. in return for devoted services. Queen Victoria took a personal interest in him and his affairs.

I have heard it stated that Sir William was the discoverer of vaccination, which is quite a mistake. A man named Jenner of another family and the Christian name of Edward was the benefactor of mankind by this discovery.

Sir William Jenner, however, established the difference between typhoid and typhus fevers in 1851.

Another leading light in the profession, Sir James Paget, came down to the Isle of Wight to see my sister once, and I met him several times after that. He had not the comfortable round-about-waistcoat of Sir William Jenner, indeed he looked as if he had no inside at all, he was so thin, and he walked leaning over the vacuum as if missing its support.

I liked to hear him talk of his early life and struggles. The high pinnacle of fame he climbed left him quite unspoilt; he was a stern-mannered, highly conscientious man, but devoid of that saving clause in life, a sense of humour. He was painfully matter-of-fact, and if by chance one made a joke, it was necessary to go through the ordeal of explaining it, and after that he rewarded by a smile that plainly said, "what deplorable waste of time." Sir James made a great name for himself as a surgeon, and was eminently a practical man.

He told me that in his practice he felt it his duty not only to satisfy himself with his physical examination; but must satisfy the patient with therapeutic value, for, he added, "what may be quite satisfactory to the doctor's mind may not be by any means so satisfactory to the patient's." Another point he considered of importance was to steer clear of patients' prejudices. He spoke with much feeling of the way doctors are often thrown down by the nurses on whom they have to rely for accurate information.

Hippocrates, the unrivalled genius of twenty-three hundred years or more, says, "Our natures are the physicians of our diseases." Not being an unrivalled genius I prefer relying on my medical man.

Sir James Paget

Sir James Paget was sent for when the late Earl of Minto had such a terrible fall in his earlier days while riding in the Grand National. The impression was that his neck was broken, yet, thanks to the great surgeon's skill, his patient recovered.

Some years later when Lord Minto went to see Sir James on another matter, the surgeon referred to the accident of bygone days, saying, "Well, all I can say is you are one of those extraordinary people who has broken his neck and recovered," adding meditatively, "It is most valuable."

Lord Minto replied, "I will leave that portion of my anatomy to you, Sir James, in my will."

"Oh, I shall be dead long before you, but the College of Surgeons would very much like to have it, I can assure you."

It was a very curious accident and a curious recovery. For months Lord Minto was practically a cripple, the muscles of his neck shrank, pulling his head down on one side, he suffered great pain in his shoulder and arm, never quite losing the latter to the end of his days. In spite of this and the entreaties of his friends he would ride again a few months later and had another bad fall in November, the first having been in March.

Then there was poor Wilkie Collins of Cadogan Place, the smart little doctor of the Guards, which regiment I forget. His name was not Wilkie really, but his initial being "W" he was known as Wilkie Collins, a sort of nickname of general liking, and after the novelist, with whom, however, he was in no way related. Dr. Collins' expenses were bigger than his banking account and this led to trouble, partly from borrowing and partly from anxiety to make some money quickly. That he helped many a poor soul in trouble I know, and after all where there is a demand there will always be a supply, try and suppress it as you may. I was very sorry for him latterly, he was in such low water before the final crash, when he had to retire from the world.

One day I was trying to remember the name of a patient of his that I knew quite well, but could not for the moment recall, so I said, "Oh, help me, do? You know who I mean quite well." He replied, "I make a point of never remembering the names of any of my patients!" There was obviously no more to be said.

Another doctor living in the south-west district spent the best part of an afternoon one wet day in a small hotel by the riverside amusing me with stories of dilemmas in which he had found himself during his medical career. Whether he was peculiarly unfortunate, or whether it is habitual to the profession, I cannot say, but I think doctors and parsons often find themselves in awkward corners. The man I am thinking of ended by being one of the learned men called to the bedside of Royalties when ill.

I knew him first in 1880. He was rather an attractive-looking person, and, in spite of the sadness of his profession, full of mirth and humour.

He told me the first difficulty he got into was with a nurse in the hospital where he was studying. He described the situation amusingly. No matter how he tried to avoid her she *would* faint in his arms just as someone came around the corner, until he made up his mind he would have to be brutal. Even that was no use, so he persuaded another student to wean her away from him and, upon his expressing his jealousy of her perfidy, he got out of the mess. He could, he vowed, have nothing more to do with a woman who did not know her own mind for five minutes together, etc. There followed tears and tempests and then out on to the open sea in calm water once more.

The next trouble he encountered was when he began practising. A young woman he was asked to attend for hallucinations thought she had fallen violently in love with him, and spent her time in writing the most compromising letters and insisted on embracing him whenever he entered the room, until at last he explained to the girl's father it would be better for her to have a fresh doctor. Meanwhile some domestic at home, under notice of leave, spent her leisure hours in piecing these letters together and holding them over his head, a sort of blackmail business, saying she would let everybody know how he behaved with his patients. Having just been married, this was very awkward and very nearly caused an estrangement between him and his bride.

With these and other stories he passed away an

afternoon for me that would otherwise have been dull, as I was doing "gooseberry" to a girl friend and her "young man," so had to be in evidence yet out of sight so to speak. None of us could go on the river as it poured with rain, and I had not the heart to take the girl home again when she was having a good time.

I must not forget that interesting character Sir Henry Thompson, surgeon, epicure and collector of old Nankin china, who lived in Wimpole Street.

He suffered from diabetes, and used to spend a good deal of time at the Royal Marine Hotel in the Isle of Wight, where I also have been a frequent visitor. He used to arrive with a large consignment of a particular biscuit he considered good for his complaint. They were most unsatisfying, much like eating a kid glove.

The doctor's dinners in Wimpole Street, or his octaves, as he used to call them, the number being limited to eight, were much appreciated by his friends and invitations sought after.

Lady Dorothy Nevill told him she would like to be asked. "Certainly," said Sir Henry, "but you will have to wear trousers."

Sir Henry was a firm believer in cremation; and had a good deal to do with forming the company that erected the crematorium at Golders Green in 1902.

An excellent cartoon appeared of him in a paper called *The Throne,* that was edited by a Royalty and run by the "Upper Ten."

He operated successfully on Napoleon III, but his patient was in too weak a state to recover from the anæsthetic.

Sir Henry was not a man of many words.   To his patients his advice to many was "Live on sixpence a week and earn it."

In spite of bad health he lived the allotted span and was a most abstemious man.

It has been reserved for me to meet the most delightful and most clever doctor of my life in my autumn days, besides being the kindest hearted and most conscientious man I have ever met, added to which he has the delicate mind of a high art magazine.

Doctors are a wonderful crowd, they spend their lives doing good with their right hands and not allowing their left to know it.   The man I am thinking of is wonderful in this respect and a delightful companion, being exceptionally well-informed and interested in everything.   He will take infinite pains to soften the blows fate loves to shower on unfortunate humanity.   I will call this friend Dr. M.   Soon after he was married, when very pleased with himself, his wife, his home and the world, Christmas came around.   What he would have liked to do was to spend it in his own home, but a patient, who was too ill to care for having anyone round her except her own people, who were all far away, was alone.   Dr. M. turned up to sit with her for a while and help her to forget the bygone days when, with health and dear ones around her, Christmas had been a happy time.

On another occasion a poor girl I knew was very ill, and there appeared to be nobody responsible. I found this kind man spending his time and energy on her day after day, and when I asked him who was going to pay him he said, "Nobody, I look upon her as one of God's patients."

Yet even this great soul could not escape some of the awkward situations that seem inevitable to doctors, especially those with kind hearts. He lives in a small country village where he is sought out by those both near and far. There came into the country one day a smart lady who rented a house a few miles from where the doctor lived, and she asked him to attend her in her approaching accouchement. This was arranged satisfactorily. No husband appeared on the scenes. This Hon. Mrs. ——, as she called herself, had only a maid with her, but soon settled into the little house she was renting for a few months.

One day the doctor was sent for hastily, as the infant insisted on making its appearance before it was expected. The lady was very ill and the doctor had an anxious time with her, added to which in the midst of everything the maid decamped and he was left alone to be mother to the lady, nurse to the baby and general servant. After washing and dressing the infant and attending to its mother, the doctor went off to telegraph for a trained nurse and a domestic of sorts. Thanks to his goodness and resourcefulness all went well, and he thought the lady very charming.

At the end of a fortnight the invalid declared her intention of going to town on urgent business. The doctor objected, thinking her not sufficiently recovered after being so ill, but she went in spite of all his protestations, taking the baby with her. She returned no more; the rent was unpaid, the doctor unpaid, and most of the tradespeople in the same predicament. What made it harder was that the nurse had to be paid by the doctor who had sent for her, also the car which brought her out many miles into the country! After this experience enquiries were made, and it was found this same game had been played before elsewhere, and everybody left unpaid.

Some time after this little ten days' wonder had subsided, the doctor happened to be in London and going somewhere by Tube. When he got out at his station he found himself face to face with the so-called Hon. Mrs. —— who had played him the trick. When he told me of this meeting I naturally enquired what he said on the occasion, and he confessed he was so taken by surprise that he said nothing beyond asking after her health!

Oh! who would be a doctor? What surprises they get sometimes! There was one doctor in India who attended me when I was so ill that it was thought I could not possibly recover. I do not remember much about it at the time, but dear Padre Adams, the V.C. parson, was by my bedside, my husband weeping on my pillow, the doctor with folded arms standing at the foot of the bed awaiting the end, when in a moment of returning conscious-ness the Padre asked me if there was anything he could do for me, if there was anything I would like to tell him.   All were breathlessly waiting to hear me say I left all my worldly goods to the Home for Lost Dogs, or some such thing, when I am told I said, "I want some shrimps!"   I remember I had been grieving before I became too ill, thinking I should never again go shrimping or paddle with my little bairns, so I suppose shrimps were on my mind.

One doctor, I forget which, told me of a poor woman he had been called in to see.   When he arrived she was propped up in a kitchen-chair out-side her cottage door.   In a moment he saw she was past any help of his.   He asked what had been done for her, and was told, "We picked her up, gave her water to drink, burnt feathers under her nose, and every other form of restitution we could think of!"

On another occasion the same doctor had been sent for to the bedside of a poor man he had been attending "for love."   He found the forbidding-looking old wife sitting by the side of her straight and stiff-looking husband who was lying on the bed with his face covered up.   She held her apron to her eyes and, when she saw the doctor coming, rocked herself backwards and forwards with more pronounced grief, saying, "He gas gorne, doctor, he has gorne."   .   .   .   (Sobs.)

"And I 'ave been a good wife to him that I 'ave!" From the bed came a feeble voice, "Pretty well, Mary—only pretty well."

It is difficult to say why some doctors are to-day distinguished ornaments to their profession. They do not know themselves how it happened any more than many learned, clever and lovable men can say *why* they are still in obscurity, except that some seem to prefer it.

One of the things that strikes me as most strange in this highly complex civilisation of which we boast, is that certain folks have to make their livings out of other people's sufferings—doctors to wit. It seems all wrong.

I have come to the conclusion that only a good man can be a good doctor, and I am more glad than I can find words to express that before the end of my days I have met so good, kind and conscientious a man as my friend Dr. M. It is an uplifting experience to meet someone you can thoroughly respect. Gifts of mind are more dazzling than sound.

Doctors are weighed in the balance as no other men are, and they get rusty more quickly than in any other profession. It is well they should remember how eagerly the sick and the feeble gather up the crumbs from the table of the strong and of those experienced in sickness.

I do not remember exactly how many years ago it was that a new medical luminary shone out in Harley Street. He became the hope and joy of the over-plump, ranging from the late King Edward VII to my humble self.   The name of this benefactor was Dr. Yorke-Davies, and although the principle of his system is now pretty well known, it struck us at the time as very novel and exciting.

Roughly outlined he reduced people's weight by letting them eat as much as they wanted, only of non-fattening foods.   Hitherto we had associated weight reducing with banting, running in blankets, or woolly jerseys and such-like discomforts.

Under the new system we were all allowed plenty of satisfying things to eat, and had the comfort of thinking we were not adding fuel to the fire of increasing weight.   We all bought the sweetest things in weighing machines under the doctor's orders, and weekly recorded our loss of weight on elaborate weight and diet forms.

In 1895, when the Prince of Wales had developed a very noticeable amplitude of figure and during his visit to Homburg, that he expressed a wish to try Dr. Yorke-Davies' weight reducing methods.   It so happened that the doctor was in Homburg at the time.

Colonel Stanley Clarke therefore wrote a note asking him if he would call, or in Royal parlance commanded him to call at Ritter's Park Hotel, where the Prince was staying.   At that time he turned the scales at 16 stone 4 pounds.

Dr. Davies visited the patient daily, advising him as to diet, with the result that during those few

Dr. Nathaniel Yorke-Davies

short weeks at Homburg his Royal Highness lost twenty pounds, and felt miles better for it.

In 1896 the doctor again attended the Prince at Marlborough House.

I remember His Royal Highness remarking to me one day that he found it very difficult to adhere strictly to the diet allowed him, saying jokingly that he was only allowed the oyster out of a mutton chop and dry toast for dinner. I said under those circumstances would he condescend to dine with us as I felt sure we could provide that simple fare! As usual the Prince did not lose the opportunity of saying something courteous and kind, asking if he might come to tea instead as he felt it would be an insult to my cook not to be able to eat the good things for which he was so famous; he would like to keep that pleasure in store for a time when not on a special diet.

A few days later I received a note from Colonel Stanley Clarke fixing a Sunday for our little tea party; his Royal Highness arrived punctually at the hour that had been named, accompanied by Sir Maurice Fitzgerald.

I have never forgotten that tea, for a dreadful thing happened. I was showing to the Prince some Indian photographs he was anxious to see. The light was not very good and I asked Sir Maurice if he would pull down a little lower the lamp suspended above my head. This was done, enabling us to see better, but we forgot to push it up again, so when the Prince stood up to take his departure he bumped his head, it was a swinging lamp happily, but gave him an unpleasant blow all the same.

The Prince laughed and made a joke of it, but I felt much distressed, and so did Sir Maurice Fitzgerald.

The first time I met handsome Sir Maurice, with his dark dare-devil eyes, was when having tea at Cowes with the Custs, where he and Lady Sefton joined us. On our return to town he came to one of my Sunday afternoons when anybody and everybody could come who felt kindly disposed towards me. It so happened that the room was very full and I was struggling to entertain, with my rather sketchy French, dear old Rustem Pasha, at that time (1885) Turkish Ambassador in London, so I had no time to give impressive personal greetings to everybody. As soon as I was free for a moment Sir Maurice came and sat down beside me, saying, "Am I in disgrace, you have not spoken to me all the afternoon?" I suggested that I could not well shout at him across the heads of other friends, and I would now make up for lost time by saying how pleased I was to see him, and that it was nice to feel he was there even if he could not get near enough to converse, etc. He was not quite happy even then and said, "I believe somebody has been telling tales about me; they have now, haven't they? I know someone has been telling you I am a rude, bold, bad man!" I told him of course they had, but that the story was of such old standing I had entirely recovered from the shock.

I remember the Prince saying to me the year "Persimmon" won the Derby, I think it was 1896, how he wished he were a plain Mr. Jones, and able to go to the Derby and have a little bet and be able to sneeze without having it all chronicled in the evening papers.

I am told that "Persimmon" was so called after the tree of that name, which came originally from America. It is rather like the cocoa palm, the bark being tessellated like tiles all the way up. The foliage being at the extreme top, like the trees we used to find in our Noah's arks when we were children.

There is a good specimen of the tree in Kew Gardens standing close to one of the temples, and the tree that was planted from the grave of the first Napoleon.

Some friends were sitting near this tree one day when a 'Arry and his 'Arriet came round the corner arm in arm, and stopped in front of the tree. 'Arry scratched his head looking long and earnestly at the name on the tree, then turning with an enlightened smile to his love said, "Well, I am blessed if they 'ave not been and named this 'ere tree after the Prince of Wiles 'orse."

The subject of Dr. Yorke-Davies has led me into others until he has been entirely left behind; it is difficult with such a crowd of memories of all sorts and kinds not to branch off to other people, who have come on my stage about the same time.

The last time I saw Dr. Yorke-Davies was at

Beaulieu in the Riviera. Dr. Lavis, an Englishman living in that little village, who had married a French wife and made his home in France, was teasing him about his figure, saying he was not a good advertisement for the theories he preached. Dr. Yorke-Davies took the chaff in good part and, while pulling down his waistcoat and holding in his lower chest, replied laughingly, "You must allow weight for age." He has also been known to give another reply when teased about his figure, "He who drives fat cattle should himself be fat."

There was really no occasion to tease the poor man about his figure, he was nothing more than "comfortable"; but he so enjoyed a good dinner that it gave an opening to his friends to chaff him.

Mrs. Stannard of "Bootle's Baby" fame was another patient who swore by Dr. Davies' treatment; he certainly did wonders for her. Besides being clever in reducing weight without drugs of any kind, he had a pleasant manner, always looked clean, smart and well dressed. He was very proud of his beautiful wife; I remember seeing her at Monte Carlo once, bicycling on her way to Nice, she was even then a beautiful woman after the stress and storm of many years.

Dr. Davies' butler used to fill me with admiration. Instead of the funeral black that is usually worn by butlers, he answered the door in exceedingly well-cut and fitting pepper and salt mufti clothes which he carried with impressive dignity as behove a person accustomed to announcing "all mighty big wigs." His tie and collar were things of beauty, *and* his boots, I have never seen anything so smart on a servant before. This beauteous person had been in the family many years, and had grown more or less confidential.

One day when Cardinal Vaughan arrived without this servant having been acquainted of his expected visit, he showed the prelate into the waiting-room in the usual way asking his name. The servant sought his master saying, "A Colonel Vaughan wished to see him," at the same time remarking (owing to the fact that the "Colonel" was robed), "I think he must be a colonel of the Salvation Army!"

Dr. Lavis, to whom I have referred, was killed in a motor accident in the early part of the great war.

The famous physician Sir William Gull, also had an amusing butler. A patient of importance calling one day to see Sir William was told by the butler that his master was too busy to see anybody without previous appointment; he added, *"We* are full up, but there is another fellow across the way whom you might see, we have a good opinion of him." The "other fellow" happened to be Sir William Jenner!

When Sir William Gull was attending the then Prince of Wales when he nearly died of typhoid, the Duke of Connaught observing him to be busy with a pencil on the back of a telegraph form asked what he was doing. The doctor replied, "I am making a sketch bearing the inscription 'Don't talk to the man at the wheel.'" The poor man while attending to his patient had evidently been somewhat harassed by too much conversation.

Sir William had engaged a special and favourite nurse for his Royal patient and had left her in charge while he prowled up and down outside to be ready if wanted; before long, she came rushing after him to say that she had observed a sudden change and that the patient was dying. Evidently her nerves were upset by her great anxiety and responsibility, for, as a matter of fact, this was the turning-point, and from that moment the Prince began to recover and quickly reached convalescence. The first thing he asked for was a glass of beer, which was promptly supplied.

I also remember when women doctors sought to become the fashion, and I asked the advice of one after a fast trotter of ours had fast trotted us into a carriage and pair. This resulted in our being all curled up in the middle of the street at Torquay, while the gee, with what remained of the dog-cart, retired into a butcher's shop that was at hand.

I journeyed to town, allowed the she-male doctor to treat me and vowed that for ever more I would pin my faith to my old friend the man, for indeed I met with very rough handling. Perhaps the lady felt I ought to carry away something by which to remember my visit—she succeeded.

If I had ever aspired to become a fashionable west-end doctor, I should have made it my business to specialise in some interesting and mentionable complaint, prescribing treatment that lent itself to dinner table discussion; for who wants to pay big fees for a treatment so unspeakably unromantic that it cannot be discussed at dinner!

If I am asked to name some suitable malady for discussion, I shall reply as some of my friends do in "The House," "I must have notice of that question." If after that I find myself in deep water I shall catch the Speaker's eye and get him to rule it out of order.

CHAPTER III

I HAD intended writing a classified chapter on the people I have met with kinks, but I find the infirmities of the human mind so numerous that I have had to abandon the idea and give only a few examples.

I had not been launched upon the world very long before I came to the conclusion that it was advisable to make memoranda of the peculiarities of the people I stayed with from time to time; it saved awkward moments. I also made notes of the subjects most interesting to my hosts and hostesses. I thought I was becoming very grown-up and business-like, unfortunately I was not sufficiently business-like to make my notes in cipher, and was horrified to find when staying with the Exmouths (fourth Viscount) at Canonteign, that I had lost the list. I had been studying it in the train, and remembered putting it back with my purse in my little handbag.   I was much worried, wondering whether I had pulled it out with my pocket-handkerchief at tea-time in the drawing-room, or what on earth had become of it.   I wished with all my heart that I had not amused myself by making sketches of some of my friends, with would-be facetious remarks and jokes beneath them.

My first evening was entirely spoilt by my anxiety in trying to remember if I had said anything very compromising about anybody.   Lord Exmouth's little peculiarities were soon recalled to my mind by his wife coming into my bedroom when retiring for the night and asking me not to stir the fire, saying, "It so worries Exmouth."   Apparently his trained ear enabled him to locate anything of this kind taking place in any part of the house.   His spirit of economy was what caused the poking of the fires to annoy him.

At one time I saw a good deal of this little man. My sister was the attraction.   I was acting chaperon.   He seldom came alone, but accompanied by his brother; the latter fell to me to entertain. The brothers were both very short (I should think under five feet high, but I am not a great judge of height), round-faced, and like Sir John Tenniel's picture of "Tweedle-dum" and "Tweedle-dee" in "Alice Through the Looking-glass," who agreed to have a battle when Tweedle-dum said Tweedle-dee had spoilt his nice new rattle.   Unfortunately, my suggestion of a likeness to Tweedle-dum and Tweedle-dee got noised abroad, and for long the young men were spoken of by these absurd names. This was, of course, before Lord Exmouth married. At that time he and his brother the Hon. William Pellew, were living with their mother, Mrs. Pellew-Bradshaw. She had married a second time. I remember thinking her second choice a very handsome man.

The necessity for being primed about my friends' hobbies, interests, and kinks had been impressed upon me very early in my married life when my husband was trotting me out before all his relations, and I was expected to show my paces. I strongly objected to these visits, but as they seemed to give infinite pleasure to my lord and master I did my best to show off nicely.

The visit in my mind was only to dine with the learned Professor North and his wife, a little family party. I had stupidly forgotten to ask what this relative was professor of until it was too late. All through dinner I kept hedging to try and find out but without success, I looked appealingly towards my husband hoping he would grasp the situation, but he was busy talking secrets about me; a fact I gathered from the way they kept looking in my direction and nodding their heads. The Professor tried hard to come off his lofty pedestal and talk down to my common or garden intellect. I tried once more, "Your work must be very interesting; do tell me something about it?" Receiving in reply, "It is very interesting to *me*. And what is your next festivity?" It was no use, so I plunged into everyday topics.

However, I had evidently made an impression, for after dinner instead of retiring to his den as his wife said was his habit, he invited me to see where he worked. At the first glance there was nothing in his study that was helpful as indicating the nature of his work. Through the open French windows looking on to a piece of garden I observed a queer edifice. To this he drew my attention, saying with evident pride: "I made that myself." It looked like a glorified meat-safe, and I congratulated him on building such a big, useful one. There was a pause, I had evidently said the wrong thing. In a voice I recognised as the kind we adopt when seriously annoyed yet trying not to show it, he said, "It is not a meat-safe, that is my observatory." He beamed on me no longer. I tried hard to put it right, said I had not meant *that* was a meat-safe, but something else altogether; he was now most uncompromising and wanted to know what other thing I meant? Wretched man! Thank goodness my husband, growing bored with his relatives in the drawing-room, came to look for his bride and helped to change the conversation, but I had the humiliating sensation of having been gauche, of having displayed my ignorance, and effaced the good impressions I had been making.

I was learning to be tactful when an old Colonel friend of my husband's came to dine with us. We were a small party of eight and sitting at a round table. Conversation turned on a curious case of cruelty to children that had been in the papers, not of a hardworked poor woman in a moment of tired exasperation beating a tiresome child, but a woman in our own class of life who systematically ill-treated a little daughter, shutting her up in a dark cupboard with her arms tied up above her head and keeping her without food until a governess or servant, I forget which, reported the case to the Society for Prevention of Cruelty to Children. My husband was saying what he should like to do to the woman in question when I saw the subject was distasteful to my old Colonel sitting beside me, so I aimed a healthy kick under the table at my good man's legs and made faces at him. All the effect my tactfulness had was to make my man ask me if I had swallowed a bone or something, and a smothered yell from the Colonel whose gouty legs were stretching in the direction I expected to find those of my husband! My man told me afterwards he had tucked his under his chair, as whenever he moved them he found himself in contact with the Colonel's. On making enquiries we found the cruel mother was a near relation of the kicked Colonel.

Kinky and tactless people make me tremble at times. I knew in India a very charming official at that time Governor of the North-West Provinces. He was the essence of tactfulness and kept all around him happy by his carefully chosen words and considerations. He married a wife who was most anxious to help him and add to his popularity, but she sadly lacked that sympathy which enables people to know what to say and what not to say. They were giving a big dinner to all the local society of the place. The chief civilian of the neighborhood was seated beside the hostess, who, by way of making polite conversation to her, remarked, "What excellent asparagus you have, Lady——"

"I am so glad you like it," she replied, "but it is only tinned. My husband said that was quite good enough for the people up here."

The unhappy husband little knew the amount of trouble the wife of his bosom was creating for him.

The peculiarities of the late Duke of Portland are common property, but I do not think it is generally known that once at Welbeck he ordered all the maid-servants to appear for his amusement on roller skates in the riding school. He was highly entertained, for most of them entered on all fours, and some even less elegantly.

When moving from one property to another he had his carriage drawn up at a side entrance so that none might look at him; the servants had to remain seated on the box, eyes front, while their master popped in and drew the blinds down or they had been drawn previously, I forget which, and away they went gaily to the station, where the carriage was moved on to a truck and thus the eccentric duke travelled.

Once the servants thinking there was no one in the carriage but not daring to look, left the coach shunted on to a siding and went off to a public-house to enjoy themselves. In the early hours they returned to the carriage to find something was being said behind the blinds and some awful threats found their way on to the air!

Sir Charles Dilke had a funny fad, he was pursued by the idea that he would one day have to fight a duel. Though quite the last person ever to dream of doing such a thing, nevertheless he spent a good deal of his spare time preparing for the event. He practised in the garden behind his house in Sloane Street, either with the foils or *l'epée*.

He had a great regard for his inner man, and was fond of inventing new dishes and eating them, which at times upset his tummy and temper. When in India his attempts to interest Lord Roberts in recondite dishes was pathetic, as well as highly unproductive.

I was talking to him once after his social upheaval, and was venturing to suggest where I thought he had made a mistake when he amused me by saying, "If the ivy will cling to the oak, what is the oak to do." I suggested the oak should at least be chivalrous if it went gallivanting. Latterly most of the society he entertained was foreign.

Then there was Lord Roberts' kink about cats. I ought in my last volume to have mentioned their predilection for him, which quite threw down my theory that children and animals always know by instinct who cares for them.

It was quite a usual custom for hostesses, when General "Bobs" was dining with them, to give orders for all the cats on the premises to be shut up in rooms, or baskets, until the visit was over, and it really was extraordinary the way they managed to get out, and always rushed for him. The story I told in my last volume of the time when he was walking up and down the deck and felt so uneasy though unable to see a cat anywhere, puss was walking step for step above his head. It was quite uncanny!

The late Sir William Fraser, a talented and remarkable man, was yet very eccentric, and used to try the forbearance of his fellow-members in the Carlton Club considerably. He was a man of wealth, but used to drive up daily from his suburban home in Clapham to the club in a shabby old victoria, with the waterproof apron, hood, and curtains beloved by our great-grand-parents. In those days they had a passion for curtains on their beds, I presume for delicacy, and quite possibly for the same reason on the victorias.

One of the habits his fellow-members of the Carlton found trying was the way he would bring a cage of dormice out of his pocket when at meals in the dining-room. He was perfectly aware of his unpopularity, describing himself as a yellow sparrow amongst black ones who were anxious to peck him.

He was not fond of ablutions, thought them waste of time. Once when staying with some friends one of the house party who was of a mischievous turn of mind, went into Sir William's room and took a five-pound note off his dressing-table and put it in his bath, where it remained until he was leaving, when it was pointed out to him proving the bath had not been used during his visit.

I have heard this same story told of other people, only in connection with their sponge. All these stories are things of the past, for people do not sit in tea-cups of water in the bedrooms to-day. Every household has a bathroom, and some boast a good many. One house I was staying in a short time ago had a most luxurious one attached to each bedroom.

Sir William Fraser repaired to the Highlands at one time in search of a reposeful spot for his remains when some such place might be necessary. He stayed for one night at Inverness with a friend. During dinner his host begged him to dig deep into the pie and other edibles after his long journey north. Sir William, who was rather deaf, still thinking of his last resting-place, replied, "Oh, certainly! I have no wish to remain too near the surface I assure you."

Once in my early married days I was staying in Yorkshire with an eccentric relative, who had all the household baths spread out on the lawn and painted them himself to avoid the expense of a trades-person doing it. It so happened the house was full for a dance, amongst the guests was a very amply proportioned old General, who was paying his addresses to one of the daughters of the house.

After receiving their first coat of paint the baths were removed into the house, and there being a shortage of the useful commodity, one of the new painted ones was pressed into the housemaids' service and was placed in the General's room. Nothing suspecting he boldly stepped into it in the morning and then sat down in it and stuck. After breakfast my relative said he was going to give another coat of paint to the baths, and invited us all tò go and view his handiwork. We followed him down the rows of baths on the lawn trying to find a suitable change of appreciative remarks for each bath as we came to it; presently we came to the big saucer bearing the imprint of feet and anatomy most faithfully depicted. It would have rejoiced the heart of any detective accustomed to tracing people by the Bertillon system.

At first we all stood speechless, gazing at the spectacle; my relative getting redder in the face and his eyes angrier and angrier. He then turned and eyed us all reflectively, as if trying from our forms to trace the culprit who had dared to use one of his newly painted baths without his permission. The beauty of the whole thing was every one of us looked absolutely guilty and red in the face. I determined when I become a judge I will never be led away by circumstantial evidence, it may be most misleading.

The General, who had given a sovereign to the head housemaid not to give him away, suggested he would like to go and see the stables—so thought all of us!

People with religious kinks are, however, far and

away the most terrifying. It is impossible to say where their emotions may lead them. There is a certain lady, living not a hundred miles from where I am now writing, who has a tiresome habit of coming up to you at garden parties and suchlike gatherings asking, "Are you saved?" This is disconcerting because one does not like to venture an opinion on anything so uncertain. While seeking for a diplomatic answer she continues somewhat in this strain, "Remember if you are not saved you are damned, there is no middle course." This sort of thing when your friends are gathering round in a ring to watch your discomfiture is trying, each answer to her leading questions is awaited in silence, hoping for something really effective. Religious kinky-folk ought not to be allowed to roam about alone at garden parties.

This same religious lady has a living in her gift. The unfortunate incumbent has a very poor time. Not long ago the long-suffering man thought he had endured enough and gave up the Ghost, but not before he had invited the parson of our parish to preach for him one Sunday. During the sermon opinions were expressed not in accordance with this lady's views; she therefore stood up and shouted, "That's a lie!" Our rosy-faced little parson continued, taking no sort of notice, so she repeated her polite statement and was requested by the preacher to sit down and be quiet and after the service if she would like to come to the vestry he would discuss the point. She agreed to this and continued mut-

tering to herself and shaking her head, occasionally making a few notes in a pocket-book. What
made the circumstances piquante was the fact, well
known to many present, that the familiar nickname
of the parson was "Lying Joe."

On another occasion when a strange clergyman
was preaching he foolishly and unthinkingly said
in the course of his sermon, "Who amongst you
are saved?"

This weird lady patroness at once jumped up
and said, "I am"; her cook in the pew behind followed suit, "And I am," knowing how much de-
pended on doing so.

After the clergyman holding this living and
chaplaincy died, a new incumbent had to be installed. A terrible time ensued. Various parsons
were tried and found wanting. One unfortunate
man came from some distance by train, having in
his letters confessed himself willing to preach his
patroness's doctrines and she had agreed to send
her carriage to meet him, the station being several
miles from the house. Owing to some mischance
the reverend gentleman missed his train, arriving
at his destination to find no carriage to meet him.
He was told it had been and gone again earlier in
the evening.

With some difficulty he hired a vehicle, and drove
some eight miles in the dark to the address on the
letters in his pocket. When at last he reached the
place it was all shut up and in darkness. After
ringing and hammering at the front door and re-

ceiving no answer, he and the driver of the cab wandered round the house looking for some window or door that might be hospitably inclined. At last a side door was found open, and a sleepy maid sitting up in a sort of back kitchen. She gave the parson a written notice that had been left for him when his hostess retired to bed. On this card was written, "If you choose to come in the middle of the night you can't expect people to sit up for you. Go to bed and I will see you in the morning. Up the stairs, first turn to the right, fourth room on the left."

The maid presented him with a smelly little oil lamp, and advised him strongly not to come to the "miserable place"; the lady was enough to drive anybody mad. The clergyman went to bed thinking it all very strange, but as he knew his predecessor had held the living for years he thought perhaps he might be able to do the same, at any rate he must try.

The following morning at breakfast he made the acquaintance of the awesome lady, who was neither young nor good-looking, and considered any daintiness in dress or personal adornment very wicked. She asked her guest to say grace; this he did, briefly, only to be told, "That is no use at all," and she stood up and in a sing-song voice half spoke, half chanted a lengthy supplication for a variety of things, including a good appetite!

It was Sunday, and the parson was to take the service, so that it might be seen if he was suitable.

In the middle of breakfast, after fixing a cold grey eye on the uncomfortable and much-to-be-pitied man, the patroness snapped out, "I can't stand that silly collar you are wearing, why can't you wear a proper one that opens in front and has no deception about it. That ritualistic thing is no use at all, it has no beginning or end."

"But, madam," replied the parson, "it is the usual clerical collar."

"It is nothing of the kind, man. I am not a fool," retorted the lady.

When the morning's service was over the parson said he was truly thankful. He was not usually a nervous man, but he confessed that morning had tried his nerves severely. He was allowed to eat his luncheon in peace, but there was a gloomy silence on the part of his hostess, and at the end of the repast she said, "You won't do at all, you can go back again at once; what do I owe you?"

The parson explained what the usual fee was and the cost of his journey, counting the cab of the night before, asking a modest four guineas. He was presented with a cheque for £3 10s. and told it was quite enough, if he chose to arrive in the middle of the night he must pay for the cab himself.

Eventually there was so much scandal about the way the numerous clergy were treated who aspired to the living in this curious person's gift, that the bishop got wind of it and put his foot down and there was an end of the matter. A parson came and stayed, whether he was approved of or not.

Some of the victim parsons took the lady's treatment of them much to heart. "Lying Joe" troubled not at all when she told him he lied. His habitual tally-diddles and inexactitudes were not in connection with Biblical history or dogma, but purely social and in amplification of his own prowess and importance. Yet everyone liked him, he was a genial amusing companion, hospitable host and kind friend. When he died he was much missed. He had held his living for many years, and in his younger days could tell a good story and drink a bottle of good port. In his stable there always stood a smart cob or two that could be relied on to bring him home safely at night after cheery dinners with old Lord Poulett the 6th Earl and Lord Bridport of the same date.

The stories the dear old parson told of those days were highly entertaining, also the accounts of some of the 6th Lord Poulett's wives, whom he knew well, being a constant visitor at the house.

Many people will remember what a rumpus there was about the succession to the Hinton St. George property and the Poulett title, and how the son of one of the earl's earlier wives (he had three) declared he was the rightful heir, but for reasons it is not necessary to state here, though they can be easily imagined, when the case came up for trial it was given against him. I remember seeing the claimant going about London with his barrel-piano, he never asked for money, at least I never saw him do so, but there was a little box on one side of the

The Sixth Earl Poulett

piano into which I have seen a good deal find its way, and I have added my mite to help to swell the grand total. Silver was often thrown to them and dexterously caught.

The musician was accompanied by a woman, whether she was his wife or not I do not know.

A large notice adorned one side of the piano giving the world to understand that the grinder was Viscount Hinton, heir to the Poulett estates.

They used to prowl about the streets, not so much with a view, I always thought, of obtaining money as to airing their grievance. People used to be sorry for them, and I remember seeing a cabman ask them into a public-house at the bottom of Park Lane to give them drinks. Nobody interfered with the poor dears, even the policemen left them in peace. Anybody wishing to find these unfortunate people and their piano could generally run them to ground in the neighbourhood of Tattersalls or the sporting clubs.

It must have been weary work wandering about, rain or shine, and I wondered they kept it up as long as they did. I always felt sorry for them.

It will perhaps be remembered that the present Lord Poulett's father married three times, his first wife being the mother of the organ-grinder whom the Court decided was not Lord Poulett's son. The secret of his marriage had been kept very quiet, it was the result of a foolish bet made with a brother officer on board ship when the 2nd Foot were coming home from abroad. He said he would marry the first woman he met or saw on landing, and he stuck to his word. The woman's name was Miss Elizabeth Lavinia Newman, and I have been told she was a circus rider, but about this I am not sure. I have always heard that the late Lord Poulett provided handsomely in his lifetime for the unhappy man who called himself, and no doubt believed he was, Viscount Hinton.

I have been told Lord Poulett, the 7th Earl, behaved generously to the piano-grinder, although the unfortunate aspirant's claim had been completely shattered in the law courts.

The present peer inherited from his parents a love for the stage, and married a pretty Miss Storey from the Gaiety Chorus, after the fashion of the young bloods of to-day. Lady Poulett's father was the Fred Storey attached for so long to the Gaiety Theatre. His forte was eccentric dancing, he appeared also, I think, at Drury Lane with the Vokes family, under Augustus Harris's management, in a show called "Belles of the Kitchen." First he danced on the kitchen table and then stood between the sisters Rosina and Victoria throwing his leg alternately over the heads of each.

The sixth earl died in 1899. He was a popular patron of steeplechasing, and scored two great victories with a little 15.2 horse called "The Lamb," the Liverpool Grand National in 1868 and again in 1871. On both occasions "The Lamb" was ridden by gentlemen riders, the first time by Mr. George

Ede, under the name of Edwards, the second by Mr. Pickernell, under the name of Thomas.

There is a curious story attached to the second race. Lord Poulett had a dream in which he saw his horse defeated, he awoke feeling very worried and disappointed, went to sleep again and dreamt he saw his horse win with Mr. Pickernell in the saddle. Upon the strength of this he wrote to Mr. Pickernell telling him about his dream and asking him to ride the horse. Mr. Pickernell agreed and the dream was fulfilled to the letter.

These two races brought a good round sum into Lord Poulett's pockets, but I fear there must have been a hole in them, for the money soon disappeared.

The poor little "Lamb" died in 1872, after he had passed the winning-post, in a big steeplechase at Baden-Baden. I should have liked to see this game little horse in the flesh. He was an iron grey with little flecks of white, the only picture of him that I know of is a family heirloom now at Hinton St. George. I believe Prince Esterhazy was riding him on the fatal day against a horse named "Monarch," ridden by Prince Kinsky.

Lord Poulett was the original owner of "Cortolvin," but sold him to the Duke of Hamilton.

Looking back over my life I have met some first-class romancers, some embroidered beautifully, others awkwardly, others maliciously. It has been an interesting study to me trying to trace the reasons and incentives for the inexactitudes. I have come to the conclusion that some people are untruthful because they cannot help it, they have no real sense of right and wrong. Others lie with a view to self-aggrandisement, and there is another class that lies from Christian charity, the white lies of charity and bowing to convention. If you know people fairly well you can generally see through them all. There is, however, one man I know, a general in the army, who romances for no reason at all as far as I can gather, but his habit has become so well known that in the army they say, "Oh, what a—Jones shall I say?" Of course that is not the general's name, but I cannot now give the name as the man is living and would scalp me. Quite solemnly once he told me he was the inventor of cart wheels, hoping I suppose that I was simple enough to believe him. At another time he told me he remembered well when a baby in arms and his nurse pinched him thinking to himself "When I can talk I will tell my mother of this woman."

This officer's son inherited his father's failing. He was quite a nice boy and used to rattle on telling most astounding stories, and then wind up by saying in the most engaging manner, "But you must not believe a word I say, I am an awful liar."

There was a certain stipendiary magistrate in Yorkshire who was superb in this line. One day when some friends were talking rather big about shooting experiences, the stipendiary broke in and we all knew something was coming that would take the gloss off any previous story of that evening. He was a huge man with a large corporation, florid, rather fat face and strident of voice. He proceeded: "My dear fellahs! that's nothing to what I did once when I was shooting with the King at Buckingham Palace." Before we had recovered from our surprise at hearing of Buckingham Palace being a sporting estate, he astonished us still more by saying, "A covey of partridges got up. I got a right and left and the recoil of the gun caused me to fall backwards on to a hare and kill it."

If we felt the man was romancing to be funny and for our amusement we should not have minded, but he was in the first place strangely ignorant, and in the second place annoying because he expected us to believe him. Nobody took any notice, which was perhaps a pity; someone ought to have tackled him and argued the matter out; only not in my house for choice!

The lies that are lied so that good may come are often rather pleasant; for instance, we may know some young man is going to make a fool of himself and we say "I am sure you will not do so and so, it would be very unlike you. I have much too high an opinion of you to believe you would do anything of the kind." In our hearts we have no such high opinion, and we are persuaded he had every intention of doing the foolish deed, but our white lie may act as a deterrent; he will wish to live up to our high opinion of him, therefore, surely this lie is doing evil that good may come, and is pardonable.

Then the little everyday tally-diddles, when our friends tell us how they have been looking forward to seeing us and how charming we look, we know it is only froth, oil that lubricates the wheels of life, and surrender ourselves to the deception that is being practised upon us just as we do when we go to a play.

I wonder sometimes is there such a thing as truth, or is it all a mirage?

CHAPTER IV

I KNOW a good deal about tempers, though I have been blessed by a sweet-tempered husband and a sweet-tempered son. It has always seemed to me that sporting people control their feelings the least satisfactorily, which is a pity. Indeed, some I have known seem to consider they are being clever and amusing when blustering and using swear words. Tradition has something to do with this. It influences people in small as well as great matters. Tradition is what makes armies particularly deadly in attack, just as successfully as it makes masters of hounds swear when naturally, and in their hearts, they are often the tamest creatures imaginable, poor dears!

There are, of course, some naturally bad-tempered men who have so grievously mistaken their calling as to attempt to hunt hounds, but personally I think that nine times out of ten the silly bluster affected by some men in the hunting field is chiefly due to the prominence accorded to that sort of thing in sporting literature.

Happily both this style and hard swearing are dying natural deaths, like the port wine drinking of the early Victorian era.

I remember my father telling me that in his young days it was the fashion to get drunk whenever an opportunity presented itself. He found this a great nuisance, being one of the most abstemious of men.

In the Northumberland Yeomanry they kept up the practice of drinking without leaving any heeltaps, which I understand consisted of drinking off glass after glass of port quickly, and then turning the glass upside down on the table to show it was empty.

One guest night, soon after the funeral of the Duke of Wellington, at which my father had been present with his regiment, when all were drowning dull care in repeated libations of port, my father, not wishing to drink more than was good for him, lifted each successive glass to his face and then shot its contents quickly under the table, naturally remaining cool-headed while his neighbours were becoming somewhat elevated or muddled, as the case might be. After this had been proceeding for some time it suddenly dawned on his guest to the right, who was, I believe, one of the North Country Cooksons, that his legs were feeling very wet and he moved his chair to enquire into the matter. My father, realising that he had accidentally been pouring the port over his neighbour's legs, thought it time to decamp with all speed. There was a tremendous hullabaloo and some unwisely gave chase, but they did not get very far.

I have strayed away from tempers somewhat. I was going to mention Mr. Carnaby Forster, at one time Master of the Ledbury. He used to be quite comic in his display of temper. I was forcibly reminded of him the other day while reading General Baden-Powell's book, *Indian Memories,* in which he described the way Sir Baker Russell, commanding the 13th Hussars, used to charge subalterns who annoyed him, and either ride them down if he managed to hit them, or crash into the ranks if he missed his intended prey.

I remember well the fierce, heavy-moustached colonel in Lucknow many years ago when I was staying with Captain and Mrs. Cuthell, my host being in the 13th Hussars. He maintained that the Colonel's bark was worse than his bite. I

noticed, however, that throughout the station there
was a distinct disinclination to bark with him.

Mr. Carnaby Forster ruled the Ledbury with a
rod of iron. When he began to be really angry, an
event for which his field did not have long to wait,
he used to fill the coverts with his admonitions and
commands. He was a small dark man with prominent eyes, and I remember seeing him gallop furiously after someone or other who had offended him,
sitting hunched up in his saddle with rage, literally
gnashing his teeth.

It was impossible at times to prevent laughing
at his exhibitions, at others it made one feel sad,
hurt one's cherished ideals of the dignity of humanity. He never wearied of abusing his hunt
servants, and they were reduced to a state of hope-
lessness from fear. One day when my son viewed
a beaten fox, for which the master was diligently
casting, and told one of the whips he had viewed
it, the man said he really dare not tell Mr. Forster,
and suggested the only thing to do was to go and
tell Lady Mary Hamilton (Mr. Forster's step-
daughter), she being the only person who knew how
to tackle him.

With all his curious ways and tempers he was
not a bad huntsman, and so keen that he used to
hunt otters during the summer months.

Lady Mary Hamilton was very popular, a big
healthy-looking girl with fair hair. Her mother,
the Duchess of Hamilton, it will be remembered,

The Twelfth Duke of Hamilton

married Mr. Carnaby Forster about two years after the Duke's death.

I remember being at Easton Park, near Wickham Market, soon after Lady Mary was born. It was a great disappointment to the Red Duke, as he was called, that the baby should be a girl. No man ever wished more ardently for a son and heir than did that good sportsman. He had been married since 1873, but not until November, 1884, did any offspring put in an appearance. At this time the Duke was rather a gouty subject and he amused me by saying his remedy was a "mixture of stout and champagne," which did not coincide with my ideas of what was suitable for the complaint.

The Duke (the 12th) was, I think, one of the most generous men I ever met. At Oxford his generosity was a byword, and in those youthful days he was a very unrestrained and wild young person: once he was nearly rusticated for playing practical jokes on a proctor. His rooms in Canterbury Quad were the general rendezvous of cockfighters, fox-terriers and rat-hunters. He was a general favourite all the same, owing to his extreme generosity, straightforwardness and charm of manner.

It was a different Oxford in the Hamilton, Lansdowne and Rosebery days from that we knew before the war. There were plenty up there then, however, as now, with money and without. To the latter the Duke was a prince of kindness. On hearing that some of his friends were borrowing money and being charged exorbitant interest by the money-lenders, he started a private business of his own in opposition to see how many bucket-shops he could close, but after a while, finding the under-graduates he had befriended never attempted to pay even the lowest rate of interest, much less the capital, by degrees he tired of the game and left the field to those who knew how to follow up and press their victims.

Birth heaped distinctions upon him, he owned many princely mansions in England and France; and was related to the Emperor Napoleon, who wished him to associate himself with French politics and ceremonies, but the Duke would not hear of it, although a staunch Bonapartist. He did not mind social court functions, but declined to have anything to do with politics.

In spite of his great inheritance, before reaching the age of thirty he was on the verge of ruin: a good many people did not know how he managed to save the situation. There used to be a diversity of opinion in my young days about Mr. Padwich, the agent. Some pointed him out as a praiseworthy good man, doing his best to husband the resources of a spendthrift, others as very much on the make.

Perhaps the chief social function of the Duke's life was the ball he gave at Hamilton Palace in Lanarkshire to the Crown Prince of Austria, our then Prince of Wales, and the Prince Imperial of France.

My old friend Sir Ian Hamilton got into trouble

at that ball. The room was very crowded, ten deep round the walls of the circular ballroom at least. He was waltzing away merrily and seeing a sort of opening in the serried ranks of spectators pulled up for a rest. Instantly about a dozen grandees fell upon him, hunting him and his terrified partner away, as they had exactly planted themselves in the front of a funnel-shaped opening in the crowd, kept to allow the Royalties who were present seated on sofas by the wall to see what was going on.

Hamilton Palace was the Duke's father's favourite abode, and was filled with marvels of art and precious books—all dispersed at the great sale!

Racing and hunting were the Duke's chief hobbies. A story is told of him in 1867, the night before the Grand National, which he won with his horse "Cortolvin." He was feeling particularly gay and full of beans at the time, and made no secret of the fact that he thought his horse would win the steeplechase on the following day. It was during the evening before the great event that he looked into the Washington Hotel at Liverpool, where all the chief book-makers and backers resorted, with the idea of either doing a little betting, or hearing the latest news of the big chase. Here he made a number of people back his horse.

During the revelry the Duke went to the bar and said to the girl attendant, "I shall put you on a thousand pounds that my horse wins to-morrow." The girl had no idea who was speaking and thought it might only be a joke, but felt elated, nevertheless, and told her master, who said, "Show me the man who said it." He was soon pointed out, and then the girl learnt it was the Duke of Hamilton who had made the promise.

The horse won, and the next night the Duke returned to the "Washington," which was again full of bookies and racing people. Instead of keeping his word by means of a cheque he went round the room collecting and borrowing the money from the book-makers and others present, in bank-notes and country notes in all sorts of conditions, dirty, clean, crumpled, pieced together with stamped paper and otherwise. These he rolled up one round the other and going straight to the bar presented the roll of notes to the barmaid. She could hardly believe her luck and again sought her master, excitedly carrying her handful of notes. Her employer locked these up for the night in his safe.

When the next Liverpool Meeting came round, the story had spread far and wide, in consequence of which many looked in to the "Washington" to see the lucky girl, but were disappointed, for as soon as the race week of 1867 was over she left her situation, married an engineer and went off with him and her thousand pounds to America, much to the grief of the hotel proprietor in Liverpool, who said the Duke had been the means of robbing him of the best book-keeping barmaid he ever had.

When racing in France the Duke was in his element, and ready for anything from pitch and toss to cock-fighting. Baden-Baden owes its success in life chiefly to him. He made the place what it was and has been ever since. In September he always had a big party there, a happy mixture of English and French friends. He won many races there on the flat and steeple-chasing, being a princely patron of both.

I was sorry he never won the Grand Prix de Paris. I should like to have seen the cerise with French-grey sleeves and cap (the Duke's colours) to the fore. Neither was he ever a winner of the Derby, or even placed in that race or the Two Thousand Guineas, but he won the One Thousand, Oaks and St. Leger. At Baden-Baden he won a race worth £2000; his mother, Princess Mary of Baden, being present made it a popular win, and I know the Duke was pleased. I never thought him lucky in his racing. Once in 1885 he had exceptionally bad luck through a mistake in allocating the weight "Miss Jummy" had to carry in the Post Sweepstakes for four hundred sovereigns at Newmarket. Marsh being the trainer it was his business to attend to such details as the weight to be carried.

That the weight was wrong was not discovered until the horses had cantered to the post. "Hotspur" of the *Daily Telegraph* (Mr. Charles Greenwood) at once flew off to the Clerk of the Scales and asked him if the weight declared overnight for the race card was what the filly was carrying, because if so it was wrong, receiving a reply in the affirmative "Hotspur" hastily found Mr. Marsh, but it was too late to send down to the post and correct the error, and away they all came, "Miss Jummy" first by three parts of a length, "Sunrise," a horse of Mr. Houldsworth's second and General Owen Williams' "Lisbon" third.

An objection was, of course, raised to "Miss Jummy" for carrying wrong weight. The objection was sustained and the race awarded to "Sunrise."

It is a most vexatious thing for an owner to find himself in such a position; and was almost an inexcusable mistake, most disastrous for many, whose long-drawn faces told the tale. "Miss Jummy's" owner accepted the situation more pleasantly than many would have done, though he not only lost the money he betted, but the stakes as well. He was a true sportsman and took the rough with the smooth, nevertheless, it was certainly one of the most unlucky days during his long racing career, which started in the middle of the sixties and ended in the nineties.

Perhaps his best year was 1883 when he won two dozen races value £12,530, which sum did not include events under the National Hunt Rules Steeplechasing.

When "Cortolvin" won the Grand National at Liverpool, I am under the impression Page was the jockey, and he received from the Duke a little present of £500. I cannot be certain it was for that particular race, but I am certain Page received £500 for one of the big races he rode in and won for his employer.

I can picture the Duke now in the Birdcage (the paddock) at Newmarket, with his full-blooded face surmounting a plentiful display of neck, with a low-cut blue shirt and more often than not a scarlet tie worn sailor-knot fashion.

He was at all times a conspicuous figure. His greatcoats were superb in their own line, being of a very coachy cut and graced by enormous buttons, which were specially made for him. Many people tried to copy these masterpieces of tailor's art and ducal taste, and I have known one or two tall slight figures look well in them, but they required a Duke or a costermonger to carry them off satisfactorily.

Once at Newmarket the Duke was having a few words with one of his commissioners about some betting transaction and was having the best of the argument. As the man turned to go he looked the Duke up and down critically and said, "Look here your Grace, a trip for to-morrow: I have just had a wire from town saying that Savernake is coming down (referring of course to the subsequent Marquess of Ailesbury, known as the coster-lord) so you be careful and keep out of the way, or he'll claim your coat and buttons!"

Custance was one of the Duke's favourite jockeys who when in 1894 he wrote his own reminiscences he presented a copy to his patron bearing this dedication:—

"To His Grace the Duke of Hamilton and Brandon, K. T., as some slight recognition of the many favours and kindnesses he has extended to me during my riding career I respectfully dedicate these pages."

As far as education was concerned Custance was quite at the top of the tree amongst his riding contemporaries. He wrote an excellent letter, and was full of humour and cheerfulness, while never forgetting himself or taking liberties.

This jockey had another admirer in Lord Chaplin, who considered him as good in the hunting field as he was on the flat. It was in consequence of his judgment in riding across a country that when the Prince of Wales (King Edward VII) was staying at Blankney, Lord Chaplin gave "Cussy," as his intimates called the jockey, the honoured post of piloting the Prince in the hunting field.

The Duke of Hamilton, knowing Custance's love for hunting, gave him a well-known old steeplechaser named "The Doctor," after the animal's racing career was finished, the price originally paid for this horse being £1200. I am under the impression that this clever and willing horse had his heart broken in a desperate finish between himself, ridden by Holman, and "The Colonel," ridden by Stevens, for the poor beast was never the same again, having been so severely treated that the Society for Prevention of Cruelty to Animals interfered, and there was a law court investigation. It ended in the case being dismissed, but it was never dismissed from "The Doctor's" mind, for ever after when in any way pressed in races he stopped and kicked furiously, revenging himself in that way.

Like many racehorses, his temper had been spoilt by his training, and when first he began to hunt on the horse Custance found him decidedly impetuous and queer tempered. Custance described the horse when first he entered his stable as "All stomach, a crib-biter, ewe-necked, and with a club foot which had a way of refusing to keep a shoe on." He was a perfect terror in the stable, and once when Custance decided the horse should have a dose of physic and everybody seemed shy of administering it, the jockey said the horse knew him and he would give the dose himself. Armed with the mixture, a step-ladder and a twitch he proceeded.

All went well as long as only linseed oil was tasted, but when aloes were recognised the horse would have no more of it and, in spite of his affection for Custance and the twitch on his nose, he sent the step-ladder flying and Custance with it, whilst the audience watching the operation fled in all directions. The horse romped round and round kicking windows, doors, partitions, everything in reach to smithereens, whilst his owner was kept a prisoner under the hay-trough until things quieted down a bit.

Captain Arthur Smith, who is still living, will remember this clever horse, one of the best over Leicestershire, where for six years he held his own in spite of being a roarer, crib-biter, weaver and club-footed. His end was sad. One day, when out with the Cottesmore, the Duchess of Hamilton told

Custance there was a lady out that day who had been heard to say she meant to cut her down, so she (the Duchess) wished Custance if on a good horse to give her a lead.   At the moment he did not happen to be on a particularly clever or fast mount, but said when his second horse arrived he would be able to comply with her wish.   The second horse happened to be "The Doctor," whom the Duchess knew well and was delighted to follow.

Coming to a fence where there were only a couple of places that could be got over, Mr. Henry Leatham jumped it first and his mount fell.   It was not a very formidable place, but had a drop of about six feet, yet there did not appear to be anything to put a horse down.

The Duchess called out to Custance, "Here is another place," but Mr. Leatham was now out of the way and it was too late.   "The Doctor" jumped the fence beautifully, but, like Mr. Leatham's horse, fell, and was unable to raise himself.   Assistance was sent for, but the gallant old horse had broken his shoulder, having landed with his club foot on the stump of a tree that had been felled and which was covered with fallen leaves, so, poor fellow, he had to be put out of his pain.   I hear that Custance gives an account of this game old horse in his book of reminiscences.

The Red Duke, as he was called on account of his red hair and reddish purple face, kept a pack of Harriers at Easton, and a stable full of horses with which he mounted many friends when staying with him. Amongst these horses was one named "Safe Coach" a sort of circus horse that knew his business so well that when out with the harriers and a hare was found knew at once what was expected of him. He preferred a rider who remained in the saddle and played the game, but failing that, would continue to hunt the hare by himself quite regardless of hounds.

Once a foreign guest, who came over to Easton from Baden-Baden to stay with the Duke, suggested he would like to see some sport with the harriers, but confessing he was not a great horseman was mounted on "Safe Coach." Hounds found quickly and away went this knowing animal, jumping neatly in and out of a deep lane. His mount just escaped embracing Mother Earth, and, abandoning the reins entirely, seized the horse's mane with one hand and the back of the saddle with the other sticking on like grim death, allowing "Safe Coach" to please himself entirely, much to the Duke's amusement, though the horse was a little too pressing at times and interfered somewhat with the sport.

The rider reached Easton again without any broken bones, but with a very poor opinion of "The Sport," and could never be persuaded to try again.

The late Lord Kesteven used to hunt with these harriers a good deal. He was a good horseman, if one can so describe a man with no hands, they being always gouty. He therefore had steel hooks fastened in his sleeves and straps across the reins to steer his useful and accommodating mount. Between them they managed to see a good deal of sport.

The Duke was certainly popular in the particular community to which he belonged, or which appropriated him. The community at times was a trifle exigent in demands on the goodwill and kindness of the Duke.

There was a sporting parson who, from the neighbourhood of Saxmundham, used to hunt with the Duke's harriers. Shortly before Christmas one year he was conspicuous by his absence, and the Duke noticing the parson was not out inquired where he was or what had happened to him. I told the Duke in confidence what the reason was, that he had been obliged to sell his only hunter to help a relation dying of cancer. The kind old man said, "Dear, dear, we must see about that." When Christmas arrived the postman delivered a letter at the Rectory bearing a London post-mark and containing two hundred pounds in bank-notes, and printed on a card, "Wishing you a happy Christmas, from an old friend and fellow-sportsman."

A little later a mare was sent over to the parson with a note, asking him if he would be good enough to give her a little work as she, past her best, was too good to shoot, but might perhaps do a couple of days a week with hounds.

I think it gave the Duke sincere pleasure to help those less well off than himself, and all his kind actions were carried out in a careless, breezy sort of way, leaving no painful sense of obligation.

No Englishman that I have ever met spoke French as well as the Duke of Hamilton. It was a pleasure to listen to him, not only was he idiomatically correct, but his accent perfect. He had spent a good deal of the early part of his life in France, which no doubt accounts for this to some extent. Mr. Labouchere thought his own accent quite as good, but he made a mistake!

The Duke also knew how to suit himself to his company as well as anybody I ever met. From his "live and let live" principles, and the way he liked everybody to please themselves, it came as a surprise to those who did not know him very well to find what a strict Scotch sabbatarian he was. Even when out at sea on his yacht, where no person's susceptibilities were likely to be hurt, he would not allow his piano to be touched on Sunday until after midnight except for hymn tunes. Even Mozart and Haydn were tabooed.

In my humble opinion the Duke was badly treated by the world, his faults were those of an unusually warm-hearted, generous schoolboy, absolutely straightforward and honourable. Yet certain saintly people who were quite possibly less straight themselves considered it their duty to blackball him at a well-known high and mighty club.

One or two people I could name loved him much, a certain egotistical young genius named Marie Bashkertseff for one, and she describes the manner thereof in her published diaries, price one franc fifty centimes.

Some years ago there was in the west-country a certain pack of hounds that hunted carted deer. Their master used to provide entertainment for his followers after the same fashion as Mr. Carnaby Forster. On one occasion he became embroiled in a heated argument with a farmer, but a small brook in flood unfortunately separated the two. Vengeance was not to be delayed by such a small thing. The Master plunged boldly in, crossed and veritably annihilated the farmer, and then waded back again. As soon as he had cooled down a little and recovered from the glow of having added another scalp to his collection he became conscious of the fact that his boots were full of water, so the affair came to a suitable conclusion by the Master standing on his head, supported by his whip on one side and second horseman on the other, until the water drained out.

While this took place he was surrounded by a silent admiring circle of followers.

In his calmer moments the Master was a delightful companion, witty and amusing. He is still alive and flourishing, I am glad to say.

He was once seen thrashing his motor because it would not start!

On another occasion when out hunting he saw a number of his field galloping off without waiting to shut a gate after them, he shouted at the top of his voice, and it was a fairly strong one, "Here you"—

something, something! "Come back and shut that gate—you . . .! . . . !! . . . !!! fellows come out with my hounds knowing nothing more of farming than wooden images and caring less, leaving gates open behind you so that the farmer's stock will get out, you . . . ! . . . !!"

Here the culprit tried to speak, but was overwhelmed.

"Holl your tongue, I *won't* have it, I tell you. Go back and shut that gate instantly." The culprit in a timid voice, "But it's my gate and I want it open!"

Here the Master's early training as a barrister came to his rescue, and he replied, without any outward signs or discomfiture, "that does not alter the principle of the thing in the least," and rode on.

I feel as if I could go on writing indefinitely about masters of hounds, but I will only mention one more. He is a dear little man who lives in Wales, hunts his own hounds and is well known to everyone who buys or sells them, as he loves a deal above all things. Although a particularly cheerful and most entertaining individual, he was very fussy about his health, being frequently convinced that he was dying. At a meet it was a mark of high esteem to be invited to peer down his throat and see for oneself how inflamed his tonsils were. His faithful whipper-in, named Davis, was long past being surprised at anything; he surveyed the world with the most impassive face I have ever seen.

One day in the middle of a run, hounds had

pushed their fox through a covert and were making for a particularly fine line of country when the Master was seen to be staring at a pocket-handkerchief he was holding in his hand. "Davis, Davis," he cried passionately and almost tearfully, "stop them, whip them off; I am going home, my nose is bleeding!"

One meets with tragedy as well as comedy in the hunting-field sometimes. I remember a very sporting little man who rode a good deal in steeplechases and point-to-points, who lived on the outskirts of a harrier country which my son was hunting with his own hounds at the time of which I am writing. The little man was well known and popular throughout the country, but no one knew anything about his home life. One day he suggested to my son that the harriers should draw his land, as it held a few hares, though being so far off was never hunted. Accordingly a meet in this new country was arranged. A hare was found and a good day's sport resulted.

Suddenly while drawing a root field, the figure of a tall wild-looking woman sprang into a bank at the side of the field and began raving and abusing the Master, his hounds and the members of the field in a torrent of most fluent adjectives. She told them passionately to be off and tongue-lashed everybody singly and collectively.

A horror-stricken silence fell, nobody knew quite what to do. The Master hurriedly took the pack away to draw somewhere else and said to the owner of the land at whose instigation he had come, "I fear someone does not like us very much, perhaps we had better move off elsewhere?"   "Don't take any notice," replied the poor little man sadly, "that is my wife, she has been raving mad for years and at times breaks away from those who take care of her."

I do not think there was anyone on the field who, before that day, had the slightest idea he even had a wife. For a thoroughly unromantic and therefore doubly real little tragedy, I think that would be hard to beat.

If Jorrock's calculation that fox-hunting represents the excitement but only twenty-five per cent of the danger of war is correct, there can be only about one per cent, or even less, of its danger in otter-hunting, indeed it would be hard to imagine anything much safer than the otter-hunter's majestic promenade through sun-kissed hay fields, bordering some babbling brook, unless we take sunstroke into our calculations.

But I remember once strolling along in just such a hay field talking to a ponderous and stately London solicitor who had come out for a day's sport as he was staying in a village close by.

In the midst of our conversation a hound came casting along the bank and ran between the solicitor's legs. Down went the poor fat man and broke his collar-bone!

After this he no longer considered otter-hunting a safe or suitable pursuit.

CHAPTER V

MOST of the theatrical people I have known have been bright and amusing. I think Mr. Corney Grain interested me the most, though he could hardly be called theatrical. He appeared certainly for many years with the German Reeds at St. George's Hall, Langham Place, but I suppose it would be more correct to call him a "high-class society entertainer!" I often speculated on how so hyper-sensitive a man could have chosen such a rôle, one bound often to irritate and hurt his feelings.

When recounting to me some of the stories he often told against himself, and which many people of that date will remember, I asked him why he de-

serted the Bar for society entertaining? He replied the latter appeared to him the "most amusing,
least sweat, and what Providence intended me to
be," adding, "It would be such a waste of material
for such a huge funny-looking man not to do tricks,
so little being necessary on top of my natural appearance to amuse the public."

For the benefit of the rising generation, who may
not remember much about Mr. Grain, I had better
explain that the unusual appearance he referred to
consisted in his size,—not only was he very tall but
he had immense depth beyond the ribs as his sporting friends would say, a big nose, fair and rather
curly hair, a very pale complexion and big blue
rather prominent eyes. His feet were a trial to
him, he said, they were always in the way.

Amongst the stories he was fond of telling were
the following: He was engaged to perform at a
house in South Kensington during an afternoon
gathering, a sort of bun struggle. Arriving as
usual in a humble four-wheeler and alighting at the
front door he was told by a gorgeous footman that
he had come to the wrong entrance, and was then
shown into the servants' hall and given a glass of
beer to amuse him until his presence was required
in the drawing-room, the servants evidently regarding him at least one degree below the chimney
sweep!

At another entertainment, this time in Queen's
Gate, while standing in the drawing-room awaiting
his turn to be funny, he entered into polite con-

versation with the son of the house, lately home from Eton. First he tried cricket, then football, to which the youth seemed quite cold, so at last Mr. Grain said, "What a charming piano you have." The youth shifted from one leg to the other, closed his eyes, and said, "Oh, it's a rotten old thing, but mother said it was good enough for you to thump on; she had the best one moved out of the room!"

Mr. Grain used to tell these stories with a great show of amusement, but it was perfectly plain that they hurt his feelings.

Dick Grain, as his intimates used to call him, was of gentle birth and well mannered (the two do not always go together), and an entertainer of the highest order. An emancipated schoolgirl once remarked, "His show is one that is quite safe to take one's mother to see!"

His brother, the well-known veteran barrister, died while I have been writing this book; he had a large practice, was full of humour, and told capital stories of himself and others, while he was never tired of talking about his brother Dick, to whom he was much attached and whose abilities he admired and appreciated.

Dick Grain's barrister brother was legal adviser to the Licensed Victualler's Board and Association. Endless jokes were poked at the legal adviser by his brother Dick.

Once when dining in De Vere Gardens with some friends, Mr. Corney Grain, the entertainer, sat on one side of me and Commander Beaumont (I for-

Mr. Corney Grain

get his ship) on the other. Mrs. George Harvey, who was staying with me at the time, was there too, she was related to our host and hostess. During a slight pause in the conversation she said that she would like to run away with a certain lamp-shade in the room which she greatly admired; also that she wished some of the beautiful old-fashioned spoons and forks were hers. We thought no more of this until the time came for our departure and we proceeded to get into the brougham, only to find all available space taken up by the lamp-shade and family silver.

This was the result of Mr. Grain and Captain Beaumont's mischief in consultation with our host! We had to wait some time to have it all returned to its proper place before we could enter the carriage for home.

All these cheery people have long ago joined the great majority except Mrs. George Harvey.

Captain Beaumont was a little lame, the result of an accident at one of Captain Eyre Shaw's afternoons in Southwark Bridge Road. If I remember rightly these were held every other Thursday when Captain Shaw and his pleasant wife (who was I believe Portuguese or, at any rate, very foreign-looking), entertained their friends and let them see the fire-brigade drill and effect rescues from top-story windows, people shot down fire-escapes and so forth. It was on one of these occasions, after the show was really concluded, that Captain Beaumont (a brother of the late Lady Swansea) thought he would show a small and admiring circle of friends what he could do, how accustomed he was to climbing great heights on rope ladders and so on while at sea.

He therefore lashed a couple of ladders together while his host and the majority of his friends were having tea in the house; the picturesque lashing concluded, the ladder was placed against a high window and Captain Beaumont swarmed up it with cat-like rapidity, unfortunately the lashing was more picturesque than trustworthy, and when nearing the top it collapsed; the poor man falling with a crash at the feet of his scared friends.

The result of this little attempt to entertain those present, and perhaps do a little show-off, resulted in his being slightly lame for the rest of his life.

At the time we saw most of Mr. Grain his rooms were in Bond Street over a shop—I think it was a jeweller's—many delightful afternoons have we spent in that "upper part," as the house agents would describe it, with Mr. Grain and his piano.

The drawing-room was large and lofty, looking on to Atkinson's "Smell shop," as he used to call the large scent shop at the corner of Bond Street and Burlington Gardens. The furniture of the room consisted chiefly of a grand piano and a "grand sofa," he said there was not room for much else when he was there. Oh yes! there was a music stool described by its owner as a "weight-carrier." Poor man, he lived a little too soon, when I think of the miserable sums he was paid for his most clever, amusing and always in good taste performances compared with those paid to-day, say, for instance to George Robey or other funny men of the moment.

I know at times Mr. Grain said he could not afford cabs to carry him to keep his engagements so was obliged to sally forth in enormous galoshes and umbrella, either on foot or by omnibus. Ten pounds was a very average sum paid to him for his services, afternoon or evening; I told him it was his own fault, he should raise his price, but he was too shy to do this, and said he felt he ought to ask less as he knew he grew less funny and would hate to be told so, he therefore preferred to jog along on the old lines. He really was quite extraordinarily shy and sensitive. A kind friend and bitter foe.

It had been arranged one year that he should join our party at Henley and lunch with us in the Isthmian Club tent; we were to be a party of eight, counting Mr. Grain. When the morning for our jaunt arrived there was a heavy shower, but not enough to prevent our going.

Just before we started a note and large brown-paper parcel was brought to me. On opening the missive I found Mr. Grain was "desolate" at being deprived of the pleasure of joining our party, but some oysters he had eaten the night before had "Gone the wrong way!" and he was not well enough to appear; as it was so wet he was sending one of his private canoes for my use, this turned out to be one of his enormous galoshes done up in the brown-paper parcel. He hoped while we were enjoying ourselves canoeing about in it we would think kindly of the suffering owner.

My young brother, who was one of the party, insisted on filling the galosh with lobster salad, strawberry ices and such delicacies, and sending it back in the evening with many kind enquiries and hopes that by then the sufferer would be able to enjoy some of the Isthmian luncheon which had been put on one side for him.

Much to our friend's annoyance he was dragged as a witness into the Labouchere-Lawson Case, which was the outcome of a row between those gentlemen outside the Beef Steak Club in September, 1879. Having been subpœnaed, Mr. Grain was bound to appear.

As it all happened so long ago, it may be well to recall the cause of the fracas.

Mr. Labouchere, the brilliant editor of *Truth,* had for some years been saying unkind things of Mr. Edward Lawson (whose original name was Levy, to which in accordance to his uncle's wish had been added Lawson, and who later became Lord Burnham and proprietor of *The Daily Telegraph*) holding him and his family up to ridicule both in *Truth* and the *World,* calling Mr. Lawson a disgrace to journalism, etc.

Both were members of the Beef Steak Club.

At last Mr. Lawson could stand it no longer and waiting outside the club for "Labby" gave him a whack on the head with his cane; he at once wished to fight a duel in Belgium, but this was declined by Mr. Lawson because he said he only fought gentlemen and he did not consider Mr. Labouchere was one. After this an abusive letter dated October 1st was sent by Labby to Mr. Lawson and the former also published it. This led to an action for libel brought by Mr. Lawson and was heard before Mr. Justice Coleridge and a special jury in March, 1881.

After a protracted trial in which Mr. Labouchere conducted his own case and cross-examined Mr. Lawson on the Eastern question and some political topics that had appeared in *The Daily Telegraph,* the jury were unable to agree on a verdict, being, I believe, almost equally divided, so they were dismissed and the matter ended for the time being, after eight days had been wasted on the trial.

The case caused a great deal of excitement and party feeling at the time. Mr. Labouchere was turned out of the Beef Steak Club, but brought an action against that club which he won, so he remained a member, but I should imagine not altogether a comfortable one.

Poor Mr. Grain had a certain amount of fun poked at him by judge and jury as to his profession, the learned judge, if I am correctly informed, pretending he did not know who Mr. Grain was and apologising for his ignorance.

Mr. Labouchere was at his best in his own home, an excellent, though at times alarming host, for

he was as full of pranks and jokes as a schoolboy. Once Sir Willoughby Maycock was dining
with him and his wife at Pope's Villa near Twick-
enham, the only other guest being old Mr. Maxwell
and his wife, the latter best known as Miss Braddon the authoress. After dinner Labby conducted
the gentlemen to the cloak room to wash their
hands, whispering to Sir Willoughby to hurry up
as he wanted to lock old Maxwell in as he was
rather an old bore; Sir Willoughby having "hur-
ried up" the key was quietly turned in the door.

At that time Miss Braddon was writing a book
about Paris during the siege, where Mr. Labouchere had been *The Daily News* correspondent
(and afterwards brought out an amusing book
over which I laughed at his account of endeavoring
to cook a portion of elephant over a spirit stove!)
Having locked in her husband, Labby calmly sat
down and helped Miss Braddon for about twenty
minutes with material for her book. Sir Willoughby meanwhile sat twiddling his thumbs in an
agony of mind, wondering what on earth would
happen; when a distant thumping was heard,
which, of course, came from the unhappy man in
the cloak-room.

"I wonder where Mr. Maxwell can have got
to," said Labby in a most innocent manner. "I'll
go and see."

Presently he returned with the poor old boy looking very cross, suspecting it was the result of one
of Mr. Labouchere's pranks, though of course he

was told the door had a tiresome habit of sticking at times, and how dreadfully concerned his host was! Labby was a magnificent humbug.

Once I asked him why he chose the name *Truth* for his paper, and said that was the last thing anybody wished to be told. He replied, "Quite so, about themselves but not of other people!"

I remember some impromptu tableaux got up one evening after dinner at our house. Mr. Augustus Harris impersonated the Prince of Wales (King Edward VII), and most wonderfully he did it. Mr. Corney Grain appeared as "Rags and Chatters" with his coat inside out showing very torn silk linings to the sleeves. After this they had a court-martial on Baron Halkett for having shaved off his moustache without Royal sanction. It must be explained that the Baron was a civilian, and had always been, we thought, extremely proud of his beautiful waxed moustache which stuck out dangerously at each side in fine stiff points. One day a girl made a bet he would not shave it off, he was too much attached to it. Behold next day he appeared without it. We hardly knew him. He was therefore court-martialed after dinner, no one being more amused than himself.

The Duke of Cambridge was presiding in the person of Mr. Augustus Harris, most wonderfully got up on the spur of the moment with a heavy grey moustache made of portions of a goatskin mat, ruthlessly cut off corners, where I was told it would never be missed, and stuck on with melted wax

candle.   Mr. Corney Grain prosecuted and Mr.
Joseph Chamberlain defended.

The amount of fun and nonsense they managed
to cram into half an hour was amazing. Mr. Grain
with puckered brow explained how pained he was
at having to prosecute his old friend for such a
heinous offence, "Not from a sudden temptation
but a premeditated crime, all for filthy lucre!" Mr.
Chamberlain with eye-glass screwed firmly into his
eye and nose looking more aggressive than ever,
patted one finger emphatically in the palm of the
other hand while he held forth on "The heroism of
the accused who had so recently parted with so dear
and close a companion that he had reared and
watched over with loving care from its infancy
until it reached three kilometers in length!" Shaking his finger angrily at the prosecutor he continued, "And why has he done this thing, gentlemen? I will tell you," here he paused dramatically,
"because after seriously mutilating the optic of a
perfectly innocent girl with his moustache while
she was walking peacefully down the Haymarket,
he came to the conclusion that his hirsute decoration was a danger to the public, and when I tell you
that the Baron will probably have to provide and
pay rent on a new eye for the young lady, may even
possibly have to keep her for the rest of his life, you
will agree with me that he has suffered enough
without the *most unjust and indecent*, yes, I say it
again, *indecent* accusation from my learned friend

opposite (Corney Grain) that the motive was for 'filthy lucre!' "

This is nearly word for word as I can remember it. The accused tried at intervals to have a voice in the matter, but was hastily thrust into a chair and told to leave the case in his (Mr. Chamberlain's) experienced hands and trust to his skill.

Then came the summing up of Mr. Augustus Harris, who with trembling voice said it was his painful duty—here he burst into tears and kept a large antimacassar he had seized off the end of the sofa to his eyes, while with the disengaged hand he produced from somewhere a black (lace) cap, borrowed from my old housekeeper, and with this hanging jauntily on one side of his sparsely covered pate condemned the miserable culprit, who had "Received so patient and fair a trial," to be taken hence and hanged till he be black in the face.

It then became the duty of the prosecutor to remove the protesting prisoner. Mr. Chamberlain fought valiantly for his client.

Mr. F. A. Inderwick, Q.C., who was also present, said if he had not seen it with his own eyes and heard it with his own ears he would never have believed Mr. Joseph Chamberlain would have so unbent, or indeed that he could have done so.

By the way, I often wondered why Mr. Inderwick was not made a judge. I think he was a little pained about it. He was certainly popular with both judges and clients and he had a pleasant voice and manner. He affirmed most modestly that his success was due to Messrs. Lewis and Lewis of Ely Place. But I have run away from my story.

It was all very silly and very funny, but refreshing to see great men frolicking, for they were great men in their several ways.

Take Mr. Corney Grain first. He certainly was great in his own line. It must be grand to be able to cheer and amuse crowds of people day after day, sending them home refreshed, with some of the cobwebs swept away by hearty laughter.

Then Mr. Augustus Harris, afterwards Sir Augustus Harris, who would dare say he was not a great man? How many have trembled in their shoes awaiting his verdict of "To be or not to be" when their plays have been offered for his acceptance, or their legs were under his consideration with a view to dancing, while the theatrical autocrat smiled that comfortable smile that seemed to say, "I have dined well and feel very happy," though at times he acknowledged he went to sleep while authors' great productions were being read to him, declaring he knew all about them nevertheless.

This great Drury Lane man, "Druriolanus," as some folk used to call him, tried to persuade me in 1889 to go on the stage. I assured him I should never be able to remember my part, and if I did' I should render it differently each day according to my mood and never give the right cue. He said none of that would matter, he would give me a walking on part, but what he particularly wanted

Mr. Inderwick, Q.C.

me to undertake was the part of Lydia Languish in
"The Rivals." At last he gave me up in despair.
If I had known him well enough I should have
liked to point out to him how his waistcoats troubled
me and to suggest his having them cut with a deep
point instead of round, it would have reduced his
barrel-like appearance, and I did not like the braid
trimming on them, but I did like his gardenias,
without one of which I seldom saw him.

He loved colour and had an artist's eye. He
designed several dresses he wished me to have made
and wear. They were really very striking, but a
little too "voyant" for me with the exception of
one ball dress in "sunset-coloured satin" he called
it, draped in grey tulle. I called it flame colour.
That dress did great execution, so much so that
when wearing it at the Wellington Club one night
before going on to a dance, I was asked by an
elderly gentleman in high favour amongst Royalties if I would try and wean a certain Princeling's
affections from an Irish girl to whom he was paying too marked attention.

I agreed to do my very best and threw myself
heart and soul into the task with such success (no
doubt owing to the flame-coloured dress designed
by Mr. Harris) that I had to call fervently for
someone else to be sent to act as counter-irritant
mustard-blister fashion, for I was fairly entangled
myself—I have never felt quite sure I did not miss
the opportunity of my life on that occasion, but
perhaps my humble rôle suits me best. I would

rather be a free mouse and roam where I like than a lioness in a gilded cage.

In his youth I believe Mr. Harris travelled for some big silk merchants; he became a great man, I always think, through his firm belief in himself. I am afraid I must allow he was conceited, but a man who has practically made himself surely has some right to be. The day he became Key Holder of the Grand Lodge of Masonry, or whatever it is termed (for I know very little about the correct terms and sayings of the craft) was one of exultation and triumph, and when decked out in Civic costume as one of the sheriffs of the City of London he was indeed proud and happy.

One day when driving in the demi-state sort of carriage allowed to Sheriffs of the City during their term of office, he was sitting well forward so that all might see and admire, when it so happened he passed two friends walking. One, I think, was a little jealous of him and said to his companion, "Bless my soul! do look at that man, I'll take a hundred pounds to a shilling one day he is King of England!"

"Give me your shilling," the friend replied. Weeks and months rolled by and no further mention was made of the bet: but one morning there appeared in *The Daily Telegraph* an announcement that "Sir Augustus Harris arrived last night at Windsor Castle, and has taken possession of the Waterloo Chamber." This was cut out and forwarded to the man who had accepted the shilling

Sir Augustus Harris

and written underneath it, "You know your bet, I told you at the time you were a fool to lay me such odds. After reading this surely you want to hedge or give me my shilling back."

Of course the true story was the Drury Lane proprietor had arrived at the Castle with his stage manager to give a performance there which had been commanded by the Queen (Victoria). I rather think Sir Augustus Harris was the first of the Drury Lane people to be honoured with a Royal command.

The knighthood was conferred on him for his civic connection with the City of London. I do not think we had any theatrical knights until King Edward VII came to the throne and placed the sword over Sir Henry Irving. The year Sir Augustus Harris was Sheriff was voted the best Lord Mayor's show ever seen.

I am under the impression, but by no means sure, that Sir Augustus was one of the original members of the Savage Club when it was started in a saw-dusty sort of back-parlour in the neighborhood of Drury Lane.

Those were days when the best actors, or perhaps I should say the most exalted, frequented what some called "pubs," others "taverns": there were no clubs such as the present generation have to shelter them.

The Garrick then stood out alone, with its own sacred precincts and halo which few could surpass or assume.

When speaking of this time at the Garrick a friend once said to me, "Actors have great pride, swank, jealousy, envy and malice, perhaps unknown to any other profession." Possibly that is so.

Sir Augustus worked very hard at anything he undertook, sparing neither money nor trouble in staging his plays well. He was wise enough to get experts to criticise at his rehearsals when putting on anything requiring precise detail. A friend of mine once saved him from making a mistake that would have been an everlasting source of regret and annoyance to him. Sir Augustus was about to produce a great racing drama and asked my friend, who was a great racing man, if he would go to the final dress-rehearsal and tell him if all the details were quite correct and to be good enough to criticise severely.

It is well his advice was sought, for there was a weighing-room scene in which many details were ludicrously wrong. When the performance was over and Sir Augustus asked if all were correct and it was pointed out to him that it was not correct for jockeys to be weighing themselves out without either trainer or owner being present, while the clerk of the scales, who was mounted on a very high stool in front of a desk like a schoolmaster, should be sitting at a writing-table close beside the scales with a notebook in which he should be entering the details.

But for this kindly criticism at the eleventh hour

the scene might have shared the fate of Artemus Ward's famous panorama when presented to the audience for their admiration and they forcibly explained they did not think much of moonlight scenes without a moon, which had unfortunately been forgotten. In consequence some rude members of the audience threw chairs and ginger-beer bottles at the moonlit but moonless scene.

Sir Augustus soon corrected his mistakes and all went well, the play having a great success.

Theatrical people live in a world entirely their own, it is a wonderful life behind the scenes. One of the chorus girls at Drury Lane once said when at work she earned two pounds a week, but often had nothing to take at the end of it, as her fines for being late or for non-attendance often mounted to more than her salary. She hailed from the Antipodes and said that when there she was known as the Australian prima donna, but at Drury Lane she never got beyond the chorus and payment on her part for non-attendance.

Naturally prima donna airs would not go down in the chorus.

Sir Augustus' sarcasms were at times biting, but he was a staunch friend, and when Oscar Wilde was in trouble he was one of the first to appear to stand bail for his friend. In consequence of this kindly act he had the annoyance of seeing in the papers the following morning that one of Mr. Wilde's greatest friends, Sir Augustus Harris, appeared to go bail for him. Poor Gus, as I have heard his friends call him, was mad with rage and some one described him to me as rushing about foaming at the mouth, and with the wings of his Inverness cape flying out behind him like some big angry bird.

Now I have come to the great Joseph Chamberlain, who looked out upon the world in amused complacency, no matter how heated people became in argument with him. The past held no attractions for him, the future was always before him written large across his brain. I think few people have had so many friends, quarrelled with them so often, and made it up again as the great "Joe." With Sir William Harcourt, for instance, Mr. Morley, Count von Bulow, even at one time with the Duke of Devonshire, with whom he served in both Liberal and Unionist Cabinets (the former from 1880 to 1885, the latter 1895 to 1903). I am sorry to say there were times when he was not always very courteous to those who differed with him in politics, being rather intolerant. Only his own particular views *could* be right.

Again, few men have played so many parts as the almost self-educated business man from Birmingham, and few men have had such an aggravating manner at times; he seemed able to sting people into frenzy while keeping perfectly cool himself. He loved argument and was an agreeable conversationalist, at least so I thought, but of course I bowed before his superior wisdom.

We all know that what he denounced with fervour at one time he pleaded with vigour at another; personally I see nothing wrong or perfidious in a man changing his opinions, rather do I think it a sign of a strong character to have the pluck to stand up and say, "I have changed my mind," in a world where the one immutable law is change. We must realise that what was true once need not be true always, and circumstances alter cases.

That he was a wrecker of two parties has often been quoted against Joseph Chamberlain, but there again I see something to admire, it surely proved party feeling had nothing to do with his line of conduct, but the good of his country, progress, and the bettering of the lives of the working classes. He cared not which side he belonged to so long as he was at one with them on these points. He was a man with the instinct of politics; his hobby was the House of Commons, which however he often defied.

I remember Mr. Chamberlain prophesying years ago the coming of the paid professional politician, and now they are here. There is no doubt he got on his colleagues' nerves at times, and once Mr. Balfour in well-chosen words reproved him, saying that he (Mr. Chamberlain) remembered too much that they belonged to different parties, but seemed to forget that they belonged to the same country.

Mr. Chamberlain was fond of children, and told me he was glad his bairns had not been as tiresome as he was when a youth, confessing he had been very troublesome, keeping his people in an agony of mind as to what he would do next.

I do not know if the following story was of a member of his own family, but it is one he was fond of telling. It was of a child with a thirst for knowledge who kept asking his mother theological and natural history posers. First he wished to know who made flies? then, who made grown-up people? and so on. To each question the child's mother replied, "God did; He made everything." There was a pause, presently the child said, "Does God make rice pudding?" Fairly driven into a corner his mother replied, "Yes." "Then I wish He would eat it," replied this precocious little person.

Once long ago when Mr. Chamberlain and I were choosing children's Christmas presents in Rose's toy shop in Sloane Street, I noticed that nothing attracted his attention but mechanical toys; he walked about winding up everything he could find, from jumping frogs to "puffer-trains," until he so seriously over-wound an engine that after a false start it declined any further action. I was interested to see what he would do, especially as an elderly spinster belonging to the shop was watching his proceedings. He said, "I should like to have bought this thing, but it won't work!" "Indeed, sir," from the attendant in accents of surprise (having witnessed the trial trip), "I have another just like it." Mr. Chamberlain then said, "Oh, I'll buy this one if you'll put it right," and so the matter ended. Having already collected a large pile of things he wished to buy for various children, some for little Dudleys, some for little sick folk in Birmingham, I suppose to over-wind one engine was looked upon as of no consequence. I noticed he did not ask the price of anything, though he examined them carefully all over before deciding, so perhaps he could read some of the hieroglyphics with which everything was marked, but which was double Dutch to me. Happy thought! perhaps the toys had come originally from Birmingham where the hieroglyphics had been invented.

I think Mr. Chamberlain's most charming attribute was his devotion to his family, he simply adored them and they him; it was very picturesque and real. This devotion was illustrated clearly when Mr. Austen Chamberlain made his first Budget speech. The strain on his father was acute, and when the youthful orator struck an attitude and also unhappily the inkstand which at once responded by emptying itself on his notes, the lion-hearted father had to put his hand over his eyes, where it remained until the oration had been brought more or less happily to its finale!

Many people will remember the dainty dancing of Letty Lind and her little pipe of a voice singing something about "Oh! Marguerite, I love thee and adore thee." I happened to know a good deal of her history; she was an engaging little person, not pretty but with a natural gentle and pleasing manner.

I was one day in a bonnet shop of one of the

fashionable ladies who were running millinery establishments, when Lettie Lind came in carrying a large canvas bag. "I have just got my wages and came to pay my bill," she said. "Help yourselves" (throwing it on the sofa), "but don't take it all, there are several others anxiously waiting for some of it." While one of the assistants helped herself, that is to say, looked up what was owing and took the amount and wrote out a receipt, Letty Lind tried on a variety of head gear, saying, "I want something very quiet or my young man won't take me out with him," and she put her head on one side with a merry little laugh, for we knew all about it. When the receipt was handed to her, she said, "Shove it into the bag, please, and tie it up, will you?" Having selected all she required and sought my advice as to what would be most suitable, she picked up her money bag and with a cheery nod to us all walked out, never having counted what was left of her wages, or troubled about the matter in the smallest degree.

Marion Hood was another "Gaiety-girl," much admired by a masculine member of my family who asked me if I would let him bring her to see me. He wanted me to know how really nice she was, and that her beautiful golden hair was "not painted!" This struck me as a trifle original. Her voice also was not a strong one, very different from the voices of Violet Cameron and Florence St. John, but Marion Hood was certainly pretty.

Those responsible for my bringing up thought

actors and actresses improper people. Not until I was married did I have the pleasure of seeing any play other than Shakespearian. A ballet I had never seen, the very word made my mother's face lengthen, while my father shook his head, his eyes twinkling as he laughed happily to himself at the memories the word recalled. In his young days he was a great deal in town and, being both handsome and witty, was made a good deal of, seeing life in all its phases.

It must have been somewhere about 1880 that I saw my first ballet at the Alhambra. I was prepared for shocking sights, I did not quite know what, but felt very advanced and delightfully wicked. What I really saw was a stage full of darling little children dressed in nightgowns which they held daintily up here and there, just enough to show pretty little pink toes and ankles while they danced about with white puffs in their hands, puffing their own and each other's faces and necks.

It was one of the prettiest scenes I can remember, and the children looked as if they enjoyed it almost as much as we did. Then I remember what I believe is unusual, namely the ballet mistress being called for, and a grumpy-looking woman in a black dress with a little cane in her hand came and made stiff little bows to us. I daresay she was feeling very pleased at the success of her teaching, but I think she was possibly one of those people who find it painful to smile, and after all what did it matter so long as she was pleased in her heart, which I hope she was.

After this I was quite determined to see more of life and the things supposed to be so wicked. I told my husband I wanted to go to the celebrated Evans' at Covent Garden, which I understood was a frisky and reprehensible club, being quite prepared to see again some lovely show perhaps after the fashion of the ballet.

My husband, after much persuasion, promised to take me if I would wear many thick veils, as he said he would not like anybody to recognise me, so tied up in gauze veils I went and we sat in a box, which I found exceedingly dull and uninteresting. We came away again having seen nothing more wicked than a few dull-looking people walking about talking to one another and drinking coffee, etc., while a band played.

But I was in good company at any rate, for the Prince of Wales was in the box next to us with Lady Molesworth (widow of Sir William Molesworth of Pencarrow), who had at one time trundled an organ through the streets of London, before Mr. Temple Weston met and married her. She married again, Sir William Molesworth being her second husband. She was a fascinating woman and became most popular with Kings and Queens.

It was really rather disappointing that the wicked world I had heard so much about should be so tame, and came to the conclusion people must have unpleasant minds if they saw harm in such pretty things as ballets and such dull things as Evans's Club, which is now no more. I soon found the dances and tragedies being played around me daily were much more surprising than anything I could find on the stage.

It has always been rather on my conscience having brought up to town one season a young and unsophisticated butler unversed in the ways of the world. My sister and I were renting a house in Cadogan Place for a few months from a very pretty widow. It was not long before we had misgivings as to the wisdom of having brought up the young man, as he displayed so much concern and appeared so shocked at anything to which he was unaccustomed.

One day he came with a white scared face and presented us with a blue document which he said a rude man had shoved into his hand at the front door and then ran away. He did not know what to do and sought our advice. On examination it proved to be a writ for the payment of a tombstone for our landlady's husband who had been dead some eight years.

Never having seen anything of the kind before he was greatly moved and distressed, being convinced he was going to be thrown into prison for debt. It was most unjust and he did not think much of London ways!

CHAPTER VI

I T may be supposed that all my remembrances are of a frivolous order, far from it. I have been entrusted with some desperately tragic secrets, which are still locked up in my memory amongst other negatives turned with their faces to the wall, which will go down to the grave with me still locked up and with their faces to the wall. I have witnessed heart-breaking scenes and taken part in a drama or two, but I am trying to avoid anything sad in this book, for surely the world is sad enough at present without my pen piling on the agony—as indeed it could if I were to write of all I remember.

But there is one case I feel I must refer to, which caused a tremendous sensation in the early eighties.

It seemed to interest the whole civilised world, special editions of certain newspapers came out with nothing else but news of the case; yet when I asked a number of people to help me to remember certain dates in connection with it, nobody remembered anything about the tragedy. A few certainly allowed that they thought they did dimly remember hearing of it; one to whom I referred being a distinguished journalist, whom one expected would be certain to remember the affair minutely.

I refer to the Langworthy case. Sensational trials are apparently very short lived in the public memory. Perhaps because they seldom have historical significance, although so full of human interest. The Tichborne trial seems to be one of the few exceptions, for it is still a name if nothing more, although at the time sons quarrelled with fathers and homes were divided against themselves in the fury of partisanship, almost comparable with that in American homes during the Civil War.

The Langworthy case was remarkable chiefly as a record of villainy that to my mind seems almost unique, and leaves one dumbly wondering at the dark possibilities of cruelty that lie in the human heart.

It also shows the apparently anomalous case of a woman who first obtained a decree nisi with £1500 a year alimony from the Courts and subsequently £20,000 for breach of promise of marriage against the same man. The law is a wonderful institution.

The way I came to know so much about the case

was through being asked by Dr. Godson, the great ladies' doctor of those days, if I would go and see a patient of his who was in great trouble and ill-health as well as practically penniless.

Of course I went, and from Mrs. Langworthy's own lips heard her pitiful story, which as it appears to have been entirely forgotton, I relate briefly.

The Mrs. Langworthy of the case had been a Miss Long, the daughter of well-to-do people in Ireland, her father being estate agent at one time to the Marquess of Downshire and later to Lord O'Neile.

She was a tall, handsome girl and gifted, as was proved by her passing in 1873 as one of the senior candidates at the Dublin University, taking honours in French, Latin, Euclid and Algebra.

Her composition on English literature was chosen as good enough to be read aloud by Professor Dowden. Fired with her success she then went to Cambridge, where she shone in Latin, Divinity, etc.

About this time her father lost most of his money, and Miss Long decided she would cost him nothing more and went out as governess. During a visit to Paris with her brother, who was staying at that comfortable old-fashioned Hotel Bedford, she met the man who was to ruin her life, namely, the exceedingly rich and not ill-looking Mr. Langworthy, with great estates in South America, a magnificently appointed yacht, French chef and all the luxuries and comforts which usually surround men with large fortunes. At the time he became enamoured of Miss Long he was a widower. His first wife, Lady Alice, sister of the second or third Earl of Limerick, died at sea in 1876, under what circumstances I do not know.

Mr. Langworthy proved a devoted if somewhat dictatorial lover, and an engagement quickly followed on their first meeting, but Miss Long was told under no circumstances must his mother know anything about it as she might disinherit him; the engagement must be a secret.

During this time he persuaded Miss Long to go for a little cruise in his yacht, having provided a suitable ballast of chaperonage. They stayed at Cherbourg for a day or two, and while there he introduced his fiancée to a number of people, including the Hon. Cecil Cadogan, Mr. Dennison and others. While at Cowes Mr. and Mrs. Vereker invited them to dinner. All was comfortable and plain sailing. One day Mr. Langworthy while at Cherbourg asked Miss Long to go for a drive with him to Caen; they looked at the cathedral and then taking both her hands said, "I want you to marry me at once; I cannot wait any longer for you and have arranged everything." She was entirely taken by surprise and objected. While he pleaded she turned over in her mind all the circumstances, and feeling there could be nothing but love to influence him, as she was penniless except for her own earnings, consented, knowing nothing about French marriage law.

The carriage was told to stop before a Catholic Church some miles out in the country from Caen. Here awaited them (all having evidently been arranged) a priest in a black cassock and a fat, disagreeable smile, who read some sort of a service in Latin. As a matter of fact the whole thing was a fraud; seemingly such things can be arranged where money and villainy are not wanting. There were many interesting features in the story at this time, much too lengthy and complicated to relate here, but various thoughts came to her mind making Miss Long doubtful about the legality of this marriage ceremony, and suggesting that she would be happier with a second ceremony.

Mr. Langworthy, having had the legal training of a barrister, knew how to turn his knowledge to account, said, certainly if she wanted another ceremony she should have one. This time the chaplain of the American Seaman's Mission at Antwerp performed it, the divine's name being the Rev. Doctor Potts, a member of the Presbyterian Church.

What Mr. Langworthy knew and his unfortunate dupe did not know was that only civil marriages are valid in Belgian law.

However, in all good faith she had taken part in two ceremonies, the one near Caen in September, 1882, the second in January, 1883, at Antwerp. After this latter Mr. Potts entered the following in his register:—

"*Antwerp, January* 10th, 1883.—Edward Langworthy, England, widower, 35 years old. Mildred

Pallise Long, Belfast (Ireland), maiden, 27 years old. Marriage ceremony by Rev. Arthur Potts."

This was duly signed by the witnesses, one being Mrs. Potts, the other a Mrs. Bailey, whom I think was acting companion, chaperon or something of the kind, I have forgotten what.

A copy of the certificate was handed to Mrs. Langworthy, but it was taken away by her husband, who said he would send it to his solicitors for safe keeping, and he would mark it private and important. He then made his wife promise to keep the marriage secret for a year as he did not wish his mother to know anything about it.

A happy time followed in the yacht; Mr. Langworthy seemed to be deeply in love with his wife; it was all glorious and the days chased each other like some love poems under sunny skies

They stayed a few days at Lisbon, where Mr. Langworthy introduced his *wife* to Lady Ashton, Lord Francis Cecil and others (this is a point to bear in mind).

From Lisbon, if I remember correctly, they sailed for Buenos Ayres, where Mr. Langworthy owned property. During the voyage his wife told him she expected to become a mother. From this moment his manner entirely changed and, instead of expressing pleasure, exclaimed, "We must put the little beast out to nurse." By degrees he now became so brutal it was forced upon her he was hoping his treatment, drugs and starvation, would kill the child, and possibly the mother also.

Driven nearly mad by his treatment, one evening she got out of her bed and went in search of her husband, threw her arms round him and implored him to say why he had so changed. He then told her not to make a fool of herself, she knew perfectly well she was not his wife and the child would be illegitimate, and as this had happened she must leave the yacht on reaching Buenos Ayres and go home again at once; if the affair became known it would be his ruin.

Without allowing her to land at their destination, he put her on board a French tramp steamer without a deck house, that having been washed away on its last voyage, and of course without either a doctor or stewardess.

Mrs. Langworthy begged for some baby clothes, and was given a box containing a few yards of flannel and calico, and £50 in her pocket and sent off home!

So back to England she came full of misery and shame with nothing to prove the story she had to tell but her wedding ring and the baby. Her pride would not let her seek her people, whom she knew would wish to help her but could not afford it. To use Mrs. Langworthy's own words to me, "When I first arrived I tramped London trying to find some clergyman to take up my case for me and see me righted; I could get help from none. One told me he had heard stories like that before and was sorry he could do nothing for me." Another, living in some state in Grosvenor Square, who preached regularly in a fashionable chapel not far from Berkeley and Grosvenor Squares, was sitting one evening after dinner before a comfortable fire sipping coffee from delicate china and toying with a gold spoon, surrounded by expensive fur rugs, books and comforts of all sorts, when Mrs. Langworthy sought his help and told her story. He did not rise from his chair while the poor woman poured forth her tale and implored him to help her. It was a wet night and she was wet through, having tramped the streets all day in hopes of finding some one to help her, her boots were worn through in places and her teeth chattered from cold and want of food.

She eventually was told he did not believe a word of her story, it was too impossible, but if it was true she must "Have faith."

Poor soul! she asked how that was going to find food for her child and herself and turned bitterly away. She described to me her despair as she once more walked along the wet pavements and meditated drowning herself and her child. Passing down Conduit Street she noticed a brass plate on a door with the name of Lumley and Lumley, solicitors, printed on it, she had not tried them, but would do so first thing next morning. She had already tried several solicitors, but she was destitute, friendless, broken in health, the law and the Church refused to help her, justice was her only weapon, while the whole force of the Langworthy's immense wealth was thrown into the scale against her.

The treatment meted out to her by the Anglican divines is a black and lasting disgrace to their Church and the system that produced them.

Her husband's relations would not listen to her, and this is the plight she was in when she entered the offices of Messrs. Lumley and Lumley in Conduit Street. They listened to her story, gave her money to go on with, took the trouble to collect the necessary evidence to prove the ceremonies that had taken place and undertook to fight the case for her. Magnificently they did it through all the courts for four years. Mr. Robert Lumley I do not remember meeting, but Mr. Theodore Lumley I am glad to have known, for he did for this defenceless, broken-hearted woman what not one single shepherd of Christ's flock would do.

Another revolting feature about the treatment from which this unhappy woman suffered, was the attitude of her own sex, the lodging-house woman where she lodged turned her out on hearing she was not living with her husband! Others treated her as if she was one of the lowest of those who walk the streets for their living. Even had that been the case, they should have shown some humanity to a suffering sister.

I did what I could for her, and by degrees one after another helped her; but that she got justice in the end and her life made possible during the long years while the case was in the courts is en-

tirely due to Messrs. Lumley and Lumley, the solicitors, and to *The Pall Mall Gazette,* who took her
case up warmly, collected money for her, published
special editions of their paper with all the details
of the case as it unfolded itself from day to day.
They also brought out a little booklet or pamphlet,
entitled *A Romance of the Law Courts, Mrs. Langworthy's Trials and Triumphs.* Anyone wishing to
read all the particulars of this extraordinary case
cannot do better than get a copy and read it, if
there are any now to be had.

Mrs. Langworthy's troubles were, however, not
yet over, though the learned judges held her marriage to be illegal, but a marriage "in fact" and
granted her £1500 alimony. Mr. Langworthy had
fled to America, refused to pay and was nowhere
to be found.

His solicitors and counsel worked indefatigably
to delay any steps taken by Mrs. Langworthy's
solicitors to obtain the money for her.

The husband's wealth was a terrible weapon. I
have been told great London papers even refused,
through the influence of Mr. Langworthy's agents,
to insert her lines in their agony columns.

Goods of his, seized to pay his debts to his wife,
were instantly claimed by his mother as her property and therefore inviolate. While all this was
taking place Mrs. Langworthy was often in great
need, and but for the kindly help of *The Pall Mall
Gazette* and Messrs. Lumley and Lumley would
surely have gone mad.

Twenty thousand pounds on paper did not help her much. Her husband was made a bankrupt, but he had made his English property over to his mother. In the end the victim triumphed, having fought hard for her child, but there was no getting away from the fact that the strain had told upon her considerably. She was aged and broken down at the end of the four years almost beyond recognition.

The end of these people was as tragic as their lives. Mrs. Langworthy rejoined her husband and forgave him, she died suddenly when in Paris with him and he committed suicide next day.

It is impossible to picture the state of a man's mind who could be so systematically cruel to a woman who had done him no wrong.

As I congratulated Mrs. Langworthy on her vic-. tory I felt a lump come into my throat, but I remembered her as she was when I first saw her in the early days of her trouble and mentally compared her with what she was after four years' hard fighting. She had won the day, but the heart, health and spirit to enjoy her triumph had gone. In a measure it was Dead Sea fruit.

The last time I saw the poor woman was when on my way to Scarborough, and she was going abroad in search of health.

Scarborough reminds me of many things and many people, Worsleys, Caleys, Sitwells, Londesboroughs, Cathcarts and many more.

Old Lord Cathcart, the 3rd earl, was a fine-looking old man with a profusion of grey hair, a big grey moustache and peculiar grey beard brushed out side ways, whisker fashion, with a funny little imperial in the middle, growing from immediately under his lip, very tall, thin and latterly very peculiar, as was the fashion in those days.

Once I remember meeting him walking down Prince of Wales' Terrace going very lame. I asked if it was gout? He eagerly repudiated the idea, saying, "No, it is my wife's hot-water bottle that has burnt a hole in my foot, and I am on my way to take rooms for myself at the other side of the town. I shall leave the whole cussed family to take care of itself!" This he did for a time, taking lodgings at the far side of the town, but not having given notice to his family of his intentions there was a hue and cry after him, but he was spotted at last and dug out.

He had married very early and was an elderly man when first I remember him. He had taken a keen interest in county matters the greater part of his life. At the age of thirty he was chairman of the Quarter Sessions and considered very young to hold that office.

The interests of the Royal Agricultural Society occupied much of his time and he was elected president. The French also paid him the compliment of electing him to the Société des Agriculteurs de France.

Horse-breeding also interested him, in fact he led the useful healthy life of the country squire, being one of the old school, so pleasant to meet, with courteous manners and kindly heart.

Lord Greenock, the late Lord Cathcart, took after his father in height, but lacked his good carriage, having a habit of walking leaning forward with his head well in advance of his body, and usually with his hands behind his back.

He was an admirer of the fair sex, and I remember once at Hurlingham, in the days when the pretty ladies of that date were known under the title of "professional beauties," we had been watching polo, and a number of these beautiful ladies happened to be strolling about. Mrs. Langtry, Mrs. Wheeler, Mrs. Patrick Campbell and Mrs. Cornwallis-West to wit. The latter passed us leaning on her husband's arm. Lord Greenock, who was standing near, followed her with his eyes, and is reported to have said, "Ah, she is his wife in this world; but she will be mine in the next." It is well for our peace of mind that we do not know all the things we are supposed to have said when young and frivolous and just as well perhaps we do not remember all we *have* said in those long days ago.

Lord Greenock's sister, Lady Cecilia, who married Captain Rose of the 10th Hussars was utterly unspoilt and a wonderful amateur acrobat. When dining once long ago with the Lyalls in Lucknow, I was sitting on the sofa talking to Padre Adams, who was much loved by us all, when someone said to Lady Cecilia, "I wish you would show us some of your acrobatic tricks." She was sitting on the

The Third Earl Cathcart

end of the same sofa as we were.   In a moment she turned the neatest somersault over the back of the sofa and came up from the other side between the padre's feet and mine all smooth and collected in an astonishing manner.   The dear padre was full of admiration but a little breathless over the surprise of this unaccustomed drawing-room performance.

At the fall of the leaf Scarborough was the fashionable resort of most of the county families, and I never think of that town, or York Station, without pictures of various people arising before my eyes, one of whom was Lady Sykes, wife of Sir Tatten Sykes of Sledmere.   They were a diverting couple.   Lady Sykes was especially remarkable and a very amusing person.   Her appearance was rather striking owing to the splendid generosity of her figure, accentuated by the smallest possible waist in the middle.   This with her extra-high heels and carrying voice helped to make her a very well-known figure of that day, and whatever country house you went to stay in there was Lady Sykes. She was very amusing and popular.

I remember once sitting opposite to her at dinner at the Newcomens of Kirkleatham Hall, Redcar. She was dressed in creamy white satin—I really hardly know how to tell the rest of the story—but the fact was the bodice of this beautiful dress was not as ample as the wearer.   I was very young and very shy in those days and felt anxious and nervous. Several of the gallant diners seemed much struck by the effect and a very young footman was so interested while standing over her that he upset a dish of beetroot and vinegar all over her shoulders and dress. It was all too terrible. I can shut my eyes now and see again the beetroot sliding over undulations and remember the suppressed shrieks of horror that went up from the table. The look of terror on the footman's face when he saw what he had done was tragic. He made a start as if to retrieve some of the beetroot but was chased away by the butler.

Mr. Clarke-Jervoise, who had taken me into dinner, said if the accident had happened to me I could not have blushed more!

Lady Sykes was quite a pretty whip and caused some sensation one autumn in London by driving a couple of white donkeys tandem in a little governess cart down Piccadilly and up Bond Street. I arrived at the door of Russell and Allen's one day at the same time that she did, and very neatly she reined up while a small "tiger" about the size of a postage stamp jumped out and went to the head of the leader. This diminutive little person was as well turned out as the rest of the equipage. His little legs encased in well-fitting breeches and the sweetest thing in boots twinkled as he ran to the animals' heads, his well-brushed hat and cockade nearly overbalancing him. It was all very smart. I told Lady Sykes she would never dare turn round in that part of the narrow street while so full of traffic. She replied, "You wait and see!" I did, and confess it was a very masterly performance, and when the small boy about the size of a postage stamp nipped up behind and sat down with a wump, folding his arms across his manly bosom almost on a level with his chin, I could plainly see he was thoroughly enjoying himself, thought it was all A.1., as indeed it was.

Sir Tatten used to complain at times that his wife was extravagant. She in return told him it was quite unnecessary to wear five greatcoats at a time, that also was extravagance. She told him once it was "a superfluity of naughtiness."

He was a peculiarly shy and nervous man. It was quite true he did wear two or three greatcoats, —and why not, if it so pleased him. When riding or walking about the estate he peeled them off when they became oppressive and handed them to a servant to carry until required again.

At one time he grew rather irritable when his wife's financial arrangements were being adjusted, and he did not recognise his signature on some of his cheques. I remember there was some bother about it, but it is a long time ago, I have forgotten the particulars. He was also displeased when Lady Sykes bought "La Fléche" at Baron Hirsh's sale, as she had not the money to pay for the horse and he did not wish to find it.

Mr. Henry Cholmondley, a nephew of Sir Tatten's, lived with him, and was in the house when the great fire took place at Sledmere. Fortunately nobody was burnt, and as it occurred in the middle of the day, most of the valuables were saved. Mr. C.

Prior, of Adstock Manor, was also there at the time. He was a life-long friend of Sir Tatten's.

The house has lately been rebuilt on much the same lines as the original.

Sir Tatten will always be remembered as a great breeder of thoroughbred yearlings for sale. The Sledmere yearlings fetched fabulous prices at Doncaster.

This well-known and liked Yorkshire baronet died at the Hotel Metropole in London in 1913 from pneumonia at the age of eighty-eight.

He certainly did embarrassing things at times, but then who does not? I can remember a number of odd things done by my friends at different times.

Mr. Glynn Vivian (brother of Lord Swansea) at a party in his own house in Eaton Square came into the drawing-room when it was full of people and Isador de Lara, or some such musical celebrity, was about to play, and walking up to his wife who was near me complained to her about a huge vase standing on the floor near us filled with towering plumes of dried grasses, red, yellow and green. These vast dyed fronds were perhaps a rather Victorian decoration and Mr. Vivian's taste evidently did not lie that way. He therefore mounted on a chair, filled his arms with the grasses and threw them out of the window. I gathered this vase and grasses had been an innovation and he did not approve.

At another time when people were expected to dinner, at the last moment something upset him and he locked up all the silver! Frantic notes were sent round to ourselves amongst others asking us to bring spoons and forks with us!

Mrs. Vivian was a very beautiful woman, a Miss Craigie-Halkett before she married. I often heard her called the "Virgin Mary" from her likeness to some of the beautiful holy pictures, and people looked out for her in the fashionable twelve-to-two parades in the Park, when we all looked forward to a sight of our dignified and beautiful Queen Alexandra, then Princess of Wales.

Some of my women friends have been quite as entertaining as the men. Lady Caroline Maddon, elder sister of the playmates of my youth, Lady May Mostyn and Lady Lina Lyndon, already mentioned in my other book of recollections,* was one of the most indefatigable match-makers and quite untiring in the interests of her family. Once when my youngest brother was giving a party conjointly with my husband and myself at the Lyric Club in its Bond Street days, Lady Caroline came round a few days before to know what eligible young men had accepted our invitations. Mrs. George Harvey was staying with us at the time and her bachelor cousin, Lord Hopetown, having been amongst the invited we enlarged upon his many advantages as an example of the elegant and beauteous young men who were flocking to our party, and Lady Caroline went away quite happy.

On the evening of our party we were asked at

* *Memories Discreet and Indiscreet.*

intervals by our friend if Lord Hopetown had arrived. He had not at the time we were asked, so Mrs. Harvey conceived the idea of keeping Lady Caroline amused and happy by introducing a very good-looking man to her who had been in one of the Highland Regiments and lately married. He was not particularly well-endowed with worldly goods, but was told he must talk very big to Lady Caroline about his yachts, race-horses, etc. This he was doing magnificently, while we nodded occasional encouragement when someone came up and asked the man how his bride was!

Another time during that same season, when Mrs. Harvey was staying with us, we were dining with the Maddons in Chester Square. After dinner our hostess asked if we would like to hear her daughter recite. The reply was in the affirmative from some of the guests. Personally, I fight shy of recitations, they always make me feel hysterical, especially when delivered by amateurs. What made this particular occasion so noticeable was the fuss that was made over the unfortunate reciter. First she had to stand against a heavy red curtain. Then Mrs. George Harvey, who was tall, fair and handsome (as was Miss Maddon), was requested to move, as Lady Caroline said, "You won't mind moving, will you, Mrs. Harvey? it quite spoils the effect two fair people being so near to one another." A general post then took place and everybody felt uncomfortable, conversations interrupted, chairs scraped about the room, and at last "Silence"

was proclaimed and the recitation began. The reciter is now Lady Cardigan, and has done her duty
by presenting her lord with an heir. We all felt
sorry for the poor girl having such a fuss made
which quite spoilt the effect that might otherwise
have been produced. Fortunately Miss Maddon
had become used to her mother's arrangements and
was not upset in any way, in fact I think she rather
liked it.

CHAPTER VII

I HAVE met some famous sportswomen at one time and another in my life as well as famous sportsmen, but as I am dealing with them in another book later, I must refrain now from giving accounts of their prowess and refer only to their personalities.

One of the greatest sportswomen I ever met was Caroline, Duchess of Montrose, sporting in every sense of the word, having owned many racehorses and three husbands. She was a great character in the seventies and eighties. Whenever I met her Emerson's clever saying, "What you are speaks so loud I cannot hear what you say," recurred to me. Pretend as much as we like, we certainly cannot radiate anything unlike our real selves, try as we may. It always seemed to me she wished the world to think her a hard, cynical woman of dashing

The Duchess of Montrose

daring character, whereas she was really kind and tender-hearted, looking for sympathy and appreciation as her daily food. While pretending she did not care the least what anybody said or thought of her, she really cared a great deal.

She was a daughter of the 2nd Lord Decies, and married her first husband, the 4th Duke of Montrose, in 1836. What her age was when she married I do not know exactly, so we will suppose it was sweet seventeen. Her second venture was with Mr. Stirling Crawford, a fine sportsman, and thirdly, with Mr. Henry Milner, M.V.O., D.S.O., who had just turned twenty-four years of age when he led his bride of some sixty-nine summers to the altar at Putney on July 26th, 1888. Mr. Crawford died in 1883.

The first two husbands left her through the decree of a Higher Power, the third she left for other reasons.

I think I may describe the Duchess as a very jolly, happy woman. She enjoyed thoroughly all the good things she was able to command and, what is more to the point, knew she was having a good time.

Mr. Stirling Crawford, the second husband, was a very popular man and an excellent shot, one of the founders of the pigeon-shooting shows which for some years were so fashionable. They were first held in the old Red House at Battersea, and at Hornsey Wood in the North of London, now called Finsbury Park. He was amongst the first also to put gun to shoulder at Hurlingham.   It was at the latter place that women first became enamoured of the sport that was christened later by one of the leading London papers "The slaughter of the doves."

The men all had their handicap distance fixed up just as you now see on golf links.   Professional betting men were not allowed at Hurlingham, though I believe this was not the case at the Gun Club.

As soon as Hurlingham became popular it was bought for the purpose of pigeon-shooting from Mr. Naylor, the owner of "Macaroni" who won the Derby in 1863.

At one time we all used to flock down to see the shooting at Hurlingham.   The women were placed on the left-hand side of the traps and were supposed to be non-betters, but did not consider it betting when the wagers were in gloves or scent!

The shooting men were ranged on the other side and had the advantage of some shade from a huge walnut tree, under which they gambled freely.   The women had to provide themselves with shade from their parasols.   These meetings in the earlier days of their fame were most instructive, simple and entertaining.

Captain Bachelor used to be the "bookie" on the Saturday afternoon for the chief prize at long odds against each individual shooter.   It was always ready money, and the secretary used to file on penny files the fiver' entrance fees much as tradesmen people do their accounts. · All betted heavily.

The highest in the land were bitten with the pigeon-shooting craze. The Prince of Wales, the Duke of Edinburgh and many crowned heads of Europe were fairly regular attendants at the meetings.

At last Queen Victoria, hearing of the shooting of the poor little trapped birds and of a certain dispute there had been over some heavy betting, put a veto on the meetings as far as any of her belongings or Court were concerned. This was a terrible blow, and all the shooting fraternity went about with long faces muttering imprecations.

Then for a short time Hurlingham felt itself out in the cold and in a measure in disgrace. The place then drifted by degrees to its present stage, trees were cut down in a neighbouring apple orchard and turned into a polo ground, but shooting was not entirely abandoned. Eventually in the zenith of its fame there was both polo and shooting.

I have strayed away rather from the Duchess of Montrose, but it was thinking of her that brought back dear old Hurlingham to my mind, and the part played there so often by Mr. Crawford.

It was here also that the poor Duchess quite unwillingly distinguished herself while looking on at the shooting. Arm-chairs, luxurious seats and lounges were unheard of in those days at these meetings; simple wooden schoolboy forms placed in rows were provided. The Duchess seeing room on one of these occupied by other lookers-on perched herself upon the end of it. All were watching Mr. Crawford's shooting with anxious eyes— it had been heavily betted on. It so happened on this particular day there was a very full attendance, the Prince of Wales, the Duke of Edinburgh and a number of royalties looking on. Suddenly great excitement was caused by Mr. Crawford's brilliant shooting and people jumped up suddenly, including the men sitting on the same bench as the Duchess, with the natural result that the bench stood on its head and so did she. Her parasol, which she had been holding over her head, took the opportunity to shut up like a candle-extinguisher. It was a nasty and surprising toss for a big heavy woman, and it was not in the days of hobble skirts and black silk stockings.

It was a great shame to laugh, but no one could help it, even the perfect-mannered Prince of Wales had to pretend he did not see while endeavouring to hide his amusement. The only person unable to enjoy the joke was the lady herself. Usually none were more ready to be amused, but for once her cheery face was clouded as she picked herself up, and turned on the man standing nearest to her holding his sides with laughter. Naturally this incensed her, and she told him her opinion of his manners. To make matters worse this individual, who happened to be an Irishman, while profuse in apologies and hopes that she was none the worse, said he had no idea she was such an acrobat! This complicated matters somewhat and while some drew forth immaculate silk handkerchiefs and dusted the good lady down she advised her laughing Irish friend to go on laughing and to hold his fat vulgar sides while doing so.

I must not leave the subject of Hurlingham without mentioning the old gardener who had been in charge for many years. When the place was converted into the smart club it became later, the poor old man was put into livery, and he had to stand at the gate as the members and their friends arrived. He was dreadfully pained. It was bad enough to be obliged to wear a long dark green sort of frock-coat with brass buttons and gold braid, but when it came to trousers with gold braid, and a tall hat ornamented in the same way, it was almost more than he could bear, his self-consciousness being quite painful.

I think everybody remembers that the Duchess of Montrose was well known on the race-course. A member of the Jockey Club once said to me in connection with the Duchess's racing, "Like most women who come racing and take an active part in the management of the horses and so forth, she is a nuisance. Crawford is old and feeble and allows his missus to hold the reins."

At this time and during the lifetime of her second husband she raced under the name of Crawford and won many classic races. After his death she ran them under the name of Mr. Manton.

As a matter of fact, I know she did exactly what

she liked and, at one time and another, caused a good deal of trouble both before and after her husband's death. As she would listen to all sorts of tales she gradually became most suspicious of her surroundings generally. She was always changing her commissioners and engaging new ones to put her money in, her chief fault being she expected all the long prices. It was over a little affair of this kind that she got herself disliked. There was quite a hostile demonstration against her at Newmarket in October, 1882, when out of a fit of pique she scratched the mare "Thebais," one of the favourites for the Cambridgeshire of that year, because she had been forestalled in the betting and could not get the price she wanted.

Mr. Crawford was at that time very ill at Cannes, where he died in February, 1883, Sir Morell Mackenzie having operated on his throat, for which he received one thousand guineas; but was unable to save his life.

This little racing unpleasantness arose through the Duchess saying if some of the long prices were not turned up to her she would not run the mare at all. Nobody really thought she was in earnest until the last moment when she adhered to her avowed intention in spite of her many friends' protests. Sir Frederick Johnson tried hard to make her listen to reason. The very night before the race several people I know journeyed down to Sefton Lodge to try and prevent her doing anything so exceedingly unpopular, or, as James Lowther ex-

The Earl of Coventry
A Racecourse Snapshot

pressed it, "Not to make a fool of herself." But it was all useless. The Prince of Wales even took the trouble to go and advise her, but by the time he arrived the mischief had been done. She had written the fatal letter and sent it to Weatherby's to scratch the mare, after which nothing more could be done, Royal or otherwise.

I do not think the Duchess quite understood what a serious thing she was doing, for she was a kindly good-hearted woman who liked people to be sporting and have a good time. Feeling naturally ran very high at Newmarket, and when in an earlier race before the time the Cambridgeshire was set to be run in, a horse of hers cantered past the stand in her Grafton scarlet, a roar of hooting and groaning went up from the general public stands, and my theory that the Duchess had not realised what she had done, was, I think, proved by her wonderment at what the row was all about, in fact she asked quite innocently in the Jockey Club enclosure what the hullaballoo was about.

When she was told briefly in the one word "Thebais," she stood still for a moment and then entirely broke down. Nobody would speak to her in the saddling paddock. I do not know what would have happened but for kind Lord Coventry befriending her and leading her out of the crowd into a horse-box. What he said to her I do not know, but she was seen no more on the heath that day.

After this there was another inclination on the part of the crowd to hoot her colours, but Mr.

Weatherby showed tact and good taste by asking the bookies to desist. This request was quickly passed from one to the other, and attention paid to it.

I feel certain the scratching of "Thebais" was not done "out of spite," as I have heard it described, but from failing to realise what it would entail, for, as I have said, the Duchess was not a malicious or ill-natured woman, and I know for a fact that she never ceased regretting that unhappy stroke of the pen.

Poor lady, it was well she won some big plums and had the satisfaction of seeing her horses win big races to counterbalance the difficulties and unpleasantnesses in which at times she found herself.

With her betting she was not always happy and got into some pretty tiresome muddles. For instance, when "Corrie Roy" was entered for the Goodwood Stakes and "Oberon" for the Lincolnshire Handicap, although both horses won she stood a loser! It was altogether rather complicated, for in the "Corrie Roy" case she lay against the mare, then backed it, then reported it a non-starter with the same threatened fate as "Thebais." However, the matter was put straight and "Corrie Roy" achieved a big performance.

It was, however, a case of the "biter bit," for the man who had the commission of backing the mare to win died in the interval of victory and settling day. Her agent had, therefore, no account and all the bets he made were invalid.

"Oberon," the horse she ran at Lincoln, was the self-same animal that Lord William Beresford took out to India with a view of winning the Viceroy's Cup, but it may be remembered that climate did not suit the horse and he proved so uncertain he was returned to England, where he proved useful at stud. But for the fact of a telegram being delayed in transit, "Oberon" would never have run in that race at Lincoln.

Once a man got a little piqued with the Duchess over a betting transaction. She had asked him to put one thousand pounds for her on a horse that failed to win. The money was not forthcoming at Tattersall's on the following Monday. Thinking this strange, he called the same evening on the Duchess and, as he was shown into the hall, she came down the stairs and said she had forgotten all about it, or words to that effect. A moment later she changed her line of argument and said she supposed the account was all right and that she knew he was a rich man and would not be inconvenienced. To which he replied, "That's all very well, your Grace, but my money is in bricks and mortar, and we don't settle with them at Tattersall's."

For years there has been a story of some lady-owner becoming irate with her jockey after he had been beaten, when armed with her orders to jump off as soon as the flag fell, come right through and win. The jockey did his best but failed to obtain notice of the judge, so he was accosted by the owner with, "Did I not tell you to come along as fast as you could?" to which he answered, "And so I did, but I could not come along without the horse." The lady was the Duchess of Montrose and the jockey little Henry Huxtable and not Sam Loates as has been at times suggested.

The Duchess built a mausoleum to the memory of her second husband at Newmarket and used to visit it every morning when in the neighbourhood. She often found an old man there also praying for the dead. His name was Potter. He frequently turned up to mourn departed sportsmen and sympathise with the relatives, receiving the widow's mite in return!

All people who through sport, or indeed in any way, become public characters have wild stories related about them, and the Duchess did not escape. One story was that after Mr. Crawford died she suggested to Fred Archer, the jockey, that she would have no objection to his being her third husband, but he had other views. I am under the impression she may have said something of the kind in chaff and had it misconstrued, but when I have suggested this I have been told it was nothing of the kind. However, I am entitled to hold my own opinion; but undoubtedly the story went round that Archer asked Captain Machell if he married the Duchess would he thereby become the Duke of Montrose? . . . Si non e vero ben trovato!!

This very sporting lady's third husband, Mr. Henry Milner, did not live with her very long.

There was no divorce or anything so vulgar, they agreed to disagree like sensible people.

In Lady Cardigan's reminiscences she says that the Duchess of Montrose "pulled" "Thebais," which is quite a mistake; she should have said "scratched." Perhaps that was what she meant to say, but what does it matter? Who thinks or cares anything about these nine days' wonders even a month or two after they have taken place, all is forgotten or embroidered out of all recognition.

After Mr. Crawford's death I am under the impression that the Duchess ran her horses in the colours of Sir Frederick Johnstone.

In November, 1894, she died, and some of her stable was sold at the Newmarket December sales. I do not remember what the total figure amounted to; but I know ten mares brought in 10,440 guineas and ten horses in training 17,215 guineas. One sale of her Sefton Stud realised the tidy little sum of £52,305. This was, however, only a small portion of her stud.

She was buried in the mausoleum she had built for Mr. Crawford near Sefton Lodge at Newmarket.

Her racing colours did not appear in the Racing Calendar from 1894 until revived by the present Lord Decies.

I once had a great discussion with the Duchess on the question of who were the greatest scandalmongers, men or women. She maintained that women were the worst culprits, saying, "They are mostly jealous spiteful cats." I did not agree, and suggested men's clubs and smoking-rooms were the places from whence came most of the scandal and gossip. I remember my husband telling me some wonderful stories dealing with men's racing trans- actions and women's morals which he had heard at "the club." I told him I had always understood women's names were not mentioned in better-class clubs. He replied, "Oh, that's all bunkum!"

It is, I know, supposed that ladies' five-o'clock teas are responsible for much scandal. I have not found it so, and I am glad my friends are not of the order who find pleasure in saying unkind things about other people; they neither like it nor will they tolerate anything of the kind. When a few nice- minded women set their faces against ill-natured gossip it is surprising how quickly it dies a natural death in that immediate neighbourhood. There are many more interesting things to talk about than our own or our neighbour's follies. It is safer to talk of things than people; except when writing Mem- ories!

I have certainly met more men with tongues that ran away with them than I have women, and a diplomatist or two who have been very clever with their innuendoes, the property of which we all know is to create an impression unawares. One man I know who is living to-day is quite accomplished in this art.

Speaking of clubs, reminds me how very unclub- able women are, which no doubt accounts for the number of those establishments that have not been successes and have had to close their doors. For years I wondered what women wanted clubs for and supposed it was to get away from their husbands, in the same way that men belong to clubs to get away from their womenkind. That, however, does not apply now, for it would be so unnecessary when we all lead such separate lives, indeed it would be considered bourgeois to know where our husbands are. I can see now that these institutions may be very useful, and in hopes of finding their utility have belonged to several. At the present moment I am a member of two.

After deep study I have come to the conclusion that many of the comparative failures in the women's club movement have not by any means always been the fault of the club managers, but rather of the members themselves. A new cult seems to have sprung up. I do not mean the Suffragettes or the down-with-everybody-and-everything-ist, we know all about them, but the club fiend is a new creation, a thing apart. I am learning to know her by sight, she mostly wears cotton gloves and sniffs! There are many of her kind and they specialise in all the vices that make club life unbearable, but their vices vary.

In one of my clubs I witnessed some strange conduct. I encountered soap-lifters who could not resist putting the soap in their pockets after washing their hands. Others who were so hypnotised by the hair-pins that they had to cram as many into their hair as it would hold. One woman, who did not think I could see her reflection in the glass in front of me, looked like a hedgehog before she left the room, she had very little hair but many hair-pins. Then the writing-paper and envelopes seem to be quite irresistible.

In the reading-room I have seen women collect newspapers in heaps and sit down on them, spreading their skirts so as to hide all traces, much as broody hens fluffle out their feathers. These club women even cut out portions of the papers when they think nobody is looking.

Women's clubs are things that have come to stay, I know, but I think most women who belong to them will allow that the club fiend eats like a canker into club life.

It is a humiliating thought, but women do not amalgamate happily, having apparently an inherited mistrust of one another, and from what I have observed in clubs, with some reason. Many will not conform to the necessary rules of club life, which is silly and short-sighted as the rules are formed entirely for their own comfort and convenience.

In fact to be an ideal club woman it is necessary not to expect too much from one's fellow-members. Women have the almost universal failing of wanting to be too intimate, of asking too many questions, and making too many confidences. They are not satisfied with the easy comradeship that exists between men who may belong to the same club for years, meeting constantly the same people, and yet not know whether they are married, single or divorced, where they live, or anything about them, their chief topic of conversation having been politics, sport, guns and such-like matters, with no personal matters introduced.

The first thing a woman wants to ferret out appears to be if the woman she meets is happy in her home life, how many children she has and all the intimate details of her domestic life. After this information is digested they are either bosom pals or at daggers drawn, and even in the case of the bosom pals, before long they often, indeed, almost invariably, end in what diplomatists call "strained relations."

Another reason why I doubt if club life will appeal to all is that instinct of "home," the beauteous word manufactured by the Teutonic people which is so deeply rooted in our hearts. Clubs are of course meant to be our temporary homes, but each individual member must not expect to run it on her own lines, for they are not in control of the establishment.

I think a little more dignity and reserve on the part of women joining clubs would lead to greater comfort and happiness all round, and I think that now women have broken away from the old-fashioned idea of its being *"not nice"* to appear in any rôle except that of pandering to man, they should try and acclimatise themselves to club life, try and be logical and prove they are at any rate capable of governing themselves.

When people used to tell me extraordinary stories of things done in "Hen Clubs," I used to think these dear kind people were trying to amuse me, never believing for a moment such things did really happen, but now I know, for one afternoon I wandered into a club and not finding the papers I wanted asked one of the servants what had become of them. He looked wearily round the room, shrugged his shoulders, and said, "Pinched!" After waiting some time and being unable to find the papers, and the papers not finding me, I went into the hall and waylaid an official, who in a piqued voice said either they were not out yet or had been carried to members' bed-rooms! I then drove off to Victoria Station and got what I wanted from the railway bookstall.

I do not trouble this club much now. In another to which I at one time belonged, but which is now no more, both sexes were allowed, and in the complaint book I read one day, "Is it the correct thing for waiters to come into the room in their shirt sleeves at eleven o'clock in the morning?" Further down on the same page, "The food is bad and expensive," to which some wag had remarked immediately beneath it, "No self-respecting chef will stay in a woman's club where they have poached eggs for dinner. No wonder he gets slack. Ask next time for larks' eyebrows devilled on toast, you will then see what a professor he is."

A member of a well-known ladies' club lately vouched for the truth of the following:

A certain lady playing at bridge there lost a largish "parcel" and had not the necessary ready to settle up, so pulled a couple of diamond rings from off her fingers and flung them down to her opponent in settlement.   They proved to be Parisian and worth less than what she had lost.

Next time these ladies met in the club the one who had been paid in Parisian diamonds went for their former owner and pulled her hair, unfortunately it had not been grafted very firmly and toupee, wig or whatever it was, came away bodily leaving a very lonely looking bald pate.

Until women as a body realise their responsibilities and observe the amenities of club life the woman's club movement can never be an unqualified success; and we must bear in mind, new ideas without the sanction of tradition must ever struggle for existence.

CHAPTER VIII

Some Racing Ladies—Stakes Given to the Red Cross Fund —Prince Soltykoff a Faithful Friend—Lord Alfred Paget Patron of the Theatre—Queen Alexandra's Interest in Racing—Her Sympathy and Enjoyment of a Joke— In Her Home at Sandringham—The Fatigue of Ladies-in-Waiting—Lady Macclesfield and Bishop Wilberforce —Lady Ely Asked her Favourites at Court—The German Emperor at Osborne—Queen Victoria and John Brown—The Duke of Connaught's Early Speech-making —Mr. Bolckow the Duke's Host at Marton—Starving amidst Plenty—A Tactful Host.

WHEN the war broke out there were no less than nineteen ladies with colours registered under the rules of racing and the National Hunt.

The Duchess of Newcastle, who is a first-rate judge of both horse and hound, and who in her youth was known as "Ta-Ta" Candy, daughter of that fine sportsman, "Sugar Candy," has played the most conspicuous if not the most important part in later day racing. Perhaps I ought to bracket Lady James Douglas with her. The latter breeds a good many horses and makes good prices in the sale-ring with her stock.

In steeple-chasing Lady Nelson comes out on top. She won the Liverpool Grand National of 1915 with

Lady Nelson

her "Ally Sloper," and gave the whole of the stakes to the Red Cross Funds. She is, I think, the only lady who has ever won that great event, and certainly the only one I have ever heard of who has so splendidly and usefully applied the stakes and winnings.

There have been fierce arguments as to whether she was at Liverpool to see her horse win, and there has been betting on it. As a matter of fact, she was not there, but in town on the day of the race. On hearing of her good luck she proceeded at once to Liverpool, arriving next day, and stood with her horse to be photographed, which no doubt led people into the belief that she was there on the great day. Her racing colours are white, light blue sash and blue cap, her husband's are white jacket with a red, white and blue sash and red cap, out of compliment to the white funnels of the Nelson line of steamers with which his name has been so long associated. Both Sir William Nelson (1st Baronet) and his wife, speak of the "sash" across the jacket, which is a very modern term for the historic "racing belt." "Ally Sloper" has not done much since his Liverpool triumph, and his then jockey is now in khaki. Both Sir William and Lady Nelson are fond of horses and racing, and spend a good deal of time at their stud farm, County Meath. They also have horses in England at Lambourne. When I congratulated Lady Nelson a short time ago on her noble gift to the Red Cross Fund, she very sweetly said, it was not only a pleasure to give it, but she considered it her duty. I wish a few more felt as dutiful.

Miss Ethel Clinton also raced and, like Mrs. Langtry, has been on the stage. That Russian butterfly, Prince Soltykoff, paid her great attention in the long agos, but she was not his first love. Regular theatre goers well remember seeing her on warm summer evenings walking arm-in-arm with the Prince along the Strand to the Globe Theatre. When she and her patrons revived "Les Cloches de Corneville" it was a very pleasant show, with much harmony both before and behind the curtain. Lord Alfred Paget was one of the patrons who shared the harmony behind the scenes; he was a frequent visitor. The chorus liked him and he liked them.

Kate Munro, a most fascinating and clever actress, was the leading lady. There were those behind the scenes who said she was befriended by a Royal personage, and I was amused at being told that one very wet Saturday afternoon when she had promised two nice little children of hers that they should come and see mamma act, but owing to the wet she thought they would not come. The nurse arrived with them, and they were escorted behind the scenes to their fond parent. When she saw them she said, "Oh, nurse, nurse, why did you bring these children out on such a wet afternoon? Dear! dear! what would their Royal grandmamma say if they caught cold!"

The chorus who overheard this were amused. They were not quite of the same standard as the chorus girls of to-day, though perhaps more easily pleased.

When Prince Soltykoff's wife died he did not marry again, as many thought he would, but was very faithful to his old friends, and at his death left his Newmarket home, Kremlin House (now in the possession of Mr. Joe Butters) to Miss Clinton; also his racehorses. She has never done anything of importance with them, but continued to race in the pronounced pink jacket and black cap so popular in the days of that sporting Russian's racing.

Racing has never claimed any of our English Royal ladies, or Royal gentlemen either for that matter, except King Edward; he was keenly interested; Queen Alexandra was not, until her King, then Prince of Wales, won his first Derby with "Persimmon" in 1896, after which she expressed a wish to go into the weighing room at Epsom and see the jockeys weighed out, and other details of that sanctum.

It was Queen Alexandra who hit upon the happy nomenclature of "Diamond Jubilee" for the brother of "Persimmon," who won the Derby the same year as Queen Victoria celebrated her notable Diamond Jubilee.

The present Queen Mother has a great sense of humour and enjoys a joke; sympathetic people often do, and she is the most sympathetic of all our Royal family, quickly responding to the mood of those she is speaking to, whether grave or gay. She is reported to have said one of the best stories she ever heard was of an old lady who suffered from an affection of the nose, that is to say the little dew-drop that comes unawares on the tip of our nose in cold and damp weather. This became a source of annoyance to the old lady, so she told her foot-man whenever he observed this phenomenon to say politely, "Thomas is waiting, my lady," so as to call her attention to it. One day, while waiting at table, the flunkey discovered it was time to obey his orders, but felt shy. At last he summoned up suffi-cient courage to say, "Thomas *was* waiting, my lady, but now he is in your soup!"

In 1885 or 1886 I think it must have been, when Monsieur Lacretelle, the portrait painter, was paint-ing a picture of Queen Alexandra and her dogs, he asked her how she would like them taken, stand-ing, lying down, or what position. She replied with a charming smile, "On their behinds," only in French it sounded much more piquante. Lacretelle drew a pencil sketch of me at the same time and made me so beautiful that I vowed I would never again have a photograph or picture taken, but some light-fingered person walked away with it during one of our crushes or bun struggles, so my pride and vanity had to suffer by appearing in a photo-graph in my usual everyday face, shorn of the beauty that had been in the eye of the beholder when the sketch was made. It was only a quite small head and shoulders, but I fancied it enor-mously.

I like to think, in my dreams, of Queen Alexandra

at Sandringham, where she is happy amongst her pets, and where she can shed a little of the fatiguing mantle of established precedent.   Where she can be the woman and the mother as well as the Queen. Where she can wander out of the big black and gold gates given to her and the Prince of Wales when they bought the place, and across to York Cottage and round to the creeper and ivy-clad little church within stone's-throw of the house.   Here for many years she has carried all her joys and woes, then back across the drive to the flower gardens on the other side of the house, where flowers bloom galore, especially her favourite flower, mignonette.   Everything about the place looks so cared for and content. The pheasants hardly get out of your way, the lodges to the side entrances all covered with well-ordered rambling creepers and roses, the model kennels where her treasures live, each division with a well-kept lawn for the pleasure of the inhabitants either to lie and bask in the sun or for gentle exercise.

The hospitality at Sandringham is thoroughly simple and homely, after the fashion of our big country houses.   The Royalties do not usually appear until midday, unless shooting is on the tapis.

Queen Alexandra is a keen observer; nothing escapes her.   I remember once sitting with Lady Macclesfield, during one of her days in waiting at Marlborough House, and in such a dull, uninteresting room, more like a station waiting-room than anything else I could think of.   She was knitting uncomfortable looking garments of strange shapes for the poor, and there she had to remain unless sent for by her Royal mistress or until she was told her services would not be required any further that day.

I did not like to ask her if she was very dull. It was such a leading question, and I am sure we would all sit day in and day out in a dull uninteresting room if by so doing we could be of any service to such a splendid Queen who has so faithfully fulfilled her rôle throughout her life, so ably filled that position into which it pleased God to call her.

When the message came that Lady Macclesfield's services would not be required any more that day, she drove me home, and on the way I asked her if she found the standing as tiring as Lady Downe did when in waiting on Queen Victoria. She said there was no getting away from the fact that it was most fatiguing, especially at big functions, but that Queen Alexandra, who was then Princess of Wales, was most considerate when able to do as she liked in her own home, being most observant of fatigue on the part of her ladies-in-waiting.

Dear, kind and good Lady Macclesfield was quite smart at repartee. Once when talking to Bishop Wilberforce, otherwise known as "Soapy Sam," who died the sudden death on the Downs near Dorking that he had always said was the one he should like, he was explaining to her about his weight and that he knew exactly to an ounce what it was when in his bath. She replied, referring to his sobriquet,

"Would that be with or without the soap, my lord?"

The conversation seems to have been of rather an intimate nature, but perhaps that was the bishop's polite way of explaining he knew his weight without any of his clothes being taken into consideration.

A story is told of this same reverend gentleman when rating a curate, to whom he said, "I do not like to hear of the clergy in my diocese galloping about after hounds and neglecting their work."

The curate, who was considerably braver than many I have seen in the presence of their ecclesiastic superiors, replied, "You go to balls, my Lord."

"Yes," said the bishop, "but I am never in the same room as the dancers."

The curate replied: "And I am never in the same field as the hounds, my lord."

This is an old story often told, but is rather a good one.

But to return to the fatigue of ladies-in-waiting. Poor Lady Downe used to catch the most terrible colds when on duty. I remember Lady Sefton bringing her to see me once when she could hardly see out of her eyes and her nose was red. I enquired how she had managed to get such a bad cold. She said it was the result of having been "in waiting" for a month, adding, "The Queen loves fresh air, and can live in a wind and thorough draught that would kill many people. She is very strong, full of energy, and can stand indefinitely herself. I sometimes find it all I can do to hold up to the end of my waiting."

Lady Ely, who was the wife of the third Marquess, was for years Lady of the Bed-chamber to Queen Victoria, and was the most charming person. Everybody who had any favour to ask from Her Majesty used to ask Lady Ely to see what she could do, knowing how much the Queen liked her and what influence she had. It was she who at Colonel Fred Burnaby's instigation asked the Queen if she would reinstate Valentine Baker in the army, and was told she had already offered to do so, but he had expressed himself as unable to accept any favour at the hands of the Queen after the way she had supported Miss Dickinson at the trial, and sent her a signed photograph.

Once when Lady Ely was asked which of the Royal Family she liked best, she said, "The Queen, she is always so courteous and expresses herself as so grateful for anything that is done for her, making it a pleasure if we can be of any service." Then when asked which she liked least, replied likewise, without any hesitation, "The German Emperor, he is so over-bearing and often rude. The only person on earth of whom he stands in the least awe is Queen Victoria, his grandmother. He behaves very nicely in her presence, but when staying once at Osborne in the Queen's later years, news reached Her Majesty that her grandson had been up early and with the gardeners, asking all sorts of questions and ferreting about. The riot act was read to him and he did not like it."

I always thought the Queen a pathetic little figure and so extraordinarily kind. Once when she heard I was in great sorrow she sent Lady Downe to see me to express her sympathy, and later commanded me to Windsor where she showed such tenderness and feeling that I quite forgot to be stilted and when in reply to a remark of hers I so far forgot myself as to say, "Happiness unshared has no taste," I think we both had to restrain our feeling, or we should have fallen into each other's arms, for tears were in her eyes and voice, as well as mine.

The Royal Family are all good at making speeches, considering how little there is that they may say. King Edward VII was of course the best. He had the happy knack of leaving the impression that he had said a great deàl more than he really had. The Queen hated having to make a speech, and seldom did so, but when it was unavoidable she spoke clearly and with no hesitation. She spoke at the opening of the Imperial Institute, but was obviously nervous. Many are still living who can remember her faithful servant-friend and adviser, John Brown, who seldom left her side. He was not a favourite with the rest of the Royal Family.

When Her Majesty was in residence at Osborne she used to breakfast in the grounds and attend to her correspondence there, the faithful John Brown in highland kit being at her side—I wonder where the garden-seat is now?—on which she always sat and which bore the following inscription:—

"To the Memory of John Brown, a devoted and attached servant and friend of Victoria R.I."

He died in 1883. A slight idea of how entirely he was part of her life and how she had grown to lean on him may be gathered from the following. When she was travelling in Scotland, and was passing the shooting lodge of the Sutherlands where they were at the time, she told John Brown, who as usual was sitting behind her in his dicky seat, that she wished to stop and call on the Sutherlands. They asked the Queen to get out of the carriage and go in and have some tea, but she declined until John Brown leaned over and said, "I would if I were you. It will warm you up." No doubt he had one eye on his own "in'ards," which were feeling cold, as well as an eye on the comfort of the Queen.

Again when at Baveno on the Italian Lakes, the Queen was in the garden of the hotel waiting for Brown. When he appeared she said, "I have been waiting for you." Instead of apologies and falling flat on his face, he replied, "Well, I must say you look very summery," she being in her usual straw hat, white Cashmere shawl and elastic-sided boots, but had on a white veil to save her eyes a little.

Cashmere shawls were always kept in stock for presents, and beautifully silky and soft they were. I had one, but it was left in India wrapped round something very tender and precious in an Indian cemetery.

At Balmoral there is a statue erected by order of the Queen to John Brown's memory, a tombstone in Crathie churchyard for which she invited Lord Tennyson to suggest an inscription, and at Osborne the granite seat with the pathetic words to his memory.

Once when driving through the gates of Buckingham Palace, a youth, named Arthur Connor, who pretended he was a Fenian, pointed an unloaded pistol at Her Majesty. He was at once seized by John Brown who, to commemorate his vigilance, was presented with a medal and a small (very small) annuity of £25.

Turning over some old notes and letters a short time ago I came across one asking me to go to Marlborough House and advise about some things wanted ·for Princess Louise's wedding with the Duke of Fife. The Princess Royal has much the same gentle manner and dignity of her mother; more so than either of her sisters. She has a little of that look of almost sad enquiry that is so attractive in Queen Alexandra.

I think I must have heard the Duke of Connaught make his first speech when he came to Middlesborough to open a park for the people, a present to the borough from Mr. Bolckow, head of the now world-famed iron and steel works.

Having made his fortune in these works, Mr. Bolckow was anxious to leave some lasting remembrance of the years he had toiled, at first with hands and then with brain while making his vast fortune.

I was a small child at the time and was taken by my people to the station to meet the Prince, who had been sent down to begin and relieve his elder brother of some of the many dull and tiresome ceremonies that were his almost daily bill of fare.

I do not know exactly what I expected to see; possibly something after the fashion of Prince Bohoo in my fairy tales, but I remember being greatly disappointed that there was no glitter, no crown, no golden wands, nothing but a rather delicate-looking nervous young man in plain every-day clothes who read a speech in which amongst other things that I have since heard many times, he said, "My beloved mother will be glad I know to hear of the kind reception you have given to me on this auspicious occasion," etc. There was a little nervous halting once or twice, followed by a little prompting from some rather funereal-looking men standing behind the Prince. Even at that early age I felt sorry for him. He had not then acquired the easy flow of language which came later, and is peculiar to our Royalties.

Mr. Bolckow, the host of Prince Arthur, was a dear old man who lived in great magnificence in an uncomfortable sort of way in a big red-brick house requiring centuries to soften its crudeness. It stood well exposed to the high road in a field or two sparsely timbered, railed in with high iron railings to protect the deer and gas-lamps that abounded in the enclosure, through which with several gates ran an asphalt drive.

The house at Marton was stored with priceless pictures, statues and bric-à-brac. I well remember Mr. Bolckow and his sweet little wife in those days. I think they were Germans and certainly spoke English with an accent and absence of aspirates. A few days before the arrival of the Prince I had been taken to see the room being prepared for his occupation where everything was white, blue and gold. The carpet was blue, crockery-blue and gold, curtains blue satin "which stood by itself" like the satin gowns of our grandmothers. (How uncomfortable they must have been.) Blue satin curtains to the bed with beautiful deep fringe to tickle the Prince's nose as he got into bed. It was at the end of the time when to lie in bed without curtains to draw round was the height of indecency.

Mr. Bolckow asked me if I would like to see the " 'orses" being drilled and broken in to make sure of their steadiness when bringing the Prince through crowded streets.   .   .

It was very exciting watching the horses learning their work; they were splendidly matched. Anyone unused to horses might have found it difficult to tell one from the other so exactly alike were the four, while the postilions might have been twins.

School children had been collected to shout hurrahs. Bands played with big drums booming in the animals' ears.

I wonder if the Prince was as elated as we were with the grandeur of the carriage and perfections of the horses. He may have been bored to tears, even longing for the horses to have a kick up to relieve his monotony, if so we never knew it.

My hand was being held by Mr. Bolckow while watching the horses and, as everything was working smoothly, we ventured quite near to the obedient animals, when an extra blare from a trumpet combined with an extra big boom from the drum caused one of the leaders to rear up and very nearly fall back on top of us. In our hasty retreat I fell down, embedded my knees in the gravel and dirtied my best frock.

Mrs. Bolckow, who had come to look for us, turned round a corner at this moment and, seeing her husband picking gravel from my knees and dusting me down, exclaimed, "Oh! my dear, what 'ave you done." "Nufing," he replied angrily; "I 'aven't done nufing."

But I must hark back to the Prince who seemed greatly relieved when his speech was off his mind.

There was a ball in the evening at which I am told the Prince danced and seemed to enjoy himself. Rather a pretty Miss Branwell was staying with my people and went to the ball with them; she was chosen by the Prince to be one of his partners, which pleased her. Next day I heard her talking about this honour and gathered she thought the Prince very charming but that his dancing did not live up to the rest of him.

It was then the fashion to dance the "deux-temps" fast and furiously, it consisted of turning round very often and very fast, followed by considerable breathlessness.

After the Prince's departure, Mr. Bolckow was offered a knighthood, but with grateful thanks declined it. I heard a small rude boy say "he had no use for it."

A great picture expert had carte blanche to fill the house with all the best pictures money could procure. They were not chosen with a view to the house, so the home had to be altered for the pictures.

A special wide white marble staircase was built with a good head light, under which on a landing half-way up the stairs stood Landseer's "Monarch of the Glen," for which 6900 guineas was paid. I am writing from memory and it may not have been that particular picture, though I think it was. I clearly remember, however, a noble stag standing listening, painted by Landseer—half-way up the white marble stairs; the effect from the bottom was grand.

The owner of all these luxuries was a kind-hearted charitable man, but in many ways careful of his pennies. I had luncheon with him and his wife in Prince's Gate shortly before he died. It was rather pitiful to see a millionaire sitting at a table laden with gold plate, delicate viands, beautiful fruits, sweets, and flowers. He was unable to enjoy any of the good things; a small fried whiting by the doctor's orders came in on a special dish for him, which he ate listlessly.   He left an enormous fortune, but having no children it was most of it settled on his nephew, another Bolckow, but the terms and wording of the will were such as very nearly to ruin the unfortunate man.   As far as I can remember a certain portion of income had to be set apart and a certain sum spent yearly on buying land.

His widow was left with the house in Prince's Gate and what most people would consider a comfortable fortune.

Latterly she had so entirely lost her nerve that she dare not drive in her own carriage, but frequented the homely and, as she thought, safer penny bus.

Some of Mr. Bolckow's expressions were amusing.   Once at breakfast, when he thought I was not eating enough, he said, "Oh, do allow me to press an egg upon you."

He was a tactful host.   One night when all the big-wigs, who always flutter round those who have acquired great wealth, had been invited to dine before a General Election that was in the offing, two big local landlords became so quarrelsome that most of those at the table held their breath wondering who would come to blows first, when, with some dignity, the little round-about, grey-haired, square-bearded host stood up and said, "I tink, gentlemen, if you 'ave had enuf vine ve vill adjourn dis meeting and join de ladies."

CHAPTER IX

Some of the Author's Loves—Old Joseph and his Ewe-Lamb—Homeless Reuben Stride—His temperament and Philosophy—Brusher Mills, the Snake Charmer—His Home-made Abode—A Temple of Romance—A Storehouse of Treasures—A Lovish Baptist Minister—His Love Letter—Author's Vanity receives a Rude Shock—Her Successor.

I HAVE had a number of loves in my life, which sounds indiscreet and exciting. Many of them have been amongst the poor, the very poor. Their patience, faith, pessimism and frugality of their lives have often appealed strongly to me. Having written of so many friends in the social world, I would like to introduce one or two in other walks of life who have interested me.

Old Joseph was one of my loves; he was a farm labourer living in one of our cottages. His unselfishness, faith and goodness taught me many lessons. He had lost both his wife and only son, all that was left to him was a little daughter barely seventeen, his ewe-lamb and housekeeper, and the same dread disease was going to carry her away. His one thought was to give her everything she wanted and to do all the work to save her strength from being taxed. Before going to his daily labour in the morning he washed the floor, cooked some potatoes ready for his daughter's dinner and his supper in the evening, besides numerous other small household duties.

I added my little endeavours, but we could not save her.

Joseph was rather peculiar and, when his neighbours offered to help him, he said that he did not "warnt any of them messing about his place." I sympathised in a measure, for he kept it beautifully clean, which is more than some of his neighbours would have done. Both he and his daughter set their faces strongly against a nurse. Here again I sympathised, knowing from experience what trouble they give in a house. In cottages I have seen them intolerable, tearing up the meagre stock of night-dresses, throwing things about and leaving everything dirty and in confusion.

So between us, old Joseph and I, we nursed the girl.

One day, when I had been some time by the bedside, I saw that the end was near, so when the old man came in at night I crept out, thinking he would like to be alone with his bairn. It is seldom there is any intermediate stage with the poor between living and dying, either they are well and live, or are ill and die; they cannot afford to indulge in any between stages. I could not rest that night and, when all the household had gone to bed, I sat by the open French windows leading on to a terrace, the moon looking coldly at me. I was thinking of things as they are and as they might be, and asking for comfort for old Joseph, when I heard footsteps coming up the gravel and on to the terrace. Joseph was staggering towards me as if his legs would hardly carry him. I was in the presence of desperate grief. Words would have seemed sacrilege. He came towards me shuffling his feet as though he did not see where he was going, and stood in front of me twiddling the blind cord, a picture of despair.

Bare-headed, his hair ruffled and untidy, his toil-bent back more humped than ever, his pathetic blue eyes filled with unshed tears that forbade him speaking, tears the more painful that they would fall back upon his heart unshed. Just for a moment the moon in pity hid her face, still he did not speak, so I put my hand on his and said, "I know, Joseph." That broke the spell, in a low husky voice he said, "S'cuse me, marm"—a pause, while he tried to moisten his dry lips, then with a burst of agony he almost screamed, "She's garn. Oh—oh—she's garn." In the silence of the night with no light save the moon it sounded like a voice from another world, where, maybe, souls are in torture. Then with another heartrending cry he threw out his arms towards the moon with uplifted face, "She's garn, my wee bit lassie"; then turned and stumbled away holding his head between his hands.

At first I thought it might be kind to leave him alone, then, remembering he had sought me in his sorrow, I gathered some flowers from the conservatory and followed him.

He was lying face down on the sofa in the kitchen of his cottage. As he did not move or speak, I went up to the sick room, thinking I would move some of the dear accustomed things it is such an agony to see when the owner wants them no more, and put them away for a while. I then made the bed straight and arranged all as it should be, laid some flowers in her hands and around her pretty fair hair on the pillow. Then, pouring out some brandy and water from a bottle we had been using for the invalid, took it to Joseph on the sofa and made him drink it.

I then led him upstairs; neither of us spoke. When he entered the room and found the pain-tossed pillows smooth, the now beautiful little face surrounded with a halo of tidy hair and flowers, all looking peaceful and comfortable, a great sigh of relief escaped him and he wrung the perspiration from his brow and flung it to the ground. I pulled him down beside me and sang softly the hymn that comes back to us all some time in our lives.

> "My God, my Father, while I stray,
>   Far from my home on life's rough way,
>   Teach me from my heart to say,
>   Thy will be done."

When I came to the verse,

> "If thou shouldst call me to resign,
>   What most I prize, it ne'er was mine,
>   I only yield thee what is thine.
>   Thy will be done."

my friend, now shaken with sobs, put out one trembling hand and stroked the soft fluffy hair, murmuring, "Aie—aie——" and I left him.

That night seemed more beautiful than any I had known before, and I rested by a gate seized with the everlasting wonder, "Why?" Why must pain, ugliness and sorrow walk ever hand in hand with joy, life and such a beautiful world? The dew was heavy and drove me home trying to find comfort in the thought "there can be no morning without a night."

Not long after this an accident laid me low. Every night as Joseph left work he came to ask for me, and enquire if I would give him the happiness of doing something for me. Most mornings he brought a fresh egg laid by his own fowls, a trout, some offering, and one day the first rose from off a little tree he and I had planted on the grave of the "wee bit lassie."

Later again, when the Reaper with the sickle visited my home, Joseph would allow no one to touch the grave but himself, and he spent some of his poor little savings on wire hairpins and other things wherewith to make the resting-place a bower of flowers and moss. He wished me to find the comfort he had experienced when he saw everything cared for in his bairn's room. This he explained to me in rough though tender words.

And now Joseph is no more, and there are no little Josephs left. I wish there were, with his heart of gold. He was one of my loves.

Another love, though a less intimate one, was Reuben Stride, whom I called the nineteenth-century philosopher. He was a well-known figure in the New Forest, and was, I am sorry to say, run over by a motor-car about a couple of years ago and killed,—at least he died as a result of the accident.

In this mind-our-own-business world how little we know of the many tragedies and dramas being enacted all around us, under our very noses. We hear of people who, by accident or disease, are bed-ridden for thirty or forty years; it is no uncommon occurrence. But it is surprising to find in England, close to our doors as it were, a man hale and hearty over seventy years old, who has not slept in a bed for more than fifty years, yet such was the case with Reuben Stride. There is something grand and pathetic in his fine old face. Look at it. Every line tells a tale of endurance, storms weathered, struggles of mind as well as body, and maybe faith, hope and charity.

Surely with a head like that there must have been brains above the average, a kind heart with that benevolent nose, eyes looking at nothing but , seeing much, hidden under that rugged moustache and beard a determined mouth and chin, the whole reminding one of a splendid rock standing out at sea all alone; mellowed and rounded by time and many tides.

You will ask how comes it this interesting study found no pillow for his head during all these long

Reuben Stride, a Nineteenth-Century Philosopher

years? He would like to have told you himself, but as he cannot I will.

That determined hidden-away mouth and chin had something to do with it, for he could brook no restraint, rules or regulations. When seventeen he entered the Navy. After serving eighteen months he could stand it no longer, and came to the conclusion the life did not suit him. The strict discipline did not appeal to him, and he saw that if he remained there it would only mean trouble and ructions, so he deserted. For some time he evaded capture, hiding here and there, always in fear of being traced, until one day it actually happened, and he was taken back a captive to be rigorously "broken in." In spite of all punishments he absolutely refused to obey any orders, and at last the authorities were thankful to get rid of him.

In recounting his experiences the old man used to say, "I tole 'em they could kill me, but I wouldn't do it." So he was discharged with what it was hoped he would consider "ignomy."

Being one of Nature's roamers, Reuben could not live by rule; his wants were few and simple, but he must be in the open air and free to roam at will amongst all the things he loved, things that count for so little to many but were great to this philosopher. The sun, moon, stars, birds and beasts all loved companions, filling his heart with peace and content, leaving no room for fractiousness.

After his discharge he wandered about Berkshire

and Wiltshire working here and there as a labourer. Then for some years he was employed as a carter in one situation in the New Forest, a life much more suited to his temperament.   During the last fifteen or sixteen years he found employment as a cattle-driver, which most people consider a trying heart-breaking task, for the poor beasts get so frightened and distracted they do not know what they are doing and have a cussed way of invariably going in the wrong direction.

This work, with occasional assistance from kind-hearted people in the New Forest, where he was a familiar figure, enabled him to subsist.

When asked why he seemed so wobbly on his feet when standing up after resting, he would explain that he "lost both his great toes an' some o' t'others through frost bite."

There is something fine in the marvellous patience of the poor, and the religious pessimism which has come to them from father to son through countless years since the dawn of time and history.

When individualism is strong it goes in search of truth and is at war with convention, leaving us all in different premises, philosophers or vagabonds.

When I asked Reuben if it were really true that he had not slept in a bed for fifty years, and if so why the police had not interfered, he replied, "Oh yes, that's all right enough.   I've slep' out more 'an fifty years, and allers kep' myself clean and decent. P'leece!   They dont take no note o' me, they know I ain't no biding place, nobody meddles o' me.   I never carries no lucifers yer know, an' if the p'leece wants to take me I sh'd say, 'Yo jess go to so-and-so,' wherever I was sleeping, an' they'd say, 'oh, he's all right, let un bide, don't you meddle along o' he.' "

When friends offered him a bed he declined, custom had heightened the spell of his quaint resting-places, he was happier under the stars or among the straw.

His face spoke of hard times but a placid resignation, that birthright of the unambitious. He argued to himself philosophically that he would rather have frost-bitten toes of his own choosing, than those ordained for him by other people. There he has my sympathy.

Some people said he was mad, but he was far from it. I have observed a tendency amongst the common crowd to consider as mad everybody they do not understand.

I was a great admirer of old Reuben, and am contemplating putting up over his grave:

"To the Memory of a dear old 19th Century Philosopher.

> "To sleep and take my rest,
>   The old sea at my door,
>   The grey hills there in the west,
>   What can a man want more?"

The New Forest teems with people, places and things of interest. I have heaps of loves there. The little ponies, children of adversity, about whom

I could write for a week without stopping and be happy all the time; the gypsies, about whom there is so much that is intensely interesting that I have never seen in print, and of whom I have the most beautiful and uncommon photographs. In fact the New Forest is one of the earth's storehouses. In it one gets very near the "Peace that passeth understanding." The glorious old trees with arms spread out and joining over our heads in benediction, the bracken waving and whispering at our feet.

The Greeks consecrated each favourite wood and grove to some Divinity. Wise old Greeks! During New Forest rambles many other intimate friendships are formed as well as with the ponies. There is something about the Forest that makes one moralise. Perhaps it is the dear beautiful trees, companions that never fail us. Nature loves them as much as I do, and deals so gently with them in their old age, covering up all their infirmities, draping them with moss and lichen, twining round them ivy, clematis and woodbine for support in their old age, in return for the help extended to them in their youth by their life-long friends the trees.

Another of my New Forest loves was "Brusher Mills," the snake-charmer. The name bestowed on him by his parents and godparents was "Harry" Mills, but he was better known as "Brusher Mills." We often hear of snake charmers in the east, but not often in the west. Strictly speaking he was

Brusher Mills of the New Forest

no charmer, but found it convenient so to describe himself, as he had to make his living somehow, and the reptiles had an attraction for him. It does not sound as though it would be a very lucrative calling, but when that stern mother, Necessity, puts her foot down, and we are thrown upon our own resources, it is wonderful what we can do.

Snake catching or "charming," as Mills would call it, as a means of making a living, would not appeal to everybody, but he was an expert and had acquired that familiarity that is supposed to breed contempt. He had no fear of any snake.

There is something weird and yet fascinating in the idea of living all alone day and night for nineteen years in the midst of that Temple of Romance, the New Forest, in a home-made hut, composed of branches and stems of trees arranged in conical form assisted with peat to keep out the wind and rain, his closest companions the English snakes, with whose whims and abodes he was so well acquainted, yet in this hut and all alone Mills lived for nineteen years.

The first thing that occurred to the mind of those interested in this strange old man was what he did with the snakes and how he caught them. He made no secret of the fact that, at one time, he made a small income by supplying the Zoo with snakes to satisfy the appetites of some of the inhabitants. Latterly he gained a precarious living by displaying his snake-charming gifts to tourists and trippers.

He did a fair trade by describing to those really

interested the difference between, and peculiarities of, the three English snakes. He was usually well rewarded. He also made and sold wonderful concoctions procured by boiling down adders and securing the fat to act as antitoxin for snake bites, cure rheumatism, and other maladies, loudly praising their virtues. Heaven alone knows what the poor souls who bought the mixture did with them, whether they drank some in their tea or mixed it in poultices, or used it as a cure for housemaid's knee; there seemed to be no end to its possibilities.

When starting out to catch snakes he wore no gloves or protection of any kind for his hands. His hunting kit, indeed his only kit, everyday and Sunday alike, consisted of a greatcoat or two, given to him by admirers and friends. They were usually worn one on top of the other, and had capacious pockets added by himself. He wore big thick laced-boots surmounted by the most wonderful thing in gaiters, made regardless of pattern or shape, which arranged themselves in concertina-like crinks and folds around his legs till they reached his knees, where they were welcomed by still more concertina-like trouser knees. My own impression is he made them both himself, got into them somehow, leaving time and chance to do the rest.

A felt hat that may once have been black and beautiful completed this toilet, but it was no longer black, rather a picturesque purple, green and grey, souvenirs from wind, sun and rain. That was all, except a many-hued handkerchief tied around his

Brusher Mills' Home in the New Forest

neck. Doubtless there were nether garments of sorts, but if one might judge by the display on washing day, when they were hung up to dry, his wardrobe was not extensive.

The paraphernalia of his craft was simple in the extreme, consisting of a long forked stick to arrest the snakes, a pair of long tongs with which to pick them up and a tall, rather narrow can or pail to place them in. This he carried by a handle.

How the snakes were killed I cannot say for certain, as Mills was not communicative as to his methods, which, however, I gathered were crude. He was clever in the way he caught hold of the reptiles, pouncing on them and catching them with his tongs just behind his head. The forcible application of the tongs obliged their mouths to be kept open, which prevented them doing any harm until he had manipulated their poisonous organ.

Moles were at times added to his bag, and as their skins sell well he probably found them lucrative. During his sojourn in the Forest he accounted for an enormous number of snakes and moles.

He was an interesting old man, and remained unmarried, preferring to live in the peaceful surroundings he knew to the possibly less peaceful life of matrimony. Maybe he was wise, for it is not every woman who would feel content and happy in such a rustic homestead, surrounded by snakes in various stages, some painfully alive and frisky, others dying in uncanny wriggles and coils, others dead, awaiting transit or to be turned into "heal-alls."

The old man's speech always left a little to the imagination, whether from living alone so many years, or from having no roof to his mouth, it is difficult to say, but it was not easy to understand him. Perhaps it was as well, for those who knew and understood him best said that when man or snake exasperated him his vocabulary was extensive and profound, in fact quite prehistoric.

He died suddenly on July 1st, 1905, from heart disease. In Brockenhurst churchyard is a carved marble tombstone to the memory of Brusher Mills. It was erected by the public. The carving on the stone is beautiful, representing Mills standing by his self-made hut, with snakes in his hand, presumably ready for his stock-pot. The workmanship is masterly and delicate. I like to think these loves of mine, Reuben Stride and Brusher Mills, are resting amidst the surroundings they loved so well.

I should like to write a great deal about the English snakes. Many people know nothing of them or their habits, but this is not the place for me to do it, and I might bore my readers.

Another love of mine, one whom I did not love, but who took it into his head that he loved me, was a Welsh Baptist minister. The whole affair was very funny. We were renting a house in Wales for shooting and fishing. While I was scrambling about gathering wild flowers on the property, this minister came down a lane close to me. He had been visiting one of the farms.   He stood and stared at me rather rudely I thought, so I walked away.

He then took the opportunity to hang about the place, which annoyed me very much, but I could say nothing as he found it convenient to try and make the old gardener and his wife Baptists, and what is more succeeded, and the silly old gardener, who had been twenty-eight years on the place, submitted to being baptised in a neighbouring pond, receiving a chill from which before long he died.

In consequence of his (the Baptist's) attention to his new converts who lived at the lodge, I seldom could go in that direction without meeting him and having to listen to his nonsense.   He then took to writing me impassioned letters full of my grace, charm, etc., and he was going to write a book all about me, in fact all sorts of wonderful things.   At last he became so annoying I put the matter into a local solicitor's hands, and that made an end to it.

His letters, partly through being in English, out of compliment to me, which was a language of which he knew little, being very Welsh, and partly through his being very uneducated, were worthy of *Punch*.   Once he wished to tell me he had waded through a field of wet potatoes to catch a glimpse of me.   This was the way he expressed it, having evidently sought the aid of a dictionary.

"Beautiful lady.   My harte been soar in me because I have not seen you late.   I spend a wet afternoon in among the wet potato boughs near the beds of the dogs hopping for a site of the gracious lady and her smile. Oh, come sweet lady were I do see you. I eat not, I sleep not for the fretting of you. Send to me 1. kine word to save your humble servant and slave, or I may do a mischief and God will forgive you not."

I thought the potato boughs rather nice. He had evidently searched for a suitable word to describe the wet potato tops, and had found boughs or branches. The dogs' beds referred to were the kennels.

My vanity received a rude shock soon after the despatch of the solicitor's letter by the lover marrying an old woman who had lived in the village who weighed a good twenty stone. She had saved a little money and shared her kitchen with a fat pig, an emaciated cow and some fowls!

My other lovers have been more every-dayish, and therefore of no interest to anybody but myself.

CHAPTER X

TURNING over the pages in the sketch-book
of my life, I find the studies in it very
varied and of unequal value, all mingled
and jostling one another. Some of the pages are
very crowded. I have been trying to recall what I
liked best about each of the figures that attracted
me most. Some I find have only interested me after
losing sight of them, after turning over another
page, then the interest lay in thinking of them in the
chrysalis stage, and trying to remember if I had
imagined any of the colours that appeared when
they became gorgeous butterflies.

Amongst the crowd passing panorama fashion

before my mind, I find the greatest conversation-alists have been undoubtedly Oscar Wilde and Charles Parnell, though on entirely different lines.

Oscar Wilde's choice of language and his gentle voice were to me much more poetic than those of the poet laureate of his time. Mr. Wilde's writing and his poetry were all real, full of feeling and beautifully expressed thought. Who can read his *De Profundis,* written in prison, without being moved? Much of it is possibly exaggerated in expression, but then he was exaggerated in feeling, and it flowed from the pen of a man in anguish, who was unable to live without a theatrical setting, with-out posing even in his own mind and for his own benefit.

I remember him in the heyday of his popularity, when women crowded round him to write in their birthday books, hostesses adding to their notes and cards of invitation one of the two inducements of that hour, either "P.B." or "O.W.," the former giving us to understand some professional beauties would be present for us to feast our eyes on, and the latter that Oscar Wilde would be there to talk high art with us.

When he first appeared in society and invented the "Howell and James Young Man" movement, he was prodigiously laughed at, but made much of all the same. His hair was long when first I beheld him, and he strolled up and down Piccadilly in a soft wide-awake hat a little on one side, an Irving-like velveteen cloak worn carelessly and always open to show a daffodil or single yellow flower standing high-artishly in his buttonhole, almost invariably on a long stalk and on one side—posing.

He went to America to preach his Æstheticism, then returned to London and recast his high-browism, colour schemes and dado ideas, becoming a Piccadilly darling, dressed in the height of fashion, short hair wonderfully arranged, and his ties quite peculiar to himself.

He was a man of moods, one day his conversation, which was always brilliant, would be brilliantly sad, another day cryptic sayings and epigrams chased each other from his tongue. No matter what subject was started, he could always pick it up and toss it back with an original note or two attached.

He did not mind being laughed at; I think he rather liked it, joining in the merriment at his own expense.

His evening dress was peculiar. I was never sure whether or no his low-cut waistcoat, fastening with three buttons on one side, was cut all in one with the funny sort of black stock he wore without any visible beginning or end. This stock reposed beneath a turn-down collar of the fashion adopted by women over the necks of their dresses. The cuffs of his shirt turned up over the sleeves of his coat.

The evening buttonhole was always white, in contrast to the yellow one worn in the daytime. He was not good-looking, his face was too heavy, his mouth was the least pleasant feature. He wore an enormous ring on the little finger of one hand, I forget which. In the distance it looked like the big splodgy seal on Government documents. This toilet was completed by a fob crowded with seals, looking like a child's rattle, the *tout ensemble* being a mixture of high art, dandyism and effeminacy.

No one will deny that he was eccentric, a genius, and I think I may add a brilliant conversationalist. I often recall one of his very wise sayings, "We should be careful how we choose our enemies."

Charles Parnell was at his best on political subjects, and his sarcasm was entertaining; he could enlarge most feelingly on the sorrows of the poor that we have always with us, but his conversation was rather spoilt for me, by not being able to rid myself of the feeling that he was not quite sincere even to himself.

Some people have been rude enough to state there never has been a woman who was a great conversationalist. I do not agree with these critics. Lady Ermyntrude Malet, wife of our at one time Ambassador in Berlin, was a conversationalist of no mean order, besides being a bright and tactful woman of considerable education and culture. There are people who consider themselves great conversationalists, forgetting monologue is not conversation, in the same way that a crowd is not company.

That great religious reformer, the Apostle St. Paul, who was also a man of the world, full of courtesy and chivalry, as well as a diplomatist, says, "Let your speech be always with grace, seasoned with salt, that ye may know how ye ought to answer every man." Herein lies the art of conversation.

Sir Edward Malet, who was a little man, charming and dignified, was very popular with the German Imperial family.

The most charming hostess I can remember is the present Lady Ripon,* whose parties were delightfully cosmopolitan.

Exclusiveness is a thing of the past. People have become bored by it, finding themselves out in the cold, while Royalties and nitrate kings hobnob. Lady White, wife of the Ladysmith man, was another charming hostess; also Mrs. Oppenheim, her salons were famous.

The most fascinating women I recall were Lady Colin Campbell and Madame Cassavetti, a Russian. I remember at Torquay one winter when the Cassavettis were there, being quite startled in their front hall by an enormous black bear, standing on its hind legs holding a tray for visitors' cards. Suddenly a brilliant yellow light appeared in the beast's eyes. I asked a girl near me if she saw anything peculiar about the bear's eyes, as I thought I might be suffering from delusion, but she had seen it before and explained, "It is an electric light that the butler turned on from somewhere in the wall."

Lady Colin Campbell, who had rejoiced in the maiden name of Blood, was a most fascinating

* Died since writing this.

woman and clever. Many loved her much. We were renting the house next to hers in Cadogan Place, when some learned bewigged people from the Law Courts arrived to find out for themselves how much they could see through certain keyholes, some doubt having been thrown upon the servants' evidence during the hearing of the divorce case. There was a little garden at the back of our house corresponding to another exactly like it belonging to the Campbells, and we were greatly amused watching one of the bewigged ones scaling the wall, while others looked on in admiration. There were some questions about whether some of the fourteen co-respondents had not entered the house by scaling this wall.

Several friends of mine were implicated in this case, poor Sir Eyre Shaw for one, but he came off with flying colours and we were all glad, for he was extremely popular and deservedly so. He behaved like a man over this case, which some did not, and we all congratulated him. He was quite a lady's man, admired all pretty people and thoroughly enjoyed a flirtation, entering into the spirit of the thing with zest. He became quite good-looking and much smarter as he grew older.

When first he was introduced to me I was much struck with his length of neck, which he did nothing to subdue, wearing very low turn down collars. I told him once he shocked me by being so *décolleté*, and that I should send him a tulle tucker out of one of my ball dresses to wear round his neck. He declared he would wear it if I kept my promise.   I was too good-natured to impose this ordeal on him.

Lady Colin edited *The Ladies' Field* for some time, and died a martyr to rheumatism.

The cleverest and most alarming woman of my acquaintance was the late Duchess of Cleveland. She was a great friend of Sir Tatten Sykes. While being desperately afraid of her, people would hover round, regardless of having their noses bitten off, in hopes of catching some of her witty sayings, and hearing *other* people snubbed.   She was at Raby Castle once when I was there in the long-agos, and I was rather surprised to find there also a sprightly and pretty woman, who was a pet aversion of hers. There had been a row between them a short time before over a bazaar (for charity!).   We were in the museum looking at the curious natural history specimens collected by the old Duchess of Darlington.   James Lowther was with us saying amusing but disrespectful things about the specimens, when the sprightly lady joined us.   James Lowther, who loved teasing people, said, "Hullo, Gipsy, you're looking very cheap; feeling bad?"   "No," she replied, "how unkind of you, that is only a polite way of saying I am looking plain."   With his boisterous laugh he turned to the Duchess, being unaware the relations were strained, and said, "I've seen her looking better, haven't you?"   The Duchess' face froze into hard lines as she looked the little woman up and down, then said, "Only wants another coat of varnish, I think."

Feeling most uncomfortable, I moved away, but not before I heard, "Another coat and a new wig wouldn't be amiss for your grace, but you should be well scraped first." Jim Lowther was delighted, and stood an amused spectator, while the ladies had their say. At times I have heard the Duchess exceedingly rude to people, at others, keep a whole room full of people electrified with her wit. She died in 1901.

The Harcourt's house in Grafton Street was a sure find for interesting people, and Lady Harcourt was a homely and genial hostess. If the walls of that house could speak, they could tell us interesting stories of important state and political secrets, of clandestine meetings between beautiful women and gay young men, not to mention a few more mature couples.

This was after the Harcourts had left the house and Madame Lili (Mrs. Pocklington) had moved into it from her shop in Oxford Street, where she had been so successful with her millinery business that larger premises had become necessary.

A great number of the "rank and fashion" went to her for their hats and bonnets. The rooms were large, and lovers found they could converse there in safety between the tryings on of head-gear. One or two forbidden little affairs matured there quite nicely.

Mrs. Pocklington, who was a very charming and smart woman, died quite early in life, and at a time when she was doing a big business. I have been

Sir William Harcourt in His Young Days

there when the carriages were standing outside her door almost as if a reception was taking place.

I could never understand why, when her affairs were wound up, there was so little money. Possibly though brimful of taste, she had no business capacity, in which case all her taste and hard work would avail her nothing. She was one of the first of the lady milliners before the epidemic set in.

For many years Mr. A. J. Balfour was amongst the most popular men in England,—partly, no doubt, because he was a statesman (we have had so few of late years), that we all leant on him, and partly on account of his charm of manner when wishing to be agreeable. His powers of being able to convince people against their better judgment has been quite unique, but few have been so respected.

At the time he was Chief Secretary for Ireland he stayed a great deal with some of my people. Special rooms were reserved for him as his own special property, where he could leave his things and come back and find them ready for use. He said rather an interesting thing one day, namely, that he considered himself to have been in every way as competent in the intellectual sphere when he was an undergraduate as when he was afterwards Prime Minister. The public loved him better than he loved the public, and he had a naughty habit when people came on purpose to see him of retiring to his rooms and refusing to be drawn.

Many will remember the time during the South

African War when Mr. Balfour was asked some questions as to what was taking place out there, and for which we were all paying. His reply was that he knew "no more than the man in the street." This was when it was his business to know,—at least, so we all thought. I do not think he has held our faith in quite the same way since. We all know he professes never to read the papers, and this is not a pose, it is true. He never does read a paper, and attends to his correspondence and business in bed before he gets up in the morning. He does not care to appear before midday if he can help it, finding, as I do, the early morning hours are the best for work. Under the shadow of the Coalition Government he has lost more of the faith of some people, judging from all I hear.

Socially, perhaps, Captain Charles Burn, the King's Messenger and member for Torquay, is one of the most popular men of my acquaintance. He is very good-looking and well-mannered, ready to do a good turn for anybody at a moment's notice. He married the daughter of Lord Leith of Fyvie, the latter's only child.

In Cairo during the Egyptian Campaign, we went in a crowd to see Captain Burn off to the front. Gerry Portal called out as the train left the station, "Good-bye, Charlie, may your beauty never be less," and we thrust a farewell bouquet through the carriage window, consisting of carrots with their bonny green hair tied up with bonny blue rib-

Sir William Harcourt as a "Retired Leader"

bons, a few trailing ferns after the character of asparagus sprengeri added grace to the posy.

The best dancers I have known were Captain Harry Lees, of the 3rd Dragoon Guards, who died while larking with his favourite charger in the Phœnix Park in Ireland, and Major Slade, of the 10th Hussars, a beautiful dancer, who was killed in Egypt, and mourned by a number of young ladies and a widow or two, who said they were engaged to him.   About thirteen put on deep mourning.

I must not forget the Rajah of Cooch Behar, who danced, as he did many other things, exceedingly well. He was one of the most English of the Rajahs that I have met, and the only one that I have seen who did not look amiss in English mufti. He became an hon. lieutenant-colonel in the British army, and hon. A.D.C. to the King Emperor when Prince of Wales. I have danced with him in India, Paris and London. His education was completed in England, and he became very English. On his return to his own country he was full of ideals for the benefit of his state and people, but this country held such attraction for him that he could not keep away for long, and this led to discontent amongst his subjects in India. Cooch Behar is small, but has a population of about six hundred thousand, spread over thirteen hundred square miles. The Rajah's family has reigned there as chiefs for four hundred years.

The Maharajah married in 1878. I liked the Ranee very much. When first I knew her she was very shy, but now has an assured and engaging manner. She is well-known and much liked in England. Her late husband was a Hindu. At one time to cross the "Kala Pani," or Black Water, would have been considered a pollution to a high caste man, but all that is in the past. Rules and observances of caste are no longer considered of the same consequence that they were even when I first went to India. It is not now necessary to pay large sums or go through all sorts of revolting ceremonies to be received again amongst the chosen or for ever be an outcast after diverging from the caste laws.

Chandra Sen came across the "Black Water," and did not seem in much fear of either his people or his Deity, and he allowed his granddaughter when only twelve and a bit, to marry the Maharajah of Cooch Behar, who was only fifteen himself at the time.

The moment the Rajah became a big man in London he dwindled down to a small man in Cooch Behar. That is the trouble with native noblemen who become Anglicised, who dance, drink champagne, and play games.

Once on the racecourse at Calcutta, when all the "Sahib log" were applauding the late Maharajah of Patiala for winning a race at a big meeting, an old Sikh gentleman looking on said in tones of disgust that the times were bad indeed when the great chieftain of the Sikhs aimed only at being a clever "Chabuk sowar" (jockey).

The Maharajah of Cooch Behar

This feeling should be borne in mind at the present moment when we have a Secretary of State for India going out to stir up the most Conservative spot on earth with a barge pole.

All sorts of nostrums are afloat, of which probably the most preposterous is that fathered by the present Commander-in-Chief in India, Sir Charles Monro, that young Indian gentleman aspiring to commissions in the Army should be educated in England, at Woolwich and Sandhurst, apparently being oblivious of the fact that under those circumstances they will lose all influence over their men, who had much rather be commanded by a Britisher than by a renegade.

In precise degree as Cooch Behar became Anglicised so did he lose all influence with his own people. At the end of his career any young British official carried more weight with the people of Cooch Behar than did their own Rajah, or his wife, Sumati Dwee.

The Rajah was a well-built man and looked very sweet in a pink dressing-gown going down the gangway of a P. and O. liner en route for his tub. The only other person I can remember who looked quite so beautiful was Sir Lepel Grifin, the political, who chose the time for his bath when the rest of us were having luncheon, strolling down the saloon in *the* most lovely things in pajamas embroidered with coats of arms and other attractive decorations, carrying a huge sponge and a bath towel of great size emblazoned with his monogram arranged so that we might admire them all. He was very good-looking at the time of which I am writing, and he knew it. He had wondrous curly hair. The more it was wet, the tighter it curled, apparently.

The Rajah was a first-rate sportsman, and his annual shoots in India were considered one of the events of the year. He was an especially fine shot with both gun and rifle, and had a sunny disposition. It took him a long time to get spoilt by the fine ladies of title who so far forgot themselves as to curtsey to him in public and "carry on" with him in private when they got the chance. Never shall I forget my surprise the first time I saw an hysterical English Countess bobbing to him. I thought he also was a little surprised, but it is part of a native gentleman's creed never to appear surprised at anything. The bear-leader even begged these ladies to restrain themselves, while the Anglo-Indians nearly fainted.

After some seasons in London, with Royal Ascots and many presents to kind friends, the revenue of Behar estate gave out, and when the great man returned to Bombay and found it was not open to him to dine at the Yacht Club the shock was terribly severe, in fact too severe.

He gave me a sweet little etching done by himself of an Indian scene mounted in a wonderfully carved frame, but one year when I let my house it disappeared, and I was sorry.

His eldest son inherited the love for England and

was a keen cricketer, but he also spent too much money and got into hot water in consequence.

Thinking of native caste, religions, and prejudices reminds me of when Captain Vigne, of the 97th Regiment, was staying at an hotel in India *en route* for Simla, and there came to the same hotel a big native gentleman with whom he entered into conversation, asking him how he managed about his food, receiving the reply, "I can eat as you do."

"But are you not a high caste?"

"I am a Brahmin of the very highest caste, but you see I am sufficiently rich to have no prejudices."

This sounded remarkable in those days. The gentleman was the Prime Minister of Rewar. Asked what his mission was to his Excellency the Governor, he replied that his master did not consider that the promises made him by Lord Canning had been sufficiently carried out.

Captain Vigne pointed out all the benefits he had received, asking what more could possibly be expected.

P.M. "Well, there is something!"

Capt. V. "What is it?"

P.M. "Oh! er! it is a little something."

Capt. V. "Well out with it."

P.M. "Is there not a little thing they call the Garter?"

Capt. V. "If that is what you want I think you had better go home again; it is useless, quite hopeless."

P.M. "What would your commission be if you could get it, 10 lakhs?"

Capt. V. "How would it be to ask for a peerage?"

P.M. "But how could his Royal Highness the descendant of kings when the English still painted their bodies accept such a thing!"

I think the man who surprised me more than anybody else I ever met was Prince Bismarck, at that time Chancellor of the German Empire. It was when Sir Edward Malet was Ambassador at Berlin. I had always pictured Bismarck as a hard, rather cruel, and disagreeable man, who would be able to speak nothing but German and be disliked by all in his own country save the Emperor.

My surprise was therefore great when I found he could speak English well, though slowly, as if searching for the words he wanted. Greater joy still, we had something in common, for I discovered he loved all the dear purposeful creepy-crawlys of the earth, and had made a study of them. They were his companions as they are mine. I think anyone with no love for or intimate knowledge of the busy world round our feet must for ever travel alone.

My world of creepy-crawlys embraces birds, butterflies, moths, dragonflies, etc., many of which are not really creepys at all. Prince Bismarck loved all nature, but especially the crawlys. He gave me a most interesting account of some spiders with yellow bodies that are of the warrior type and fight fierce battles. Once he put two on a bush to see them fight. Their tactics were full of subtlety and once, when Bismarck interfered, one of the spiders swelled out his body and tried to frighten him by making little rushes in his direction and giving what he presumed were stamps with its feet, after the fashion of rabbits when they wish to warn others of any danger. The Prince loved trees; they spoke to him as they do to me. He loved beetles and spiders, so do I. We became so engrossed comparing notes that I forgot for a time I was engaging too much of his attention to the exclusion of more important people waiting for a word with him.

I met the great man only once again some years later when in Paris, having luncheon with the Rothschilds. We greeted one another with affection born of our mutual loves. He was quite excited at our meeting again, and wished to introduce a friend of his to whom he had often spoken of my love for animals and all the underworld and things of nature. A fierce-looking little German was introduced and out of compliment to me they spoke English. I will not attempt to copy their accents, but this was the introduction. "This is the lady of whom you have heard me speak who loves *bugs* as I do!" A little shiver ran down my back and I was almost frightened out of my best Sunday manners, but as nobody seemed surprised at my love for bugs I gradually recovered.

Long after this I found that scientific men, when

they cannot locate and name any particular microbes, classify them under the sort of slang appellation of bugs, so I hope that after all it may have been understood in that sense and not that I loved the on-board-ship variety.

Bismarck's face gave the impression of great determination, amounting possibly to obstinacy. His face was big and square, heavy eyebrows grew low over his eyes. His jaw was cruel and determined, slightly contradicted by his chin. The general effect was one of squareness. It seemed strange to look at this powerful man, both mentally and physically, and think that his recreation, his pleasure, was amongst the mysteries wrapped round the little crowds of which we know so little, all full of earnest purpose, working untiringly, and patiently through their little span of life. The amount of knowledge the Prince had acquired could only have come from close observation. Books give us so little information or insight into the lives that fill one with admiration, wonder and respect. I love all my little fellow travellers.

Bismarck died in July, 1898.

CHAPTER XI

REVISITING one's old home after an absence of some years is always a painful
pleasure when some of the loved tenants
have gone. Lady Sophia Cecil experienced this
when, after a long absence, she happened to be
staying near Bogner, and decided she would like to
go over her old home at Goodwood and show it to
her companion who was with her.

It will be remembered Lady Sophia was the
widow of Lord Thomas Cecil, and daughter of the
Duchess of Richmond who gave the famous ball at
Brussels on the eve of the battle of Waterloo.

Not knowing on what days the public were allowed to view the place, she thought she would try

and get in under any circumstances, so hired a cab and drove up very humbly. The housekeeper received them grumpily, saying, "You should come on the proper days if you want to see the place," but condescended to take them round, telling the visitors to "hurry up."

On entering the drawing-room the housekeeper remarked, pointing to a picture, "That is a picture of the Duke and his wife, the host and hostess of the Waterloo Ball, alluded to by Byron in "Childe Harold" when there were "Sounds of revelry by night." Turning to her companion Lady Sophia said, "We never thought it a good likeness of my dear mother." The astonished housekeeper became servile at once, apologising for her curt manner. No notice was taken of this, but before proceeding to her cab Lady Sophia said, "You have showed me over my old home. I only hope you are more civil to the tourists who visit Goodwood than you have been to us. Good day."

Lady Sophia and her sister, Georgie, Lady de Ros, never could agree as to the locality of the ball-room in Brussels, but Lady Sophia always said she was the most likely to be correct as her sister was older and too occupied with her partners to pay much attention or remember, while she was only a child looking on and taking notice of everything as children do. Lady de Ros had been a constant partner of the Duke of Wellington at the ball and had buckled on his sword when the officers ran away at full speed to Waterloo, Napoleon having arrived a few days before he was expected.

Latterly Lady Sophia Cecil lived in Granville Place, where she kept up the old-fashioned custom of having sucking-pig for her Christmas dinner, that being her favourite *pièce de résistance*. Many of her guests would doubtless have preferred a good Norfolk turkey.

We do not come across many sucking-pigs now, I am glad to say, but it was a favourite dish of my maternal grandfather's. When alone he liked his children to come and sit at the table while he ate his dinner. They had to bring their books which they were expected to read to themselves or look at pictures and not dare to breathe a word unless spoken to by their stern parents. About the time of which I am thinking a new litter of puppies had been born in the stables. These were a source of great joy to the children, especially to one small boy who had singled out a puppy as his favourite.

My grandfather was enjoying his sucking-pig, served up as was then considered appetising, full length on a dish decorated with pickled walnuts, apple sauce and beetroot. Suddenly he looked up and noticed one of his small sons with bent head glancing furtively at the dish, growing redder and redder in the face, whilst one or two big splashing tears fell on his book. When asked what was the matter, he replied, amid choking sobs, "Poor little yellow puppy!" The griefs of our childhood may have been brief, but they were very real.

I wonder what makes trivial happenings of long ago so fixed in our memories? While turning over in my mind some of the great moments I have experienced, I find a number of silly and quite unimportant affairs will push themselves forward. Why, for instance, at the present moment should I think of the following?

My husband thought he would like to spend his short leave fishing in Scotland. We agreed we would have another honeymoon all by our lone selves, "Far from the madding crowd," this being suitable to cooing and fishing combined. A bachelor friend offered us his cottage near Nairn, which he was not occupying, and said he had ordered "a trap of sorts," the only thing to be had in the neighbourhood, to meet us at the station.

It all sounded delightful. My man implored me to travel very light, as he did not wish to "drag a ton of luggage" about with us. I did my best and thought I had made a very modest and wise selection of "wanteds."

When the luggage stood on the platform I really felt proud and superior, for I had only one portmanteau that I could easily lift, and two rods neatly done up. My husband's luggage consisted of a huge portmanteau bulging out at the sides, and surrounded by a collection of fishing-rods, landing nets, reels, guns, great coat, etc. He was rather apologetic and burbled something about its being wise to take plenty of boots, but "the beastly things" take up a lot of room you know.

Being a reasonable and well-conducted wife, I agreed it really was marvellous how he had got so much into so small a space, and I was rewarded by being told I was a "sensible woman."

So in this happy frame of mind we sat close together, hand-in-hand, and looked out of the railway carriage window, hunting the country in imagination as we passed through it. We had great arguments as to how we should negotiate certain fences which look small when viewed from the window of a train, and often so formidable on closer acquaintance.

We arrived safely at the cottage so kindly lent to us after a rather exciting drive behind a wonderful grey mare of many summers. She had one ear that stood up and flickered while listening for any instructions, the other lying down and flopping about as she moved, a veritable scarecrow on four wonderfully useful clean legs.

The vehicle,—for what else can I call it?—had once been a dog-cart, no doubt of "high degree." One spring was gone, which gave it a rakish appearance, and no step was left of any kind, so my husband gave me a leg up as if I was mounting a horse and landed me on the back seat, telling me to "hang on." It was well I did, for evidently the bump I gave on landing was a signal to the grey mare, for off she flew, hard held by the country bumpkin driving her. My husband came tearing along behind, holding on to all the pieces of string and strap he could find hanging about. At last he clambered up by me with the aid of one foot I held out to assist him. I could not spare a hand; and from the back seat he scrambled over to the front by the driver, which effort resulted in his hat falling off.

I heard him conversing with the Jehu on the subject after this fashion, "Can't you see I've lost my hat, you fool? Stop when I tell you!"

Reply—"Don't you be a fashing of yourself. Ye can gang the morrow and be afther for fetching of it, for stop the varmint I canna!" Then came something about tempting Providence. However, all is well that ends well, but we saw the hat no more.

We did not have the best of weather, but had a glorious time all the same.

A minister of the kirk near where we were asked us to tea with him one afternoon. We had never seen him before this visit, and I have never seen him since, but he found we had many mutual friends so had a fine long pow-wow. He apologised much for his rooms, saying that being a bachelor he was rather untidy, and had nobody to put things straight for him, and so on.

Tea was brought in on a big black tin tray by his housekeeper, a stout woman with a healthy soap-shiny face, especially polished I think for the occasion, her skirts fulled in well round the waist, back and front alike, surmounted by a spotless apron. The lady did not smile upon us and we felt rather awed. Presently she left the room and we breathed again, for she was a dour-looking dame.

We were having an excellent tea with honey, bilberry jam and other good things, when our host suddenly rang the bell, explaining that his house-keeper had forgotten the slop basin. She arrived in response to the bell. We were then deep in conversation, so, almost without turning his head he said, "Mary, you have forgotten the slop basin." There came no rejoinder; she retired and shut the door. After waiting a while the bell was rung again and answered as before. "The slop basin, please, Mary, I am waiting for it."

A loud and piqued sniff was the only response and the door shut with emphasis. We continued our conversation, but no slop basin arrived. I assured him I liked the dregs of my tea, that all the "best families" did, but no, he would ring again.

This time Mary appeared with a red face and glittering eyes, and when asked why she did not bring the slop basin she, with arms akimbo, and nodding head, shouted, "Go on wi yer. It's all along o' yer own arkardness, for yer know yer h'ant got one!"

Tableau!

During that honeymoon I had some fine fishing. One cloudy day, when the water was dirty and rapid, I started fishing with a blue doctor I had tied myself. After fishing patiently for over an hour with no result I fortified myself with some damp biscuits and changed my blue doctor for a minnow, best of all dull day baits, I was soon rewarded, but had hooked a brute who sulked in a big pool. Nothing would persuade him to leave. I pulled steadily with rod low for the best part of an hour. Presently a tug or two warned me he was thinking of changing his tactics, and down he rushed, with me after him, rod up and reeling in as fast as I could. I wanted to get opposite to him when the fight would soon have been over. This he seemed to know, for he kept me racing up and down the bank, and then wading recklessly after him, fearing I might inadvertently in my scrambles lower the point of my rod when, of course, the show would be over at once and good-bye to the fish!

Just when on the point of tears from fatigue and excitement my fish began to weary too, and by degrees I got him into shallow water, keeping up a steady haul. He came splashing up on his side close under the bank.

I laid my rod down with nearly tight line, handle uppermost, and made a detour to avoid his head, crept down and tailed him. Such a beauty, about twenty pounds, the largest I had caught, but oh! should I be able to hold him? He kicked with all the life left in him, with the result that I ended by falling on my face but still holding him with both arms. I nearly lost him, but spread myself out as much as I could, determining that sooner than lose him I would lie there till one or both of us died.

Fortunately my lord, growing uneasy about me, came to see where I was. He had been fishing further up the river. Hearing his "coo-ee" with which we called one another when apart, I answered with what breath I had left, and when he arrived how pleased I was to see him. He soon settled the matter.

I had another quaint drive once at the end of a shooting expedition. We had been after snipe, my husband, Colonel Reginald Sartorious, V.C., Mrs. Dutton, a great friend of mine, and a first-rate shot, and myself. Our return journey brought us through Cawnpore, about which I must speak before relating my curious drive. None can surely visit that city of melancholy fame without memories surging through his brain of the heroes who shared in the agony of that time—Havelock, the gentle Outram and stern Sir Colin.

The story of the massacre is old history, but I happen to have a photograph of the house and well taken at the time under great difficulties while the blood of the women and children was still wet on the walls and floors, and as I have never heard of or seen another taken at that time it may be of interest. It was taken by a Doctor FitzGerald, with the relieving forces, and given to me by Colonel E. W. Shaw of the 27th Madras Native Infantry, who also was there with his regiment and is still living, enjoying life though eighty years of age, and I believe he is the only surviving officer of that regiment who were present at the time.

The three windows seen in the picture are those of the room where the five butchers carried out their ghastly work, the shrieks and scuffling telling its own pitiful tale. The horrors commenced at 4 p. m. one day until too dark to see, when the key was turned in the door and dying and dead were left mixed up until the morning, next day the work was continued, all being over by 9 a. m. except for a few little crazed children running round the well where their mothers' bodies had been thrown. The poor little souls were seized and thrown in alive with the rest. The historic well lies between the tree and the building, commencing near the trunk of the tree where the decorative tiles are visible on the broken wall and extending to where they are seen again on the left.

In a letter received from Colonel Shaw after reading my last book of "Memories," he says, referring to my description of the historic rooms and well, "The house was exactly in the condition you have described." Later he adds, "I also went to see where our poor countrymen and women had made so gallant a defence. The entrenchment was so low anyone could have jumped over it, and it is wonderful how they were able to hold out so long."

But now about the drive, though after thinking and writing of the Cawnpore days it is difficult to write of frivolities. We decided to stay at an hotel while passing through the city, as we were hardly presentable enough for putting up with friends. I retired to my room, the men went off to drink pegs with one of the Regiments stationed there at the time, I rather fancy it was the 95th.

After a while the men came back to say they had

The Well at Cawnpore; Photographed During the Mutiny

promised that we would all dine at their mess that night and a carriage would be sent to fetch us. We had no evening garment suitable to the occasion with us, but made ourselves clean. During the cleansing process in my room, which opened on to a verandah, one of the crows, so bold and cheeky in India, insisted on coming in. I shoo-ed it out several times, but it came back again and made tracks for a tea-tray standing near my bed. I then threw a brush at it. Beyond hopping to one side no notice was taken of my hostility, so I picked up a teaspoon and threw that, which the bird promptly picked up and flew away with it. I never saw the treasure again, and it was a treasure for I greatly dislike the taste of metal in my tea and when travelling always carried this old silver spoon with me, and now it was gone. The crow scored and I felt annoyed both with the bird and myself. It was a much-travelled spoon.

Being told the carriage was waiting my pleasure, I emerged clean but ruffled.

The carriage turned out to be a bullock cart, a low sort of affair with high sides. The seats ran omnibus-fashion down each side, comfortably cushioned in Turkey red. The steeds were two milk-white bullocks with humps on their backs, or "humfs," as my very English bearer called them. The servant who had brought this equipage was not allowed to drive, as Colonel Sartorious declared he was proficient in the art of driving such cattle. The gentle-eyed beasts of burden resenting a new driver refused to start until their usual driver spoke swear words to them, then we got under way, Colonel Sartorious driving without reins as is usual under the circumstances, the guiding and urging being carried out entirely by twisting the animals' tails. Presently, without any warning, we came to a full stop, and the steeds lay down in the middle of the road. The servant running behind thought Colonel Sartorious must have been giving an extra twist or perhaps a twist too little and this was the result.

We were growing very hungry and our hosts were waiting for us, so we were firm and refused to allow the Colonel to drive us any more, though he protested, saying he had often driven the same sort of animals in the same sort of cart belonging to his own regiment, the 6th Bengal Cavalry.

We arrived late of course, and threw the blame on to the broad shoulders of the driver who had so fancied his own powers in bullock-driving.

We passed the guardian angel standing over the historic well as we moved homewards the following day, and it was just the hour when long years before the Agony of Cawnpore had begun, 4 p. m., the time when those murdered ones had been in the habit of "eating the air," as they say in India, when people emerge after the heat of the day. I suppose I had become very silent, for I was asked if anything was the matter. My husband replied for me, saying, "She always gets the dumps in Cawnpore!"

I used to enjoy talking over Mutiny times and Indian days with Sir Owen Burne. He seemed to have noticed so many things that had escaped others, and our views often coincided. He was another of my friends who were present at the murder of Lord Mayo, and he had enjoyed a little jaunt on the Suez Canal with my friend, Monsieur de Lesseps, though in his case it was before the canal was opened to the world. He was also a great admirer of Lord Lytton, for whom he had acted as private secretary.

It was after Sir Owen's return to England, when Lord Mayo was killed, that Queen Victoria sent for him to tell her all about it, he having been private secretary to the Viceroy at the time of his death.

I was an admirer of Sir Owen's. He was so persevering and so plucky, having no one but himself to thank for arriving at the top of the ladder. He was one of nineteen children and started in the world with twenty-five pounds in his pocket, the only sum of money he ever took from his people, who were not rich and had so large a family to bring up.

I have had many discussions with him over volunteering for Active Service. He disapproved strongly of men "volunteering for medals and fame." I told him what he was saying was really disapproving of ambition, which is such a splendid attribute and without which neither men nor women do much good either for themselves or other people, and I was surprised at his expressing such views considering ambition had been so great a factor in his own life. He replied, if the country wanted men they would be called for without any medal-hunting on their own part.

From Sir Owen's earliest days I could gather he had been filled with ambition, and to me it seemed that his ambitions were amply fulfilled, but much of his life was spoilt by feeling his endeavours were neither fully appreciated nor rewarded. Yet from an impecunious subaltern with a shy manner he became military secretary to the Commander-in-Chief, Sir Hugh Rose, for which appointment he was very young, and he felt most keenly that when some cases with which he had been dealing were reported in the usual course of events to the Commander-in-Chief in England, he expressed disapproval, laying the blame on "the very young Military Secretary." The Duke of Cambridge having approved of the appointment at the time it was offered to Sir Owen. The latter felt annoyed and pained, he therefore resigned, feeling rather bitter and very disappointed. He appears, however, to have taken it in the right spirit.

He worked hard all his life, passing from one good appointment to another, amongst them political A.D.C. to the Duke of Argyll, Secretary of State for India, head of the political and secret department of India Office in London, etc., never doing anything epoch-making or particularly brilliant, but some of the pictures in life that are in subdued colouring are the most pleasing and remain long in the memory.

I think the private den of Sir Owen's, when in Sutherland Avenue in London, and Mr. Grant's, secretary to the Yacht Squadron at Cowes in the Isle of Wight, were amongst the most interesting I can remember, being full of souvenirs and gifts from kings, queens, and people of interest, historically, famously and infamously great. I delighted in wandering round the rooms of these two friends and hearing the histories attached to the treasures.

Amongst the amusing stories Sir Owen told me was one of the time of the Shah of Persia's visit to England. He was rather a troublesome person to control, and could not understand why he must not do exactly as he liked. For instance, once when told he (the Shah) must take the Queen in to dinner he absolutely and flatly declined explaining there was another lady of very ample proportions (but whose name I must not mention) who appealed to his taste much more, and he intended to take her in, and Sir Owen must see to it that his wishes were respected. Sir Owen turned first one big official and then another on to His Highness, who eventually did as he was told, but very sulkily and with bad grace, fairly dragging the poor Queen in to dinner.

After this had passed off without undue comment, the Shah informed Sir Owen he wished to see a boxing contest "with lots of blood!" Not wishing to again offend, Sir Owen, feeling very uncomfortable at having to arrange anything of the kind to take place on the royal premises, and wondering what would happen if it was found out, arranged with Lord Queensberry and, I think, Sir Claude de Crespigny, to have a garden performance in a quiet corner somewhere near the Royal stables.

Unfortunately things went wrong, there were so many appointments to be made and kept. Somehow the bishops in lawn sleeves and frills, who were awaiting an interview with the potentate to beg him to use his influence to protect Christian Missions, got mixed up with the fight. The dignitaries turned tail and fled, feeling strangely out of place in their robes and frills.

It was most awkward, for barring this accident the fight might have passed off without many people knowing much about it. Lord Shaftesbury, however, who was acting as spokesman for the Bishops, was furious and, spluttering with rage, asked Sir Owen what he meant by arranging fights in the precincts of the Palace. When calmer he addressed the Shah on behalf of the Bishops in suitable language. In reply His Highness said curtly in Persian, "Oh, hang the Christian Missions." It was Sir Owen's privilege and duty to repeat the Shah's words in a beautiful form that would appeal to the prelates and make them happy. This he succeeded in doing.

When it was all explained to the Queen she was quite placid and calm, understanding the arrangement had been made purely for the entertainment of her guest at his own request, but some of the Court officials bristled with indignation as if they had been personally insulted. It was hard on Sir Owen as the very last thing in the world that would have afforded him pleasure would have been a fight of any kind, yet he was treated by some as if he were a naughty schoolboy who had been caught stealing lollypops.

The prize fight having been cut short by the entrance of the Bishops, the Shah now suggested that he would like to see a cock fight, but by this time neither Sir Owen nor anybody else felt the least inclined to humour the foreign guest—Shah or otherwise.

Lord Sydney, the then Lord Chamberlain, wrote a very indignant letter to Lord Queensberry, asking him how he dared turn Buckingham Palace into a boxing-saloon. Lord Queensberry by way of reply enclosed the letter he had received from Lord Knollys asking him to get up the show, adding, "Might I ask my lord to what department of Her Majesty's Government I am to apply to be refunded the £25 which I paid the pugilists?"

No reply was received to this.

All the officials in any way connected with the Shah's well-being and happiness during his sojourn on our shores were thankful when the day came for his return to his own country. His demands were without precedent, and all matters connected with Courts and Royalties are ruled by established precedent.

For instance what was to be done when he gave orders that the whole of the Alhambra ballet, also Cornelie D'Anka, were to be purchased for him and his Grand Vizier sent to bring them along.

Nobody dare break the news to the potentate that this was not feasible. At last the Grand Vizier looking crestfallen returned to announce his failure in carrying out his orders. "All right," remarked the Shah, "wait until we get back to Teheran and then off comes your head."

It was arranged amongst other things to amuse this foreign visitor that he should be taken to Epsom races. He was pleased with the idea. The first race was won/by Lord Rosebery, then Prime Minister, the second by the Prince of Wales. "Ah! I see," said the Shah, "you arrange the races the same as we do in Teheran, only the Shah and Grand Vizier are allowed to win."

One day when he was driving through the streets with the Queen, there was considerable cheering. He remarked to the Queen, that this must be very expensive. Her Majesty rather indignantly replied, "Certainly not, merely the latent loyalty of my subjects."

"Oh," replied the Shah, "when I want to be cheered in Teheran I have to disburse much largesse!"

It has interested me watching the way that the treatment children and young people meet with affects their characters. Some who have been harshly treated and had to struggle for themselves become harsh and take their revenge when their time comes, meting out the same treatment that they have received with interest, the harder from having conquered single-handed and not forgetting to impress that fact on those under their thumb. Others it makes helpful to young ones going through the mill. This was the case with Sir Owen Burne. He was most kind and at all times helpful to young ones "coming on." His own small family adored him. He married twice, his first wife was a sister of Lord Kilmaine, his second was Lady Agnes Douglas, daughter of the Earl of Morton.

I think I can best describe my friend as a dainty man, dainty in speech and in choice of his friends, more particularly his women friends.

He died in 1909.

CHAPTER XII

THERE are few of us I suppose who at some time or other in our lives have not been really frightened. I have been in a railway accident and was not the least alarmed; certainly it was more funny than serious, but we did not know at the time how it was going to turn out. Hunting and carriage accidents I have had galore, and I do not remember being particularly frightened; I have also slept in a haunted room all alone, feeling very brave and not the least frightened, possibly because I saw no ghost; but I can remember twice in my life being petrified with fright and thoroughly ashamed of myself for being so.

230

Once was when the pantechnicon in Motcomb Street off Lowndes Square was on fire.

My mother and I were staying with friends in Lancaster Gate while my wedding garments were being prepared. One afternoon between tea and dinner an old friend, Mr. Fred Verner (son of Colonel Verner, who married Mrs. Hamborough, of Steephill Castle), came in and told us there was a big fire on, somewhere in the South-west district, and he thought we should be able to see the flames and smoke from the upper windows of the house we were in.

Never having seen a big fire, I expressed a wish to go and have that experience, so we all bundled off in hansom cabs, telling the drivers to take us as near to the fire as they could. Naturally, we all got separated, each cabman having views of his own as to the shortest route. I was in a cab with Mr. Verner, and we got comparatively close to the scene. Great crowds had already collected and, what I had not counted on, fresh crowds soon hemmed us in, and the flames were advancing in our direction in leaps and bounds. Sparks were falling on the horse's back and on the people, who tried to get out of the way as we did, but were unable to do so owing to the crowd behind us.

The horse grew wild and so did the crowd; the cabby lashed with his whip at the men who interfered with his horse's head until it was seized from him and broken up.

Those around us were now growing hostile, and

things looked serious, when their attention was diverted by a livery-stable keeper close to where we were, trying to get his horses out of their stables, which were now on fire.

Nothing would persuade the animals to come out until a goat was produced and handed in from some back premises, after which a few of the horses followed it. The rest, I fear, were burnt.

The smell and the heat combined was overpowering. Our cabby relieved his feelings by airing his most telling swear words. Mr. Verner was fervently wishing "to God I had never brought you out," when our horse after one more futile effort to frighten the crowd, fell down on its side with a crash, breaking both shafts. At first we thought it was dead so still did it lie; but I think the number of people who promptly stood on its head and all over its body was the cause of its quietude.

Happily for us, a policeman walking on the roof of the stables saw our danger and directed the hose to be turned on the crowd behind us, which led to our being escorted from the remains of our cab into a house in Lowndes Square, where we remained for a while before making our way home. I escaped with nothing worse than a badly bruised arm, where I had been forced into the iron thing the window shuts down on.

Mr. Verner handed some money to the cabman with his card before we left him, and we saw the poor little gee get on to its legs again looking much older, and so did we. In addition to having added to our years we were wet through from the water that was played around us to clear off the crowd, and I could not get the smell of burning out of my hair for a long time.

I never wish to be in a crowd of that description again, and I now take care to avoid fires if possible.

I believe the goat that was fetched to induce the horses to follow it was the one belonging to the Duke of Cambridge, which spent its life wandering unmolested between Gloucester House and Piccadilly from end to end.   Long after the fire I was told that the goat belonged to the Duke; if so, it was probably the one I remember some years later when we were in Park Lane.   Its staple food seemed to be newspapers, which it ate with avidity, what else it had I do not know.   Billy managed to thrive, being fat and comely, while dignified and majestic, friendly with all except errand boys, who, however, were not interfered with unless they spoke words of endearment or made chirrupy noises.

My next fright was on board ship going out to India, when the *Eldorado* was wrecked off the coast of Portugal, the sea was running mountains high, and there was a nasty fog.   We had been signalled to pick up some of the passengers, and got into trouble ourselves.   It was evening, and we had been sent to our berths for safety, as the sea was washing everything off the deck.   We were allowed light, however, so that we might amuse ourselves as best we could.   Judging by the thundering of the seas smashing on to the deck matters were not improving. We could hear amidst all the noise anxious voices shouting words of command on the deck, bells ringing to the engine-room, and general excitement.

We had been having some excitement ourselves in our endeavour to remain in our berths, when with an extra roll, which we all thought was bound to be her last, the ship heeled over to such an extent that all lights went out, swinging water-bottles turned somersaults, crockery from one end of the ship to the other seemed to be smashing, passengers screamed and groaned, water rushed down the companionway into the saloon with such force that it burst my cabin door open.

I had been thrown completely out of my bunk with mattress and bedding on top of me. My portmanteau bobbed about in the water on one side, having broken loose from under my crib, and pieces of crockery and books were flying about my head. I do not know what besides, for it was as dark as ink.

Presently someone came splashing down the saloon shouting that we were all to dress at once and go on deck. Go on deck, indeed! Easier said than done. Personally I was so petrified with fright that not to save my life could I have walked a yard. I think the screaming of the women and children in the other cabins, combined with the darkness and wealth of water in the cabin, must have been what deprived me of my power to move.

I said to myself, "This is ridiculous.   I must not give way and be a fool."   An extra sluice of water brought something with it that gave me a bump on the head.   The water was in my ears and everything buzzing and a long way off, and then I was to all intents and purposes dead.

All my life, since I began to notice things and think, I had held a firm belief that death was not a thing to dread, on the contrary, that it was rather beautiful, and that many confused the process of dying with death.   The actual dying, paying the last penalty for having lived and for all our shortcomings, is often painful, at times an agony; but death is not; I have felt ever since that voyage that I have experienced dying and tasted death.

When I became conscious again I was in a nice dry bunk and the stewardess sitting beside me.   I was told I was not to talk, but she gave me some details of what had eventually happened.   A little child in the next cabin to mine had suffered a good deal, its arm and one thumb being broken.

The ship had at the last moment decided to right herself, but nobody had been allowed on deck as everything was in a mess and had to be cleared up.

As soon as I was able to appear, I was asked if I would see what I could do with a Calcutta merchant who had refused to get off the floor of his cabin, where he lay on his tummy groaning at intervals.   We had been great friends up to the time of our fright, so I went and asked him what he thought he was doing.   On hearing my voice he pushed one hand along the floor in front of him saying, "Oh! is that you? I am saving my soul!" I told him if he would get up and come with me into the saloon, or better still, on deck, where I felt less sick, I would help him with the task. After a while he consented, but he was terribly shaken and quite childish, bursting into tears at intervals.

Like a good many more on board, I was very brave when it was all over, and able to help in clothing the passengers from the *Eldorado* that we had picked up, by lending and altering clothes for them, they having arrived on board with nothing but night garments, waterproof cloaks and such-like things.

After this episode I meditated a good deal on courage, and tried to comfort myself with the thought that it is not a virtue at all really, as it may and can quite easily become the servant of great villainy! After this reflection my self-respect returned in a measure.

Perhaps the two ceremonies that have impressed me most were King Edward VII's Coronation, with all its pageantry, and a funeral at sea, grandly and painfully simple.

The former was a great gathering, all glitter, pomp and stateliness, but a most fatiguing day for all concerned. The morning was cold and cloudy. Everyone had to be in his place in the Abbey by 8 a. m., though the King and Queen did not arrive until 11.15. Some people sat in their places all night for fear of being unable to find their seats.

There was, however, plenty to occupy and amuse the mind during the waiting hours, by watching the seats filling up. It was a wonderful scene, from the south transept the altar could be seen and the seats where the King and Queen knelt to receive the sacrament. In the north transept sat the peeresses, in the south the peers. Galleries were thrown across and further back for members of the House of Commons and their wives.

All were beginning to feel as if they could take in a reef about their waists when the procession was heralded by the singing of "Ein Feste Burg Ist Unser Gott," accompanied by trumpets. Heard from the distance by those in the galleries it sounded soft and sweet, and our emotions, which were many on that day, had begun. Then, as the procession filed in, came the exultant fanfare of trumpets and as they died away the Westminster boys, hidden away somewhere near the organ, suddenly and startlingly burst forth with "Ave, ave, ave," followed by a verse in Latin and winding up with a shrill and most effective "Vivat, vivat, vivat."

The beautiful and stately Queen, as she moved holding the King's hand, showed as well as did the King, signs that the emotions of their subjects was shared also by them. Many, both old and young, were moved to tears.

The poor old Archbishop of Canterbury, after administering the oath and the actual Coronation, (when he nearly dropped the Crown), found his strength considerably taxed. The King and Queen took their seats near the altar to receive homage, he was the first to render it, and found he was unable to rise again, and had to be helped by the King, who took him kindly by the hand.

King George, at that time Prince of Wales, was the next to kneel in homage, and the King put his arm round his son's neck, kissing him affectionaïely. It was very touching, and Lord Spencer, one of the most conspicuous figures at the Coronation, found an inconvenient tear or two trickling down his nose.

All was so real and yet so like a dream. Many thoughts filtered through one's brain, while for some reason the refrain of that old song, "For the Fashion of This World Passeth Away," kept haunting me. Truly a great "tomasa," impressive and splendid, and yet for what a little while—and then —all present on that historic day would be as one family, doing homage at the throne of the Most High.

Dr. Temple, the Archbishop, who so nearly dropped the crown through feebleness, said he considered the greatest compliment ever paid to him came from one of his Rugby boys, who said, "Temple is a beast, but he is a just beast."

At times Temple could be quite witty, and once when looking on at a cricket match he overheard one boy say to another, "Do you know, Jack, I have entered for the Confirmation Stakes."

A voice they both immediately recognised came from behind them.

"Well, you had better consider yourself scratched."

At the end of that tiring impressive Coronation day one was left with a feeling of sadness and depression. I could not shake it off; when the service was over it all seemed still more unreal and dreamlike, and a number of "whys?" would keep cropping up in my mind. I was glad to fly back to the country, where the placid sheep hide their faces in the hedge-row, and the trees whisper of things less transitory. Here I could feel again the calm and content that such things bring.

The funeral at sea struck me as one of the most profoundly grand and profoundly sad ceremonies I have ever witnessed, and the day has never been forgotten.

It was in the Red Sea, and the heat almost past bearing. A dear old Indian Civil servant, who had spent all his best years out there to provide education and comforts for his children and wife at home, was on his way to the moment that he had dreamed of night and day for long. The great reunion— and then the remainder of his days in peace— amongst all his dear ones. As he was out of health his eldest daughter had been sent to take care of him on the way home, but all her care was of no avail, and he slipped away one very hot night.

I was desperately sorry for the daughter. She was no longer young and rather retiring and shy. I pictured her sitting alone in her cabin facing all the dread details necessary to this occasion, and no one to hold out a hand of sympathy. I wrote a note and pushed it under the door asking if I could do anything either to save her pain or help to bear it. I received a reply thanking me, but she would rather be alone.

The next day at sundown the Captain read the service that brings comfort to many (but drives me frantic) over the pathetic figure done up in sacking and heavily weighted, over which lay the Union Jack. All were gathered close up to the side of the ship, and the gangway let down. When it came to the moment of committal the ship stopped, the paddle ceased churning the water, and there was not a sound of any kind. I shut my eyes, for I could not bear it, and there was an awful splash, followed by a piercing cry of anguish from the cabin just below. I can see the swirl of the water and hear that cry now as if it were yesterday. The engines continued their work, and in a few minutes the spot was left far behind.

But the moment I heard that cry of anguish I fled down to the cabin and entered it without knocking, saying it was not right she should be alone, and folded my arms round this comparative stranger, and began to cry from sympathy. She lifted her face from the pillow with her hands still over her ears and looked at me stonily and coldly, and as I took her cold clammy hands into mine and then put my arm round her neck and drew her head down on to my shoulder, she found relief in tears.

We were friends until she died, not a great number of years ago.

The world is sad enough already without my piling up the agony, and now again I have fallen away from my resolve, and must not transgress any more, but turn to brighter subjects, marriage and giving in marriage, for example. Some of the affairs of which I have known have arranged themselves in an uncommon manner. There was old General Brownrigg, a great frequenter of ladies' society and five o'clock teas. He took considerable interest in a girl whom he thought was making herself too conspicuous with a man he knew something against, so he spoke seriously to her on the subject, advising her not to marry him. She answered him thus: "My dear General, I have never thought of him in that way. If there is a man I should like to marry it is yourself." "Dear me, this is very sudden!" he replied. "I must take time to consider and entreat the Lord." He went home and on to his marrow bones.

They were married!

Rather a curious thing happened once when I was at the Academy with a man in the Carabineers. He stopped dead before a picture of a nice-looking girl, not particularly pretty, but very lady-like and with a sweet expression. He stood lost in contemplation for some moments. I asked him if he admired it very much, and he replied, "Yes! look at the book and tell me who she is, will you?" I did as I was asked. He had never seen the original in his life, but said she was the girl he should like to marry, and he did before he was much older.

I have noticed how some of the ugliest of men have been the most successful with women. Mirabeau established this fact, in spite of his ugly scarred and pox-marked face crowned with a head of untidy black hair, he not only found a woman to marry him but had a considerable number of liaisons as well. But then we are told beauty is in the eye of the beholder. How often men flutter about amongst the pretty and handsome girls and then marry a plain one!

I am now supposed to have arrived at years of discretion and have definitely come to the conclusion that the happiest marriages are not those where man and woman are passionately in love with one another, each believing the other perfect for about a fortnight, after which one or both fall from their pedestals. The carefully thought-out marriage of convenience has a much better sporting chance of happiness. Too much is not expected, and each respects the other's reason for making the arrangement. I have known one or two of these end most happily.

The different methods and ways that men make love would make an amusing chapter, and if the names of the individuals were given it would be more amusing still, but that would not be fair.

There is often something rather ridiculous about old men flirtations and love-making, but when women become lovish in their middle and old age it

is tragic.   One of the saddest sights in life is a
frisky frump!

It is astonishing when you have been behind the
scenes for a while to find the number of people
whom you had considered as the acme of straight-
lacedness and virtue who deviate from the straight
path.

Some elderly men make love quite nicely.   I remember one experience of my own, when quite a
girl.   A dear Old General, then at the War Office
honoured me by asking me to be his wife.   His son,
afterwards in the Scots Guards, likewise did me the
honour.   The former used to say, "Don't let that
young cub of mine make an ass of himself.   I'll cut
him off with a penny if he does."   The son, in his
turn, used to say, "The poor old governor is getting
a bit childish.   If he bores you, let me know and
I'll put a stop to it!"   The General was rather pep-
pery and most people were frightened of him; so
when he popped the question I did not know how
to get out of the difficulty of saying I regretted I
did not see my way to oblige him.   Amongst other
rather lame reasons that I brought forth was that
I should see so little of him as he would always be
at work in the War Office.   I was at once asked if
I thought he was a clerk who went to work at
eight a. m., and returned home at eight p. m.?   I
hastily said of course not, though I had not formed
ideas on the point.   He then with a pained smile
said, "I go to work about twelve and return about
four!"   It obviously would not do to say that under

these circumstances I should see too much of him perhaps.

I ended in making such a donkey of myself in my endeavour not to hurt the feelings of the good man, who had been very kind to me when only an awkward school girl, that I left him in the seventh heaven of delight thinking I was going to make him happy for life and be a mother to his son!

My father had to readjust the matter.

Bishop Warburton says the last of our lives is "a losing game." I do not quite agree with him. It is true that we only learn how to live when we are likely to be called upon to die, but the last half of our lives is one of more contentment, our ideals no longer beckon us as we gather up the threads of the past which we have learned to look upon with unimpassioned eyes, the days when everything seemed so overpowering by contrast to to-day. We all set out thinking and expecting to be amused by life, not grasping that until we have obtained life's satisfaction we are not in a position to be amused at all. It requires a stout heart to sing in exile.

I remember an elderly man, who was known to have many loves, once asking my young brother if the Lyric Club (after it had moved from Bond Street, and where fortnightly dances were then being held) was a place where he could take ladies.

My brother replied, "Well, that depends whether you mean ladies or lydies!" The old boy looked uncomfortable.

CHAPTER XIII

PERHAPS the pluckiest man I ever met was the late Lord Queensberry, the eighth Marquess. A wonderful sportsman, nothing came amiss to him; he did not know the meaning of the word fear and would tackle people stones heavier than himself.

At one time in his life he was utterly infatuated with a beautiful actress, who was married to a huge bully; his attentions and admirations led to a difference of opinion between the men. The bully not having the courage to tackle the smaller but more courageous man, hired a professional pugilist to hammer him. So one day when Lord Queensberry happened to be out for exercise in Maida Vale he found himself in a cul-de-sac, when up came the pugilist saying, "My lord, I've got to give you a hiding." "Right," said Lord Queensberry. In a few seconds a ring was formed, but no policeman. Inside three rounds Lord Queensberry had his opponent out.

Apparently the man bore no ill-will, for when occasionally he met his conqueror in Piccadilly, he always gave a somewhat exaggerated salute, saying "Good-day, my lord!"

I saw a good deal of Lord Queensberry's first wife, who divorced him; she used to come and sit with me and talk about her sorrows and many disappointments.

Sir Claude de Crespigny, who admires pluck in anyone, be they man, woman, or child, told me not long ago that "Old Q. was the bravest man of my acquaintance; he laughed at odds."

Admiral Grenfell, who was, I believe, the strongest man and hardest-hitter in the Navy of his days, was once asked if he had ever boxed with Lord Queensberry, who was considered a good man at the game. "Certainly I have." "Could you beat him?" "Beat him! I should have to kill him first." The Admiral was at least two stone heavier than Lord Queensberry.

One of the reasons why the latter so often came out on top was owing to his fitness; he was always in hard training, and it was noticeable the way those he conquered became great friends and admirers.

Once at Warwick when Lord Queensberry who

The Eighth Marquess of Queensberry

had finished second in a steeplechase (he subsequently disqualified the horse that finished first) was on his way with saddle and weight-cloth to weigh in, a huge man in the ring called out, "Well pulled, my lord." Down went the saddle and bang went the fists between the bookie's eyes. He was removed by the police, yet Lord Queensberry had made a friend for life.

What made the incident the more remarkable was that the man was about the best pugilist in England, and in training to fight the following week. His admiration for a man of Lord Queensberry's weight and inches tackling him knew no bounds, and the following day when his assailant took a bad toss on the far side of the course at Lichfield, he left his stand and ran across to where Lord Queensberry was lying, picked him up, put him into a fly and packed him off to the town.

The following day to continue his attentions the bookie sent a present of some famous bone oil, in hopes of accelerating the recovery of the game and sporting lord.

A wonderful sportsman he was too. During the five seasons that he hunted hounds he never missed a single day, though at one time he had strained a muscle in his thigh so badly that he found it impossible to ride astride; nothing daunted he rode in a side-saddle!

He was a lover of animals, horses especially, and was kind to them, but they had to do some work. Once after hunting with Lord Wemyss close to the

North Sea, he rode the horses he had hunted thirty-five miles towards home, then hired hacks from the Duke of Buccleuch's tenants and rode right across the Cheviots to Kinmount, where they had to cut off his boots and breeches, but he was out with his hounds next day. I think the first pack he hunted was the Worcestershire from 1870 to 1871. He was not altogether popular from all I can gather, but it was before my hunting days.

He was not a first-rate man on a horse and, as far as racing was concerned, never did anything wonderful. In fact his ambition as a rider was greater than his ability. He had become known as a gentleman-rider, and had registered the crimson and black cap as his colours in the Calendar, but latterly his riding was chiefly confined to the meetings round London.

His name has been more closely associated with boxing than racing, and he was considered a good light-weight boxer. Who is there who has not heard of the Queensberry Rules in connection with boxing, yet he did not draw them up; they were drafted by a Mr. J. G. Chambers, who, I believe, owned *Land and Water* in its sporting days. He also rowed twice for Cambridge in the University Boat Race, but be that as it may he it was who drew up the rules and submitted them to Lord Queensberry.

In 1910 an exhaustive treatise was written on the Queensberry Rules of boxing by Mr. Frank Bradley, the best ever written both for amateur or professional.

In the early days of boxing, when it was forbidden that railways should carry passengers to see prize-fights, no gloves were worn, but even after prize-fights became the fashion, the orders for the railways still held good for a time. The "Queensberry Rules" were originally drawn up for some amateur challenge cup Lord Queensberry instituted to be won three years in succession, and these cups were what gave rise to the ever after popular Queensberry Rules, eleven in all.

Lord Queensberry and that great athlete Fred Cotton, who Sir Malcom Fox inspector of gymnasia described as the most perfect specimen of an athlete that he had ever seen, decided to run a four-mile steeplechase over the Bogside course. The race looked so close towards the finish that Lord Eglinton and his brother held a driving whip by way of a tape. Lord Queensberry fell, completely exhausted a couple of paces short of the winning-post and Fred Cotton fell the same distance beyond it; the former characteristically said, "Never mind, I came to before old Fred!"

Considering that neither of these sportsmen had been in any special training beyond a round of balls in the neighbourhood, it was a severe contest.

Lord Queensberry might always be relied upon to do original things.

Once when hunting the Croome hounds they made a line over the Severn, Lord Queensberry and

Fred Cotton alone followed. The war made the breeches of the former so slippery that he said he fell off at every fence until he killed his fox; adding, however, "The swim cured me of a bad cold."

On another occasion after dining with Lord Coventry, 'Old Q.' to save his horses three or four miles, drove a short cut to a ferry. Finding the boat was at the far side, and the ferryman evidently tucked up safely at home in bed, he undressed in his phaeton, swam the river, and walked half a mile up the street to the Ferryman's house. It took a little while to waken the good man, who was enjoying his first beauty sleep.

Having at length succeeded in attracting his attention, it became necessary to convince the man if possible, that he, Lord Queensberry, was not a raving lunatic. Eventually succeeding, the river was recrossed in the ferry-boat. The dumbfounded ferryman watched his late companion re-dress in the phaeton and all once more started across the river; after which the drive home was accomplished, not, I am sure, without a thoughtful remembrance to the ferryman. At all times Lord Queensberry was liberal and generous. He was an amiable man and loved a fair fight.

Fred Cotton was also a man of many parts. I have a hunting-song he wrote once and sent to me with kindly messages from the composer; which reminds me I have not seen it lately; I must look it up.

Lord Queensberry was on board a steamer once

at Rio Janeiro en route for Montevideo when a huge Yankee came on board, and during the voyage made a nuisance of himself. The way it was described to me was, "He was always more or less in liquor and gratuitously insulted everybody."

At one halting-place, I forget which, Harry Grenfell, subsequently an Admiral, came on board to give some instructions regarding a number of birds he was shipping. Shortly before this moment he had been refused a championship heavy-weight boxing cup because he slogged so hard and did not box.

While in a stooping position (which doubtless looked very tempting) examining the lashings with his head close to the birds' spurs which if they were frightened and kicked out might have found the embryo Admiral's brain-pan, he remarked to a seaman that he must be very careful of his ostriches. Suddenly a heavy hand dealt him a resounding smack, at the same time saying "You ——— liar! they're not ostriches, they're emus."

Then the fun began, and to everybody's delight the bully was soon lying senseless in the scupper. Lord Queensberry, always alert, immediately had him carried sideways over the gangway and took him ashore in a boat with his head hanging over the gunwale, thinking a little rest on shore again would be good for him!

When first I can remember Lord Queensberry was soon after I married; he was then about thirty-five or six, clean-shaven except for the little fuzzy side-whiskers then considered chic. When wearing a tall hat his black wiry hair stood out under it like a frill, especially as his hats were invariably a size or so too small for his head, and he indulged in very curly brims. He was a small man, smart in his own way, but with curious theories on dress, women and a variety of other things. I wondered at any-body with such a pronounced nose daring to box.

He was a good friend and kindly to all. He used to be laughed at a good deal, and very many were the weird stories in circulation about him. He died January 31st, 1900, the same year as his great enemy, the man he disliked most in all the world, Oscar Wilde.

I once heard a woman say that Lord Queensberry was an atheist. I was pleased to be able to say that if he was he went to church all the same, as I knew when he was hunting the Worcestershire hounds he regularly attended the services in the cathedral, sitting behind the choir in the prebendary stalls.

After thinking over all I knew of him and his life not many years before he died, I came to the conclusion that he had become his own father too soon. A little more discipline in early years was all that was wanting. He had been at Eton and six years at sea, but he became his own master at the age of fourteen. He was a descendant of the grand old stock of Douglas famed in song. There has been a good deal of money amongst them, not always spent wisely.

A whole crowd of great sportsmen were on the stage, so to speak, doing brave and daring deeds when first I left the schoolroom, and having a great love for horses, dogs and all the great works of the outside world, I found a heap of people to interest and teach me. A few of the many kind friends with which I have been blessed all my life, caring as I do for the natural world described by Goethe as holding the "Open Secret" for all to see who feel so inclined, but which so few care to study. God's work is so infinitely more wonderful than that of man.

It has become the fashion to say England is not the country she was, that we are all going "to the dogs" and degenerating, but I do not agree with this theory. It seems to me England is a much better country to live in now than she was even in my early days, to say nothing of one hundred years ago. It is no longer the fashion for men to get drunk and boast of it, as if it was a clever achievement, neither are they so frivolous as they were. When airing this view to a friend a while ago he said, "Don't you believe it, dear lady, everything goes on just as it always has done, only we don't hear so much about it."

I suggested that even under those circumstances we are moving up the scale. It is a step in the right direction if we do not proclaim our misdeeds and mistakes from the house-tops, calling all to come and admire our audacity. It is something to have learnt discretion.

One of the most remarkable results of our advanced civilization has been the evolution of the bachelor woman. There are no old maids now. The last thirty or forty years everything has moved so rapidly that we seem to have skipped a generation or two and landed on our feet an entirely different people.

Women now have other things to think of besides love and marriage. The day is gone when the unwritten law of our lives was "Thou shalt not think!" We do think now, and the result is, we have emerged knowing our own minds, needs, and our own hearts. Self-reliant we refuse any longer to lead the artificial life that thirty years ago was considered "good form."

There is an old song that tells us,

> "There are still some few remaining
> Who remind us of the past."

I know one. She is a relation, and when a great friend of mine, a bonny girl, was going out to Russia to nurse the wounded, she held up her hands in horror, saying:

"Oh, but how dreadful for her. A nice young girl like that. She may have to wear pyjamas and all sorts of terrible things like that."

We are all busy people now, and have no time to scream or faint if we have to wear pyjamas, indeed we think them much the most modest and suitable things to wear when travelling. Neither do we now sit down and lapse into premature old

age and bitter thoughts for want of something better to do, and then resent the somewhat logical
conclusions of our artificial education and lives.

We do not grow old now as we used to do, for the
face does not betray the years until the mind has
given its consent.

Women are ceasing to be parasites, house-keepers
and useful commodities. They have learned to forget their sex and mix amongst the workers and
thinkers of the world in equality, and are doing very
real work in a number of branches of usefulness at
one time closed doors to them. Among other things
they are now capable private secretaries to busy
men.

Not long ago I was talking to one of the leading
business men of the day about something he wanted
my advice on in connection with sporting garments,
etc., and I could hardly attend to the matter in
hand, being so taken up with the competency of his
secretary. She stood by his side, and in a calm
methodical manner handed him all he wanted as
the occasion required, without having to be asked
for anything. One time it would be a book, at another some notes, patterns, or brochures, then reminding her chief of his next appointment, following him wherever he went making notes of everything to remind him later.

She ran through a short résumé of the points to
be remembered before each interview, drove people
away when they had been long enough, keeping
everything up to time, no hurry and no fuss.

During an interval when she had been sent on a message, I remarked on his secretary's efficiency, and he said he had been able to get through twice the amount of work since he had secured her services. The girl was quite nice-looking, no giggling, smiling or by-play, entirely composed, collected, and very quiet. I felt quite proud of my sex.

Girls are free to-day to move about the world as they like; the consequence is that they are natural, not always posing and pretending. They can meet men and be friendly and enjoy their society in a way that was impossible even a few years ago.

The most delightful relationship in the world is the platonic, between man and woman *as long as it lasts*. Everyone should have a really great platonic affection for one of the opposite sex, it gives zest, and keeps up self-respect. It is a charming relationship, no pretence or humbug, neither have any claim on the other, it can come to an end at any moment, only one thing is necessary, mutual tastes. Under these conditions people can be sane, which is more than anybody can be when in love. Another great advantage, there is none of that intimacy so death-dealing to all our finer feelings.

Platonic affection is simply confidential, kindly companionship, nothing expected but comprehensive and loving kindness.

This relationship is going to be the order of the day. It depends on a woman's tact and cleverness whether she can keep the relationship on a working footing. She must bear in mind that all interest ceases when the object of a man's liking becomes familiar and the problematic and elusive elements have disappeared.

Certainly some of nature's laws are open to criticism. Life is made up of so many things, too much of one, too little of another, stitches dropped, edges frayed, all incomplete, but we are getting nearer the solution of some of the big problems.

Amongst the noted sportsmen of whom I was writing before I ran away on the present-day emancipation of women, I should have mentioned the Duke of Westminster, I mean the first Duke who owned so many celebrated horses, the most noted that recur to my memory at the moment being "Doncaster," "Bend'Or," "Ormonde," "Orme" and "Flying Fox."

"Doncaster" was a lucky deal for the Duke; He bought him from Mr. Peck, his trainer, for £10,000, why this low price I do not know, as Mr. Peck had bought him from Mr. Merry, the Iron Master, for £14,000.

"Doncaster" was the head of a wonderful family, "Bend'Or" was his son, "Ormonde" the son of "Bend'Or," "Orme" the son of "Ormonde" "Flying Fox" the son of "Orme."

The Duke had a special palatial home built for "Doncaster" at Eaton, each of the above horses occupying it in turn, except "Flying Fox"; I think the Duke died before seeing him in it.

"Ormonde" was the Duke's favourite; many people thought he would ride the gentle beast in the

Queen's Jubilee procession, but he never for a moment contemplated anything of the kind. The horse was not, however, left out in the cold during the festivities, the Duke having a box specially erected for him in the grounds in Upper Grosvenor Street and the horse was installed there during his great Jubilee garden party. Many horses would have had their heads turned with the amount of adulation he had bestowed upon him by guests. Never before did he receive so much patting and caressing, but he appeared in no way perturbed; even condescended to eat a scarlet geranium presented to him by an Indian Chief, who had gathered it from a flower-pot standing near.

The Duke liked rearing his own horses and watching their triumphs. He rode "Ormonde" once round the paddock at Kingsclere, just to say he had been on the great horse.

There were various tragedies connected with the Duke's racing, the greatest being the poisoning of poor Orme, who was intended to do such wonders. It was a great scandal and nobody was supposed to know who did the deed, but I have always thought the Duke had a fairly clear idea who the culprit was; and unless I am very much mistaken I know too.

The Duke was absolutely straight in all his racing matters. I never heard a breath against him, even when the fuss occurred over the 1880 Derby when "Bend'Or" won, and the owner of the second horse, "Robert the Devil," lodged an objection with the Stewards of Epsom Races and claimed the Derby Stakes. The owner of "Robert the Devil" was Mr. Charles Brewer, bookmaker and commissioner. He maintained "Bend'Or" was not "Bend'-Or" at all, but a colt named "Tadcaster" by "Doncaster." Such evidence as they had rested on the testimony of a stud-groom, who had been discharged from the Eaton stud, and two other employés.

They declared the two colts had got mixed up in the course of their transference from Eaton to Newmarket, or some such thing. As a matter of fact they had got their birth-marks entered up wrongly. Both horses were chestnut, and when "Tadcaster" was foaled he had a dark patch on one quarter, and it was over this marking the discussion arose.

The mistake Mr. Brewer made was in going down to Eaton and persuading the groom to show him the stud-book, for the Duke would have raised no objection to showing it to anybody. Then followed an awkwardness, the stud-book got lost! but turned up eventually again, and though the case never went into the law-courts it was thoroughly handled by Mr. James, Mr. Craven and Sir George Chetwynd, who, with the help of Lord Bampton, who examined the stud-book and gave it as his opinion it showed so many errors that it could not be relied upon in any way, and that in his opinion "Bend'-Or" should remain the winner, this was the final finding of the Stewards.

In a quiet sort of way Lord Bampton was for years legal adviser to the Jockey Club. It was the popular impression at one time that he was a severe judge. He may have been, but he was a very pleasant companion, full of wit and humour. I must refer to him again later.

I know that some years after the rumpus over "Bend'Or's" Derby, Mr. James Lowther said that additional facts which had subsequently come to his knowledge disposed him to think that the Stewards had come to a wrong decision, but it was of course too late to reopen the question.

However, Mr. Brewer had his revenge, for in the following September "Robert the Devil" beat "Bend'Or" in the St. Leger at Doncaster.

The Duke was a good deal upset over the Derby occurrence and, shortly after, sent twenty-three of his horses to Tattersalls, "Tadcaster" amongst them fetching only 160 guineas.

While being a just and kind master the Duke did not throw his money about. Like others I have met he lived in the greatest luxury, spending huge sums on horses, racing, etc., but was most careful and economical in small matters and I seemed fated to catch him in the act of some of his little economies he did not care for the world to know.

Once when I was taking a short cut through Seamore Place from Park Lane to Grosvenor Square I met Lady Chesham in South Audley Street. It will be remembered she was a daughter of the Duke by his first wife. Suddenly from round the corner came the Duke with a brown paper parcel under his arm, which he at once tried to suppress. Naturally neither his daughter nor I made any remark about the parcel, but he was obviously uncomfortable and quickly left us. He continued his errand and we both laughed, for we knew quite well he was off to a little cobbler in Shepherd's Market to have his boots mended; he thought nobody knew anything about it, as very few did.

I first made the discovery when one day I had been asked to go and see the old cobbler who was ill. He lived in a squalid little building, renting one room with a window looking on to the pavement, close to which he worked, and it was always open. He interviewed his customers through it. As I was coming out through a narrow passage, which was the exit, I came upon the Duke at the window claiming his mended shoes and paying the pence demanded. I hastily turned my admiring gaze on the neighbouring telephone and telegraph wires attached to adjacent chimneys, as I knew it would be very gauche to see what was happening, but the Duke was upset and galloped away without waiting to have his footgear done up in paper properly. As he was hurrying along out fell one mended shoe with a plop upon the pavement. He picked it up looking furtively behind him, but had not gone more than a couple of yards further before the paper carried away entirely. I could not well efface myself entirely as the paper had done, so went to the rescue and poked one shoe in one pocket and one in another

as best we could.   Entering into the game I offered
to take them home with me, have them done up in a
most scientific manner and sent home by one of my
household; but no! he would not trust the shoes out
of his sight and carried them off himself.   He was
a lean man and looked quite funny with bulging
pockets.

Lady Chesham often asked me to help her about
her headgear; it was difficult to make her look
smart for big occasions for she wore her hair cut
short like a man's.   This is comfortable and grand
for hunting or any form of sport, but does not look
well at Buckingham Palace garden parties and such-
like entertainments.   It always gives one rather the
look of a horse laying his ears back.

Another daughter of the Duke's was the Marchioness of Ormonde, and when his horse "Ormonde" won the Derby, Archer had attached to his
yellow satin jacket a prettily worked little medallion
said to have been worked by her.

CHAPTER XIV

I T is rather depressing to reflect on the number of kind and hospitable people who have suffered financial distress, or at any rate lost more money than was convenient over racing combined with all its associations.

The late Lord Guildford for one, the seventh earl, who died in December, 1885, the result of a hunting accident, his horse catching his feet in a binder of a newly laid hedge, either in Somersetshire or Dorset, I forget which.

He was a rather headstrong, determined person with a quick temper, and once when he fell out with the Dover Racing Authorities, said he would never have anything more to do with them, and started a rival meeting of his own, which was held in the park at Waldershall, his place near Dover.

The first meeting, to judge by the crowds attending it, proved an enormous success from a sporting point of view, but financially it was a "big drop." He had a good deal of worry over the meeting altogether, not the least being in connection with the gipsies and caravaneers he had allowed into the park and whom he told he would never have on the place again. The expenses in connection with the making of the course, building stands, stables, etc., had been heavy, and the caravaneers had not been respectful of the outlay.

The following year Lord Guildford determined he was going to do everything on his own lines, and be advised by nobody. He would make some money and have no nonsense.

Train-loads of sporting people came from all parts, promising even a greater crowd than the previous year, and amongst them a load or two of Welshers and other undesirables who had quite a good time.

The Mayor of Dover, being of a Christian spirit and wishing to bury the hatchet, had come in his robes of office to the show; he was relieved of his watch. Sir George Chetwynd, who was acting as judge, lost a pocket-book containing interesting and valuable things besides money!

Sir George's sister had married Lord Guildford, and this meeting was to be quite a family affair. The butler even had been pressed into the service, and fastened into a box to collect the gate money.

Feeling much impressed at the numbers in the stands and overflowing into the park Lord Guildford went to collect some of the enormous sum of money that must have been taken at the gate and remove it to a place of safety.

With this object in view he went singing and whistling to himself *en route* to the gate and asked cheerily for the money, and was handed £3 10s. There was a pause, his lordship being evidently deprived of his breath for a time. After the money had been turned over in his hand a few times as though nothing of the kind had ever been seen by him before, breath returned, and Lord Guildford said, "What the—something—something do you mean? Look at all those people," waving his hand in the direction of the stands. "Oh!" replied the butler, "those are all the Press, you said I was to let them in free."

More language followed, indicating he had arrived at the conclusion "races run in the 'family way' were no good," and the butler was a blithering idiot as well as a blood-shot fool or something like that.

Strict orders were issued that no more "press" people were to be allowed through the gate.

A number, however, I happen to know, found their way in through an undefended part of the park.

Caravaneers were conspicuous by their absence this second year, and some one enquired why they had not asked permission to do a little business. The head showman replied, "Ask for permission! No fear, his lordship had said the year before that if ever they came again he would turn his —— dogs on to them, and passing the house a short time before the second meeting they had seen that his lordship was in earnest for there as large as life were two b—— mastiffs painted up on a board hanging against the house as a warning."

This is what the scared showman saw:

The late Lord Winchester, the twelfth earl, was also very unfortunate with his racing. He used to live at Eastwell Park, now belonging to the Gerards, "but went broke." He was a great racing man and wit in the days of Lord George Bentinck, and married a relation of mine.

In his hard-up days he was glad to accept the hospitality of many people he had not known before his difficult times.   Amongst these he became acquainted with a Mr. Beddington, a Jew, son of Moses, the inexpensive tailor who used to have a shop at the Oxford Street end of Museum Street, with a revolving window to show his goods to advantage.   Both Moses and his son had retired from business and bought a property called the Beddington Estate, and there the idea had occurred to papa Moses that he might do well to change his name to that of Beddington.

Young Beddington bought a yacht and was anxious to make friends with society.   He therefore invited Lord Winchester to go a short cruise with him.   On their return they put in at Ryde, and Lord Winchester, out of compliment, took him into the Royal Yacht Club.   During the course of conversation Lord Winchester said, "By the way, how came you to adopt the name of Beddington?"   Receiving in reply, "Well, you see, my father being fond of the antique, purchased the ancient estate and changed his name at the same time."

Lord Winchester exclaimed, "Great heavens, man, wasn't Moses ancient enough for him!"

It is well perhaps for our peace of mind we do not see ourselves as others see us, yet it might be very wholesome.   So many of the men who threw their money away on racing and betting thought they were being very fine fellows and cutting a great dash, while everybody was calling them fools behind their backs and laughing at them.

How good it would have been for Bulwer Lytton to have seen himself as others saw him. He was before my time, but I have heard a great deal of him from those who knew him and his wife well, and his son was Viceroy in India when first I went out there.

Bulwer Lytton went about looking much like a rag-and-bone man, his hair long and untidy, his face unshaven and dirty, his clothes tattered; it must have been difficult to believe he was the author of so many *chefs-d'œuvre* of literature. His features, my people tell me, were remarkably fine, and could not be entirely hidden and spoilt by his untidy habits. He married a pretty Irish girl, which displeased his mother, who had brought the property of Knebworth into the family, and she cut off supplies. He therefore found himself with about a couple of hundred a year and unable to live at the rate of less than £3000. I have been told this as much as anything turned him against his pretty and witty wife, and he determined to get rid of her, and I do not think it is generally known in what a disgraceful way he tried to do this.

They had talked over the question of parting, and his wife agreed. He thereupon said, if she would attend at a certain house in Brook Street on a given day two solicitors would be there to discuss with her the questions of separation maintenance. On arriving in Brook Street she found the two "solicitors" were medical men prepared and engaged to certify her insane, and she was carried straight off to an asylum. Fortunately her own doctor, Roberts by name, who always attended her, got wind of this treatment, and immediately went to Lord Lytton and informed him that unless he at once gave immediate orders for his wife's release, all London should know the facts. She was at once released, but never forgave the insult. For many years she used to hang a widow's cap over her bed and called it her "liberty cap."

I think if Lord Lytton had been able to see himself as others, who knew of his disgraceful conduct, saw him, he would have felt chastened. The fact of his mother being annoyed over the marriage and stopping supplies, however, seems to have obliged him to work, and it is astonishing to see the list of books he wrote during this time.

When he died at Torquay, in 1873, I am told he looked so splendid in his coffin with clean shaven face his son hardly recognised him. After his burial in Westminster Abbey, the late Dean of Westminster preached a most eulogistic sermon referring to the dead. Lady Lytton, remembering his treatment of her wrote to the Dean, presenting her compliments, saying, "The Devil could not tell the truth when he was dead."

Whether there was any difference between her and her Viceroy son I cannot say, but she refused to accept any income from him.

There have been some quaint stories told of her

son, one being that he had a habit of kicking under the table any lady he took into dinner, in consequence of which hostesses used to place a wooden box in a handy position to intercept the kicks. I never went in to dinner with Lord Lytton, so cannot speak from experience, but I find it difficult to believe, for though undoubtedly a person of moods, he was the soul of chivalry and courtesy.

It is easy to acquire bad habits without being aware of them, and if perchance we are "stars," nobody dare tell us of them.

Bulwer Lytton's wife was sparkling with Irish humour, always ready with repartee. Once when she was growing stout and panted for breath when going up the steps to the opera at Covent Garden, one of the gilded youths present said, "You want a change of horses, Lady Lytton." She replied, "I could get a change of asses on the spot."

The late Marquess of Exeter (the fourth) was rather regardless of appearances, but he was wholly delightful and did not care the very least what anybody said or thought of him. He confessed that he was never more happy than when, owing to reduced circumstances, he decided to rent a place at Shanklin in the Isle of Wight, and indulge in his favourite hobby of sea-fishing. He walked into the Castle and County Club one day in muffler, sweater and hob-nailed boots to the horror of the secretary, who did not know who he was and protested at "such a ruffian" being allowed in the club. He must have felt uncomfortable when told "the Ruffian" was the Commodore of the Royal Yacht Club at Ryde.

The Rev. E. Burnaby, brother of Fred Burnaby, the Ride to Khiva man, was in the Isle of Wight at the same time as the Exeters, and, as he was trying to get up a Primrose ball, asked if he might add the names of the Marquess and Marchioness of Exeter to his list of patrons and was told, "If our poor names are any use you can have them, but we have no money."

It is said that the Primrose League was founded in remembrance of Lord Beaconsfield's partiality for the flower, yet as a matter of fact he cared nothing for it, which Lady Dorothy Neville, at whose house the inaugurating meetings were held, was obliged to confess when asked on her word of honour if she had ever heard Dizzy express his regard for the primrose. Mr. Gladstone remarked he thought the gorgeous lily was more in his line

The way primroses became connected with Lord Beaconsfield was through Queen Victoria, who had an admiration for him, sending him boxes of the little flowers gathered from the slopes of Windsor Castle or from Osborne, I forget which. Lord John Manners, who succeeded to the Dukedom and who was a member of Disraeli's Cabinet and formerly one of the young England party, took great interest in the Primrose League movement. Lord John it was who wrote those never-to-be-forgotten verses:

"Let arts and commerce, laws and learning die,
    But leave us still our old nobility."

When the present duke's uncle was owner of Belvoir, overlooking the Vale of Grantham, dinner used to be announced by the private band playing "The Roast Beef of Old England."

A friend of mine was being taken into dinner there one night by a member of the French nobility, who asked what the tune was. She replied, "The Roast Frogs of Old France, out of compliment to you." He bridled with joy.

Mr. Evelyn Burnaby, who is still with us, has had an interesting and full life, beginning with law, continuing in the Church (owing chiefly to there being a family living awaiting a Burnaby), varied with much hunting and endless social engagements and attached friends. He is clever, as all the Burnabys have been, and is a kind friend. Like his brother Fred, when annoyed he can hit hard. He fell out once with the "Pious Fraud," the soubriquet of the late Lord Kinnard. This was how it happened. Both were of one party looking on at a Lord Mayor's show. Mr. Burnaby had just come up from hunting in Leicestershire. During the fitful conversation indulged in on such occasions, Mr. Burnaby turned to Lord Kinnard and asked him if he thought he could get him the vacant stall at Westminster? Lord Kinnard replied it would not be possible as he heard Mr. Burnaby had been seen at Cremorne, adding, "You had better stay in your horse-box, to which you are more suited."

This was throwing the gauntlet with a vengeance, and quickly picked up by Mr. Burnaby, who re-

The Rev. Evelyn Burnaby

plied, not much to the point stingingly, "I am not surprised you take such an interest in the ——— Hospital, considering you help to fill it."

Mr. Burnaby was generally to be seen in the distinguished strangers' gallery when any important debate was on. He was a friend of old Denning, Chief of the House of Commons police, also of Mr. Inglefield, who is still, I believe, chief attendant in the Lobby.

Denning it was who, as Tipstaffs in the old Queen's Bench Court at Westminster, conveyed the claimant to Newgate after he had been sentenced to fourteen years' penal servitude in the celebrated Tichborne case.

Once when leaving the strangers' gallery, Mr. Burnaby accidentally put his foot into the hat of another visitor and was walking away with it on his toe when a plaintive voice behind him said, "When you have quite done spoiling my brand new hat will you please return it, as I can't afford a new one!" Poor Mr. Burnaby felt crushed when he became aware of his carelessness.

Apropos the Tichborne trial, it is illuminating to see what can be done in the way of fraud. The letter I am reproducing from the original written by Arthur Orton is an excellent copy of the real Tichborne's writing. It must have required considerable practice before being able to write such a letter. I never saw the man, but my father, having been a barrister, and knowing counsel on both sides, took great interest in the case, and he said months must have been taken in perfecting the writing over which experts were divided in their opinions.

The history of the letter was a dinner the Claimant gave when staying at the Waterloo Hotel, and the five pounds referred to was sent to the man who provided amusement for Sir Roger's guests.

He was taught to shoot pigeons in the same way he was taught to write, and he lost a lot of money over it at Hendon, it being a fashionable amusement at the time and a good way of advertising himself.

The Welsh Harp at Hendon was a sort of suburban home for the Claimant. He spent a good deal of time there, promising all sorts of things to everybody when he came into the estates. One of his victims was the proprietor of the hotel, whose brother is still living at Kew, and he often laughs over the circumstances *now,* though at the time it was very serious when the Claimant went to prison, for so firmly had the proprietor believed in the man that he had built a new part to the hotel, which was christened the Tichborne wing and was to be paid for by Tichborne money. Warner was the name of the hotel-proprietor, and he firmly believed in the man until about the end of the civil trial, when he received a shock in rather a curious way.

One day Warner was called away from the dinner-table just when a large sirloin of beef had been put on it, so Sir Roger offered to carve for him during his absence. Before the proprietor could

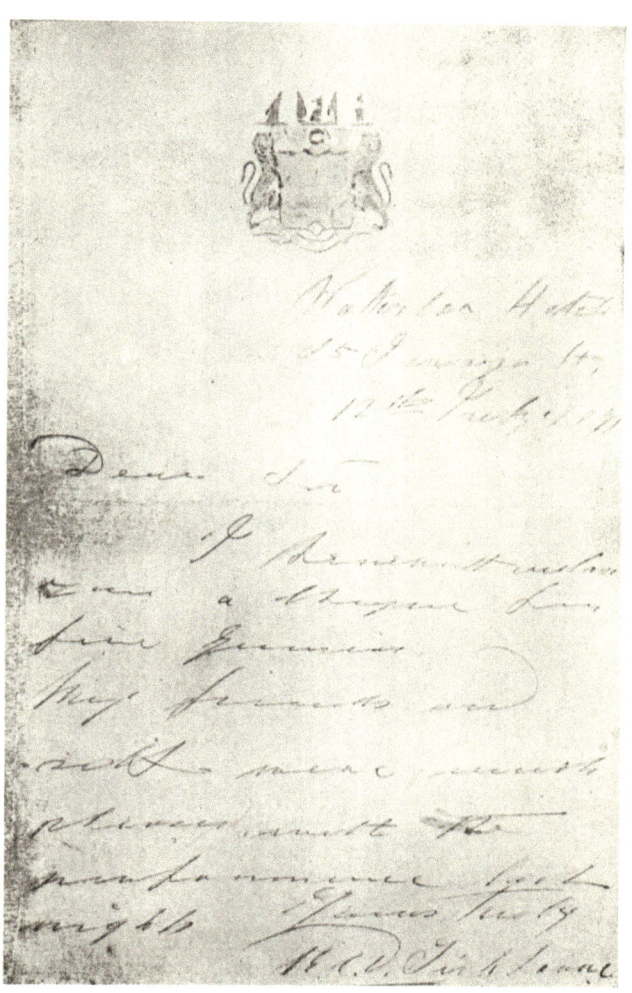

The Claimant's Letter, Taken from the Original

get out of the room Sir Roger was sharpening his knife up and down the steel in such a workmanlike manner that it gave Warner a real fright and he was overheard to say as he was going downstairs, "By God, he is a butcher." Which is what Sir Henry Hawkins so ably proved him to be.

His trial was the making of the then Mr. Henry Hawkins, later Lord Bampton. It may be remembered that Dr. Kenealy defended the claimant, his speech lasting from December 2nd to January 14th, in 1874. Henry Hawkins' reply lasting from January 15th to January 28th, Chief Justice Cockburn summing up from January 29th to February 25th.

I should think this must have been one of the longest trials ever heard in the English Courts. The defending family won of course, Orton getting fourteen years with hard labour, but it cost the estate £92,000.

It is a curious fact that during the earlier part of the hearing of the case, Mr. Hawkins firmly believed in the Claimant, and expressed his views amongst some of his sporting friends, in consequence of which there was a good deal of betting on the Hawkins' opinion. Mr. Lambert, who had owned some successful horses, put some £500 on it, the betting then being about even. One day, however, Mr. Lambert received a messenger from Mr. Hawkins, who had been told, "Go and find Mr. Lambert and tell him if he had invested any money on my early opinion at *once* to get out of it, as I shall not only prove him an arrant fraud, but also that he is none other than Arthur Orton!"

The advice was of course taken, and both Mr. Lambert and another friend were winners over the result.

It was difficult to believe that Lord Bampton in the courts and Lord Bampton in the street or on the race-course were one and the same man. In the courts presenting a dignified appearance in wig and gown, his clear cut features, clean shaven face and quick eye, which seemed to collect evidence in a glance. On the heath at Newmarket, in a curious yellow tinted, black banded top hat, dark blue pilot coat, snuff coloured tight fitting horsy pants and a rough ash plant stick, his loosely tied neckerchief flying out on either side of his face, giving the idea more of a horse-dealer than a legal luminary.

Those who did not know him often wondered who on earth he could be, as he was to be seen talking with all the celebrities, trainers and bookmakers. Once when he was standing talking to the ever popular John Corlett, of *The Sporting Times,* otherwise known as the "Pink'un," the following conversation was overheard by a friend, from two men standing by.

A. "I say, Bill, who's that funny looking old man over there talking to the master of the *Pink'un?"*

B. "Why, you ought to know, that's Hawkins, who gave you your 'time' when you were up at the Old Bailey."

A. "S'truth, so it is, but don't he look different without his wig, oh my!"

Lord Bampton used to bet a little, but never heavily. At one time, while still a Q.C., he was doing a little quiet betting with a bookmaker named Frank Lees, who for some time did not know the name of his client. The bookie remarked one day, "Oh! you win too often," or "you come too often for your money." To this Mr. Hawkins replied, "Never mind, Lees, if ever you get into trouble, you can come to me and I will get you out of it."

Lord Bampton was rather amusing, and once when Fred Archer was giving evidence in the witness-box, he with a very grave face asked, "And what is your Christian name?" The Court could not control its mirth. The judge used occasionally to send little jokes to Mr. Corlett for the *Pink'un*, and once when on circuit in the summer at Leicester something occurred which he thought would do nicely for the paper. Anything from Lord Bampton was accepted without enquiry or demur. Unfortunately the joke was omitted or lost and all that was received by the *Pink'un* was a note:

"Dear Corlett,

"The enclosed occurred here in court yesterday. I thought it would do for your front page.
"Yours,
"HENRY HAWKINS."
"P.S.—It's very warm here. If it is hot for me what must it be for the prisoners."

This tickled some of the readers nevertheless, as the judge was considered to be severe.

Lord Bampton was a great friend of James Lowther, and gave him the benefit of his legal knowledge in connection with racing difficulties and the Jockey Club.

I suppose Sir George Lewis was the most famous lawyer I ever met, or perhaps I should say the most successful I ever met, for he was not really a great lawyer, but was great in common sense. He was the man of whom it was stated that "he knew sufficient of every family to hang half London." He was staying at Scarborough once during one of their gay weeks when there happened to be rather an extra number of grass-widows disporting themselves. Sir George was having quite a good time amongst them, and at a ball held in the Grand Hotel was one night prancing along to the "Holly Bush Polka" with a young lady of his own religious persuasion, when some kind friend, wishing to be funny, said, "You will have them all as clients, Sir George." It had a very sobering effect on both the widows and Sir George.

Well-bred people accept their husbands' infidelities with calm. The late Lady Harborough was a wonderful example of this, and in spite of some strange experiences with her first husband married a second time, the last being Major ———.

Very little was seen of her during her first husband's lifetime; people used to say she was kept in captivity. During his earlier years Lord Harborough had what the papers termed an "illicit attachment" with an actress, and two children were born.   By the will of Lord Harborough the estate of Stapleford would go to one of these children after the demise of Lady Harborough.   One of them, named Mr. Kennedy (for convenience), when he grew up came to preach one harvest festival at the church attended by Lady Harborough. He was somewhat dramatic in the pulpit.   After the service the vicar asked Lady Harborough what she thought of the sermon.   She replied quite pleasantly, "He has inherited his mother's dramatic talent."

Stapleford was one of the mansions the Prince of Wales viewed when looking for a home before he finally settled on Sandringham.   Eventually the place passed into the possession of Mr. Hornsby, the Grantham agricultural implement maker, and I have been told that now on its portals there is a Latin inscription indicating that it was built by the Earl of Harborough in the fifteenth century, and completed by Jacob Hornsby in 18— something, I forget what.

Thinking of sermons reminds me of when my friend, Mr. Evelyn Burnaby, was taking a service once at Longleat while on a visit to Lord and Lady Bath.   He, being young and nervous at the time, inadvertently prayed for King George IV, and was teased about it in the drawing-room after church. He got out of it by saying it would not do any harm, it was a long time since anyone had prayed for him.

George the IV, by the way, was an intimate friend of Lord Erskine, who was leading counsel when Queen Caroline was prosecuted, and when passing through the park one day with His Majesty the latter noticed a new corps being trained. On hearing they were a corps of lawyers, he said, "Call them the Devil's Own," which name is borne to this day.

Longleat, the Bath's place, many people think, is spoilt by being built in a hollow. Personally, I prefer the hollow, but it has been suggested the adjacent hill known as Heaven's Gate would have greatly enhanced its beauty.

Frequenters of Bath in the olden days will probably remember Guinea Pig Jack, who stood on the road between the station and the town with his box of guinea pigs who performed tricks at their owner's command. Here the Italian daily made them "Die for the Queen," and recover immediately on hearing "The bobby's coming." I have been told the man made thousands of pounds in pence given to him and his pets by visitors to the city, and that a Roman Catholic priest advised him to part with it, and, being a Catholic, he meekly obeyed. So the poor little guinea pigs' daily tricks did not benefit their master much. Mr. Burnaby once asked Jack if he and his guinea pigs would be photographed with him. He consented for a fee of five shillings for the honour he was conferring on my friend.

I never think of Bath without remembering an exciting drive I had coming home from there one day with a tipsy chauffeur. It was a big powerful open car, and I was responsible for the well-being of some ladies I had invited to luncheon with me at the Empire Hotel. When we came out after luncheon I thought the chauffeur, who had been with us a year or two, was looking rather strange, so I asked him if he had got all the parcels I had sent to be put in the car. He leaned over and began counting, "Thershe one, thershe two," then with a silly smile and wag of his head, said, "thershe a good many." Evidently the young man had lunched. I had never known him make such a mistake, and he had driven the car up to the door of the hotel and turned it round safely, so it must be my fancy and, at any rate, he evidently could drive, but to make sure I asked him to turn the car round. This he did quite scientifically, so I decided we must venture.

I had been making some rather extensive purchases for a party I was giving, and had a salmon, strawberries, melons and all sorts of things in the car.

The moment we started off we flew at about sixty miles an hour, swishing round corners, between trams and pavements in a horrifying manner. Police ran after us shouting, people stood still and stared. I knew it would be worse than useless to speak to the man as long as we were in the traffic. It would only mean a smash. After many squeaks and hairbreadth escapes we left the town and shouting policemen behind. I therefore suggested to the man he had better drive a little slower or we should be killing somebody. He replied, quite civilly, "Oh, yes," but continued at the same speed.

Presently on the rather narrow road in front of us I saw a carrier's waggon crawling towards us, the driver evidently asleep inside. I thought there was nothing for it but an almighty smash, so planted my feet firmly that I might be shot clear. Instead of smashing into the waggon we darted down into a grassy ditch, and before we knew where we were found ourselves out again, past the waggon, and careering down the road once more. I thought every spring must be broken and could not imagine why we were not overturned during our journey in our exit out of the ditch, for we had been shot off our seats right into the air and down again.

The salmon, strawberries and new felt shoes for the housemaids, to make them quiet in the morning, were dancing about together naked in the bottom of the car amongst our feet. The papers had all flown away, and so had our wraps. We had some very awkward corners to turn before we reached home, and at Wells an archway to go through and then turn short and sharp to the left close up against a big stone wall. I held my breath as we neared it. There was a grating noise of one wing against the wall as we went under the arch, and we balanced on two wheels rounding the corner, and then a fairly straight run home.

A special Providence must have watched over us, for we all arrived safely, and I must allow that while the driving was highly dangerous it was masterly. We all got out, and I made no remark to the chauffeur until next day. When he came for orders I spoke like a father to him and said of course he could never hope to drive me or anybody else again. He said, "No." He knew he had taken too much and was truly thankful he had not killed us all. He then went away into the village, had another drink, and shot the owner of the public-house. I came to the conclusion we had come rather well out of our exciting drive, and truly thankful I had not attempted to argue with him while at the wheel.

One of the regrets of my life has been not having seen Lord Beaconsfield in his bath, which sounds very indiscreet, but his devoted wife always said that "Anyone wishing to see a true specimen of manly beauty should see Dizzy in his bath." I ought to have done so out of politeness, and it would have made such an unending source of conversation between us!

I think Lord Beaconsfield was fully alive to the fact that he owed much of his fame to the beautiful old Lady Sykes, of Basilden Park, Reading, who died at the age of one hundred years in 1844. She was known as "The Norfolk Centenarian Peeress." She introduced him to Lord Lyndhurst, and is supposed to be "Zenobia" in his novel.

I think he also knew why she took so much interest in him and his career.

It is not generally known, I believe, that Lord

Beaconsfield in his last moments when under the care of Dr. Kidd, and with Lord Barrington in the room, raised himself in bed into the attitude he was known to adopt when about to address the House, and while, no doubt, mentally doing so, passed away.

His devotion to his wife was touching. He once said to me that if there were more wives in the world like his it would be a happier place to live in, or words to that effect. She was a very careful person, looking after the crumbs and pence to a remarkable degree, for which he was grateful and proud of her thrift and carefulness as well as for her tender care of himself.

I met his heir, Mr. Coningsby Disraeli, in Ireland when with the Ridgeways, and felt he was overshadowed by the greatness of his uncle. It is so hard to be expected to live up even pictorially to the aloofness of the great!

When annoyed Lord Beaconsfield was without doubt the rudest and worst mannered man I ever met, and I am glad I never came under the ban of his displeasure.

CHAPTER XV

VICTOR HUGO did not consider our English
judicial system as good as the French; he
explained this once in Paris when in 1877
a *cause célèbre* was being heard in the Palais de
Justice. The court was crowded with men and
women, the latter attired in the latest creations of
Worth. He expressed it as his opinion that our
English system is litigious and not inquisitorial.
The French trial is the final act, every circumstance
has been investigated previously by a body of officers and the accused examined by them privately.
In England the judge hears the evidence for the
first time and addresses the jury upon the facts as
they have been proved in court. I was asking Sir
Howard Vincent his views on this subject once.

He said the French was undoubtedly the one by which to arrive at the truth but it would never be tolerated in England. The late Sir Fitzjames Stephens who presided at the trial of Mrs. Maybrick in 1887 also agreed that the French system was the best, considering the desired object was the truth, therefore the inquisitorial system was bound to be the superior, but added that the great love of fair play that was our natural characteristic would prevent its ever being introduced into England.

Victor Hugo was the only poet I ever met or heard of who was able to combine poetry and business. He was a "cute" man of affairs, if I may use the slang expression, and what a wonderful but melancholy personality; I think he dreamed of tragedy, he certainly showed his taste in that line very early in life, being only fourteen when he composed and produced a tragedy, when at that age he should not have known what the word meant. The thing that struck me most in conversation with him was his melancholy and entire absence of humour, but he was a genius and knew it. The worst of being a genius is they have to pay so dearly for it, the privilege is to sorrow more bitterly and torment themselves more utterly over matters they are powerless to control or alter, than falls to the lot of the ordinary everyday individual.

Like Ruskin striving after the impossible, unhappy and discontented because he could not make the world the beautiful place he wished it to be, and could dimly see in his dreams.

Carlyle's unhappiness took another form; he could not tolerate anyone greater than himself. But I must go back to the people of my own time.

Sir Fitzroy Kelly, whom my father used to tell me about, called Apple-pip Kelly, in consequence of his having been counsel for Fawcett, the Quaker, tried for the murder of a man at Slough who had died from a dose of prussic acid. Sir Fitzroy made a powerful address to the jury suggesting the deceased might have died from apple pips which were known to contain the properties of prussic acid.

It was an ingenious defence, but I fear did not save the Quaker.

Kelly was a wonderful old man, for when his years were nigh four score he still liked to pay his addresses to the fair sex, whom he greatly admired. Unfortunately on one occasion when driving out from Lewis to say pretty things to a widow of his acquaintance his carriage was upset and he sat down in a puddle of water, which so cooled his ardour that he went home, returning no more to the comely widow.

He had a habit latterly of falling asleep when the case he was hearing became dull. Once when trying a case involving the loss of a ship's cargo the chief baron was in a condition of somnolence. It so happened that he was a firm believer in the wholesomeness of dates and was particularly fond of them, and on Counsel mentioning the word dates, the judge awoke with a start, saying, "What did you say the ship contained?" "Dates" was the reply.

"Most important," said the judge, grasping his pen to make notes, and slumbered no more.

He succeeded Sir F. Pollock and was the last of the chiefs of the now obsolete court of Exchequer.

Judges can really be very funny sometimes, though it behooves all present to laugh even if they only think they are.

The following is quite neat, I think.

Some years ago when Lady Rollo, on her husband's death refused to let the hounds go out, a sergeant-at-law asked Lord Chief Justice Tindal whether he thought there would be anything indecorous in so doing, if each hound had a piece of crape round its neck or tail. "I hardly think," said the judge, "that crape would be necessary, surely it would be sufficient if they were all in full cry."

Even legal folk manage to make mistakes sometimes, I have observed. A jovial Rivett Carnac cousin who was administrator-general in Bombay at one time was staying with us, and our dear old friend Sir Charles Lowther was dining amongst others. Though blind, his eyes, at least one of them, had a way of roving round, but this had not been noticed by the man from Bombay, and when asked to sing one of his comic songs for which he was famed he sat down to the piano and sang a silly thing with a chorus in which all were expected to join, something about

> "And one eye looked up at the ceiling
> The other looked down at the floor."

Sir Charles clapped and encored, but we all felt uncomfortable, and I smiled the emotionless smile of kings and queens, my eyes not smiling at all.

Conventionality dies an easy death in war time, and in consequence I have been amused many times. Naturally everybody worth their salt has wanted to do their bit. It so happened that practically every male that was sound, and some that were not in the neighbourhood of my home, had found something useful to do shortly after war was declared with the exception of one man a little past mark of mouth and consumed with his own importance; he felt it looked odd his being left the sole unemployed male element in the place so wrote to the Military Authorities offering to do any work that would not take him far from home, as he could not really be spared, the estate (about 100 acres) and the village could not possibly be left without his guiding hand, he also kept a strict eye on the morals of the place, but he could spare a little time every day to cut bread and butter for soldiers or something useful of that kind.

Various forms of usefulness were suggested but so many obliged him to be mixed up with women workers that he declined; he felt too shy and did not think it at all proper or *nice!*

At last, from very shame, when he was asked to take night duty in a voluntary hospital near, he accepted it, without having quite grasped all the post entailed. There had been a good deal of joking amongst the nurses about this prudish per-

son who fancied himself so enormously; he felt
no woman nurse or otherwise could be near him
without proposing to him or something worse, so
they determined to give him a lesson. When he
came on duty the first night a pretty nurse explained
to him minutely his duties. All was going swim-
mingly until she said "and in case of emergency
you must come and awake me, I am always so tired
I sleep very heavily."

Night Nurse. "But hum—er—how do I call
you? do I knock at your door, and which is your
door? Oh, really!—I think that would be a mistake—would not do at all."

Day Nurse. "No?" (sweetly, with head on one
side). "Why not?"

Night Nurse. "Well—oh—er—don't you see er
—it might—er—lead to—er—really this is very
awkward, to (*in desperation*) misinterpretation."

Day Nurse. Cheerfully, "Oh, well we can't help
that, can we?" She began to move away, calling
back, "Don't forget to call me *well,* your only
chance really of awaking me is to pull me out of bed
by my legs!"

Night Nurse. Pale and trembling, muttered to
himself, "This will never do—impossible situation,
never be able to hold my head up again—what *will*
people think—and *say!* I must find the head doctor
and make some other arrangement," and he did.

Another rather sporting married man of a certain
age, wished to be useful and wrote to the War
Office saying he had been accustomed to hunting

all his life and the handling of horses if there was anything in that line he could do? Then in a weak moment he poked some fun, or what he thought fun, at the Government officials by saying he was A.1. at managing mules.

In consequence of which before he was much older he found himself responsible for hundreds of biting and bickering mules at the front and wished himself dead.

There has been much marriage and giving in marriage since the outbreak of war. One of the victims, though a· willing one, has been a very young friend of mine just out of the schoolroom and rather bonny. A naval man spirited her away, and put her in lodgings at a place on the South-East coast where he could see his bride occasionally.

Being absurdly young, bright and nice-looking everybody was kind to her, and when there was a Zeppelin raid over the town where she was staying many were the people who flew to protect her. She had not been long in bed one night when the bombing began, window panes and roofs were flying about in every direction. The landlady was the first to dash into her room, pull her out of bed and hustle her down the stairs to some safer place, she met several people on the way to save her, others went to her room to find her flown. A frantic messenger came from her husband saying the only safe place was with her face to an inner wall and a corner for choice, she was therefore hustled into a dark corner on the stairs with her face to the wall.

Not having been allowed any voice in the matter she now plaintively suggested she was chilly with bare feet and only her silk night garments, but she told me it was not much use complaining as all the people who had come to save her were attired in her things, the landlady was in her dressing-gown, her slippers on another, a third her great coat, a fourth her eiderdown, etc., and the poor little bride had nothing left in the way of wraps.

This war, so dramatic in achievement and so vital in all its bearings, has obliged many of us to alter some of our preconceived ideas, we are shaken to our foundation, hardly now knowing what we believe to be right and what wrong.

I was talking to one of our present-day soldiers about this not long ago and chiding him mildly for his change of front on certain points, conscription being one. Once he did not see the necessity of it for the English people, but has now of course changed his views. When I asked him how he reconciled his mind to the various changes, his answer struck me as worth considering. He said, "You must not forget I am a paid servant of the Crown, and so long as I am that my own private views have nothing to do with my work, and must not appear in it. I am there to do as I am told, to carry out the views and instructions of my employers. If one master employing me says, 'Let us scuttle out of Egypt and abandon those we have led into danger,' I abandon them, and scuttle, doing all in my power to facilitate the scuttling. Another employer may say, 'At all costs we must hold Egypt and rescue those who are holding their lives in their hands and waiting for us,' here again I endeavour to carry out my orders, but I do not consider myself the weather-cock you seem to imply that I am. I am obeying orders, my opinion is not asked, and if it was my advice would probably not be taken. My first duty lies in unquestioning obedience. If I found that I could not keep my own views under proper control I should no longer be of any use to either party and should most certainly chuck it."

These views are perhaps what may be expected from the old army reared in red tape and forbidden to think or have views of their own, but it is very wonderful that the new army who three years ago, and some only a few months ago, were doing mental arithmetic with pens behind their ears in the city or measuring out yards of silk to lady customers and bamboozling them on to its properties and worth, should fall into line as if they had been all their lives at the game. Yet we hear little of insubordination. The old order hath changed nevertheless in more ways than one, which was bound to be the case with mixed cosmopolitan crowds of soldiers. For instance, a relation of mine out at the front heard a Canadian Colonel addressing his men prior to an inspection from the King, Lord Kitchener or some such bigwig, he was imploring them not to call him "Sammy" before the chiefs.

At first the accent of the Canadians and Australians puzzled me; I am growing used to it now, but acclimatised as I am becoming I was rather upset a while ago at being asked if I had noticed some fine lice on the altar-cloth in a certain church, in time I gathered it was the lace being referred to by my Australian friend.

General, now Field-Marshal, Lord French was always a very keen and dashing cavalryman, he, to use a latter-day expression, was fairly "putting the wind up" the Somerset Yeomanry during one of their annual trainings years ago when he went down to inspect them.

It was in the good old dreamy pre-war days, when the few who could be tempted into joining the irregular forces felt they were really being very decent to their country about it and were sometimes rather insistent that this should be borne in mind during their time in camp. Many of these staunch yeomen were hunting farmers mounted on their own useful horses, but there were others who seldom, if ever, crossed a horse at any other time and were on hirelings, so that military evolutions carried out at a faster pace than a slow trot were a matter of the utmost delicacy and not to be lightly undertaken.

When the day of General French's inspection arrived, the Yeomen turned out, a blaze of splendour, and all went famously until the General wanted them to do a "charge." Anxious to oblige him, they charged in the restrained manner they had found to be the most desirable, especially as they were crossing country they did not know very well.

The impetuous General French, however, was not satisfied and galloped after the squadron shouting, "Faster! faster!! Gallop! gallop!!"

Stung to frenzy by his shouts, the doomed squadron flung all discretion to the winds, and really let themselves go, with terrible results. All vestige of formation was lost, while an ever-thickening trail of equipment and fallen yeomen was left in the wake.

When this uncontrolled living avalanche had reached its wildest point, a sunken fence suddenly yawned before them, representing a drop of at least four feet. The first ranks strove madly to stem the tide, but those behind drove them blindly forward. Really, the horrors of the Balaclava charge paled before this story!

By this time none but the most consummate had more than one foot in the stirrup, and those who had not fallen off, passionately envied those who had. On they charged, and met their doom over the sunken fence. Some jumped it with their horses, others without; a few slid in.

It was too terrible to watch, for it looked as if there had been a severe battle, the far side of the fence littered with fallen warriors and their horses. The air was thick with deep and agitated voices swearing before Heaven they had done with soldiering for ever; some of the horses had come to the same conclusion.

After it was all over General French spoke honeyed words to them, even referred tactfully to the little matter of the sunken fence which he had not noticed when he ordered "the charge." There were a good many resignations all the same!

One yeoman told me he could never hear the tune the band played that day without breaking out into a perspiration.

Music really plays a large part in our lives, much larger than many of us are aware of. Under its influence we become heroes and heroines in imagination, and who can say it does not at times make us so in reality. Think of the dear old street organ that we paid to go away, why? Because it played tricks with our memories and emotions which we could not face. Then scent, another powerful messenger,—but I must not stray from my yeoman, for really he ought to have had a medal after surviving such an ordeal, but it was before the days of "the monkey and the goat," which I hear is what C.M.G. stands for. Perhaps he agreed with Sir Robert Peel that the distinction of being without an honour is becoming a rare and honourable one, but then Sir Robert was thinking and speaking of the hunters after titles and honours, of which we hear so much to-day, ready to pay large sums into the party funds, the amount being regulated by the honour conferred. As far as our soldiers and sailors are concerned to-day, it seems as if all had deserved medals for bravery.

In these stressful times, when we walk about

metaphorically with our hands on our hearts and a great dread in our brains, it takes very little to make us laugh, which sounds paradoxical, but is a living fact, one's nerves are at high tension, both laughter and tears are very near the surface.   On this account all were much amused when a trifling contretemps occurred to poor Lord Breadalbane during the early part of the war when taking a party of the Grenadier Guards to shoot at Byfleet. They had to change trains and cross a bridge at East Ham, West Ham or some such place, I have forgotten the name of the station.   It had been raining and the platform was slippery.

Everybody had turned out to admire the beauties, who perfectly understood the amount of attention they were attracting.   The nursery maids and errand boys left and forgot their babies and parcels to get a better view of the clanking soldiers crossing the bridge with chests thrown out and a would-be detached expression.

Suddenly, when all had negotiated the slippery steps satisfactorily and were forming up ready for the next train the hob-nails in Lord Breadalbane's boots played him a dirty trick and with a mighty splutter he fell flat on his face in front of his men and the admiring crowd.   The clatter was stupendous, it seemed almost impossible one man, even if tall and lean, could make so much noise.   His sword flew out of its scabbard and executed a "fox trot" all by itself, his ammunition-bag sat on his head wrong side up, cunning drinking-cups and field glasses hobnobbed in an out-of-the-way corner, head gear fell over the platform on to the line. It has taken some time to describe the scene, but it all happened so quickly it was difficult to guess exactly what was taking place, no one looking more utterly bewildered than the men, who with protruding eyes of horror and open mouthed from shock continued doing goose step, marking time until the commanding officer was right side up again. Unfortunately the moment he was rearranged and preparing to give words of command in a huffy ruffled manner another side slip sent him flat on his back.

The first fall had occasioned ejaculations of "Oh, my, 'ope 'e 'asn't hurt 'isself" from the nursery-maids, but when the second acrobatic evolution took place there were shrieks of laughter from the gallery, on the bridge and the other side of the station. It was a silly little thing to make us laugh but I have laughed for less at well-performed pantomimic displays.

The faces of the men were such studies, the first disaster and clatter disconcerted them, but the second really frightened them, they had never seen any account in their drill-books of what was the correct thing to do under the circumstances. The only person who saw nothing funny about it at all was poor Lord Breadalbane.

I begin to feel quite ancient when I think of General the Hon. Sir Julian Byng, who has done so well in this war, as I first saw him with the tenth Hussars at Lucknow.

I have been refreshing my memory of what he was like in those days by looking at a photograph I have of him taken at that time in a group. In those days he was a very junior subaltern, shy and retiring, but gave one the impression of being like the sailors parrot "thinking the more."

A good many years have passed over our heads since then and the shy and retiring youth has blossomed out into a general with a witty and forcible vocabulary.

When Lord Kitchener consulted him as to what was the best to be done at the Dardanelles, in November, 1915, his answer is worth recording, it was so true. "Either," he said, "we must get on, or get out,"—hereby putting the problem in a nutshell. A very high and mighty person who seldom allows himself any freedom of speech was talking to me about this a very short time ago and he said, "Byng was right. Had the Government been able to make up its mind they must 'get on,' and had they sent the wherewithal the war would have been over in the early summer of this year, but they could not, therefore the only alternative was to 'get out,' but for a long time they could not even harden their hearts to do that."

I miss the cynical and drastic pen of Mr. Labouchere. No one has arisen to walk in his footsteps with the same daring disregard for consequences and personages, no one has the courage of his convictions to quite the same extent. How much more he would have told us of the little whispers we hear from the front!

Mr. Gibson Bowles, judging by a letter he wrote a short time ago, is "fighting all parties in the House of Commons in the interests of the State." Perhaps he has his eye on a few little things that want looking into. I have known him speak some home-truths at times. In days gone by when he, Fred Burnaby and a friend owned *Vanity Fair*, I remember some of his remarks were not always flattering.

On one occasion when the mother of a well-known baronet gave a ball, the following week *Vanity Fair* held a paragraph saying, "The liquor was not of the highest order, as it much resembled gooseberry wine." This, if he had been one of the guests was not good taste, but quite possibly he wrote from information received. The hostess' son said he intended inflicting summary castigation on Mr. Bowles's latter end. Fred Burnaby said, "What will he care, he's told that every day."

CHAPTER XVI

COLONEL FRED BURNABY used to say the three grand dames of his generation were Jane Lady Ely, Lady Waldegrave, and Lady Molesworth, widow of Sir William Molesworth of Pencarrow, Cornwall, mathematician, philosopher, and at one time Secretary of State for the Colonies.

Lady Molesworth was a remarkable and highly talented woman. Talent, no matter in what form, and that illusive undefinable quality we call charm, for want of some better definition, are undoubtedly great factors in life, and always make themselves felt. Take, for example, two characters of diametrically opposite temperaments reigning at the same period, both gathering in a rich harvest of admirers—Lady Molesworth and the notorious "Skittles," I do not know her real name, and can find none who do, though plenty who remember her well. Both these women started life in the streets, the former as a musician, the latter with a basket of oranges and watercress at the top of Sloane Street. Lady Molesworth became the leader of all that was best in society of her day, the friend of kings and queens, and holding political salons of importance. The notorious "Skittles," with the face of an innocent child, became the most famous charmer of male hearts in England, a byword in the shires as well as London.

Both were dazzling successes in widely different ways. I think everyone will admit that nothing but talent that rose above all handicaps could have enabled Lady Molesworth to win and hold, as she did to the end of her days, such a position as she made for herself.

People are prone to underestimate the talents of the "Skittles" of every generation. They say, "Oh, that sort of success is easy enough for a pretty woman by those methods!" But is it? I think not. That is a great mistake. If it were true what crowds would make themselves rich in the social history of the times. I maintain there must have been real talent in "Skittles" besides good looks and easy ways.

The careers of both these interesting women are worth a passing thought. Lady Molesworth was a Miss Carstairs, and when trundling her organ in the streets of London attracted the attention of Mr. Temple West of Mathon Lodge, Worcestershire. It was a case of love at first sight, and honourable love. He took her under his wing, had her educated, and married her. That her education was not wasted she amply proved later in life. At the death of Mr. Temple West, who left her well provided for, she married Sir William Molesworth. There is little doubt she made both men happy, and they left her considerable fortunes. Sir William died in 1858. She survived until 1888, dying rich and respected.

Her time was spent between Pencarrow and Eaton Place, her house being the last at the corner of the south-west side. To be asked to stay at Pencarrow was like getting the "Blue Riband" of society.

At the time I married she was no longer young, but still a leader of fashion, giving recherché dinners and entertaining royalty, much envied of many of the blue-blooded.

She was supposed to have a marvellous cook, and judging by her dinners she certainly had, but I have been told by someone who ought to know that these dinners were cooked by a charwoman called in for the purpose. It seems incredible, but here again it may have been a case of talent making itself felt, and there may have been family reasons why the char-lady was unable to maintain the high position her talent deserved.

It is surprising that no life or memoirs of Lady Molesworth have been written, for from a social point of view her knowledge of society and her power in the political world were greater than that of, say, Lady Dorothy Nevill. In Lady Molesworth we see a woman who appealed to all that was best in men, their honour and chivalry.

She was a very kind woman, but had the "selective" and "exclusive" instinct strongly developed, and she was not to be "got at" easily by ordinary society. To struggling musicians she was especially kind, ready at all times with a helping hand, remembering, no doubt, her early years.

Charles Dickens was to have dined with her the week he died at Gadshill.

She was an exceedingly clever and delightful woman. The Prince of Wales (King Edward VII) admired her, and found her excellent company. Once when she was in a box with him at Evan's Supper Rooms, Paddy Green, the old "walker-round," who used to wander from table to table greeting the visitors all as "dear fellahs!" with his green silk handkerchief and snuff-box, went up to her and claimed acquaintance, reminding her of the days when they had been on the stage together, and from his pocket produced an orange play bill, on which their names appeared. Quite naturally she said, "Show it to his Royal Highness, Paddy," and he did so. She seemed quite amused and pleased about it.

Providence had bestowed upon "Skittles" an

entirely different temperament from that of Lady
Molesworth, and she graduated from the top of
Sloane Street to the Panton Street crowd, Cremorne, and the well-known places of amusement.
From there to a beautiful home of her own, that is
to say, it was occupied by her, and into the shires
where she hunted with the pick and flower of the
land. Who taught her to ride I do not know, but I
do know who introduced her to the shires, and I
have heard much and often of her deeds and
prowess there. There was also the echo of a famous
rumpus she occasioned there fifty-five years ago
when out with the Quorn, at the time Lord Stamford, the seventh earl, was the master. Naturally
I was not there, but friends who were said there
was a terrible scene.

"Skittles," mounted on some of the finest hunters
money could buy, chosen for her by one of the
friends responsible for her presence in the field,
had for weeks been wiping the eyes of all the women
out hunting, and a good many of the men. One
day she hailed Lady Stamford, the wife of the
master, as an old acquaintance of Cremorne. No
notice was taken of the salutations, so "Skittles,"
emboldened by her triumph and success, again addressed the master's wife, who had been recognised
by society and much liked.

Lady Stamford then complained to a whip to rid
her of the presence of so objectionable a person, and
"Skittles" was asked to "move on," but flatly declined to do anything of the kind. The master was

appealed to and asked to take the hounds home. This he was reluctant to do, feeling that the hunting field was open to all who cared to support it, but he said that if "Skittles" made herself objectionable to other women in the field he would be obliged to ask her not to come out, and if she did he must take the hounds home. The particular friends of "Skittles" then begged her to go home for the day and thus restore peace. To this she eventually agreed, but not before enjoying the last word, which was shouted for all to hear.

"All right, you fellows, I'll go. I won't spoil your sport, but what the hell is the good of Lady Stamford giving herself such airs? She is not the head of the profession, and never will be. Lady —— is the head of our profession! Good morning, gentlemen."

A friend tells me that she looked as if butter would not melt in her mouth, but the vocabulary she used on the occasion was surprising to those who did not know her well, or who had not seen her displeased before.

I have gathered that "Skittles," the leading *reine de la main gauche* of her time, was very pretty and owned a beautiful figure. The photographs I have seen of her certainly verify this.

How the name of "Skittles" attached itself to her I do not know; there have been several versions of the story, but she was the original "Anonyma" of the "Belgravian Mother's Lament" in *The Times,* which in course of time expanded into a social phase. These society mothers wrote to one paper deploring the "degrading taste of the *jeunesse doré* of the period," noting the "disgusting and de- praved" way they thronged at the park railings to see Anonyma during her usual parade down the Ladies' Mile with some of her beautiful ponies, while the virtuous daughters of Belgravia stood neglected in the background, practically wiped out of the picture by the popularity of the London lassie.

I have been told, but with what truth I cannot say, that this clever little woman later in life mar- ried one of her long-suffering and deeply attached swains, who had been in attendance for some years, but that they separated very shortly after the tying of the knot.

Lady Stamford made a splendid wife and was a most benevolent woman. After her husband's death she took interest in horse-breeding and in selling her yearlings. She was well-known at New- market and, in later years, often seen there, still retaining some of her youthful good looks with the added grace of a sweet and good expression and lovely snow-white hair.

The poor around her old home at Enville in Staffordshire loved her. It was her husband's favourite place, and it was there he took her soon after their honeymoon.

It was reported after Lord Stamford's death that his widow was about to marry Robert Peck, the first trainer to the Duke of Westminster. They would have made a good-looking couple, but perhaps it was only one of Girton's stories, the one-time valet to Mr. Christopher Sykes. Before he started his hotel he said Robert Peck had seriously contemplated the marriage and had asked him (Girton) to be manager of their household affairs, adding he could put "Robert" up to a thing or two. This I can quite imagine. I have always been under the impression that his servants had quite as much to do with ruining Mr. Sykes as his guests. Everything was carried out on such exceedingly generous lines and so many dependants filled their pockets while Mr. Sykes' were emptying.

The marriage did not take place, however. Girton started his hotel—and later Mr. Robert Peck married someone else.

Lady Cardigan, who was a Miss de Horsey, was certainly a highly entertaining woman, but owned the most bitter tongue. There were, of course, reasons why she felt bitter, but that is an old story and well known. When she was entertaining me with astounding racy stories, I always felt I had only to wait long enough and I should be brought into her list. The moment she was piqued with anybody she appeared to remember some astonishing stories about them. It would be difficult to make a list of any length of well-known people whose names she left in peace. Her black list ranged from our royalties, against whom she was intensely bitter, to Cardinal Vaughan, of whom she said some very pithy but very naughty things, probably children of her own imagination.

Neither Lady Cardigan nor Lady Stamford were ever presented at Court. The former was going to be and all was arranged even to the dress, but an order was issued cancelling the introduction. She felt this very much and was an embittered woman ever after.

Once when she and I believe "Skittles" also, were guests at a special dinner given by some members of the extra smart and fast set, Lord Cardigan, the hero of Balaclava, was responding to the toast of his health and making some reference to the Light Brigade charge when his wife placed cannons to the right of them and cannons to the left of them by loudly declaring her noble lord had never been in the charge at all. However, much must be forgiven a woman who has spoilt her own life, and felt all men's hands were against her. Occasionally really good and kind-hearted folk, when hurt, say things they do not mean.

The last time I saw Lady Cardigan she must, I think, have been doing the "post-impressionist" business, for she was driving down Piccadilly in orange hair and an emerald green coat.

Mrs. Postlethwaite was another lady of considerable notoriety in my early days. She was very beautiful. Every shop window was full of her pictures. I heard men rave about her. Then one fine day her husband unkindly refused to pay for her lovely clothes, and the shock turned her into a religious enthusiast! She had religious meetings at her five o'clock teas and gave "the kiss of peace" to her old friends, Mr. Gladstone receiving one I know, and many others who wished to share her religious enthusiasm. Disraeli and Gladstone were both favourites in the race and waxed wrath with one another over her.

I feel that not to mention these ladies who played so large a part in the history of the years I have lived in would be a mistake. No one is all good, no one all bad, and all these women were undoubtedly clever.

> "In men whom men condemn as ill
> I find so much of goodness still;
> In men whom men esteem divine,
> I find so much of sin and blot,
> I hesitate to draw the line
> Between two men when God does not."

Life is a huge puzzle, but each piece is meant to fit into its place, and will do so in spite of all our failings. If we were all virtues or all vices we should cease to be interesting. It is those who live in spasms between the two that interest us and fire our hearts.

It is not really necessary for a woman to be beautiful to be attractive. There are not many irretrievably plain women. It rests a good deal with themselves. Antoine Berrager, the French Advocate, who considered himself rather a judge, said, "There are no ugly women, only there are women who do not know how to look pretty." There is comfort in the thought! Some day I shall have to write an essay on "Voluntary Ugliness" when I have time, for a happy face has a beauty all its own.

The present-day fashion of there being no old ladies is rather nice, I think. They no longer envelop themselves in dowdy black cloaks and mantles with bonnets tied under their chins. Instead of this, we find them with their bonny grey hair nicely dressed in the fashion of the moment, wearing smart hats with wobbly ospreys, frisky little coats and skirts with regiments of dear little buttons, pretty shoes and big buckles, and then their figures! Is it that they have renounced the good things of the flesh-pots, or is it that they now allow their figures to be natural, I wonder? Whatever it is, it is pleasing.

Some stories of the past are like dear old songs to be softly sung, for once they were tender, very tender, and now are fragile with age. A few of these are to-day drifting through my memory and making me feel sad. There was poor, fragile, witty and emotional Mrs. Grant of Glenmoriston, whom I remember as Miss Davidson, dancing at Inverness during the gaieties of the "Northern Meeting" in 1886 or 1887, just before she was married. She and her husband were utterly unsuited to one another, but she was not very happy at home, she told me, although "my man is fond of me and says I may have my own way in everything." But that was not all she wanted and did not satisfy her.

One day what I feared would happen came to pass. She came in to see me and told me that the man she loved so dearly was to be made happy, she was going to run away with him, and she did. Her husband behaved splendidly and followed her to Paris to try and persuade her to return to him, but it was no use. She asked him to set her free, and he did. The moment it was possible, her lover married her on June 26th, 1894, and she died on July 22nd the same year, pitifully short-lived happiness after the long struggle with herself as to whether she would or would not, could or could not. How true it is that we all have to suffer for our mistakes and pay for our happiness in this world, and yet what do I mean by this world? There are so many; we all create our own.

The little blind god "love" plays very cruel tricks with us, and in charity we must all bear in mind:

> "And to love or not, we are no more free
> Than a ripple to rise and leave the sea."

It is only when our nerve cells are acting in unity that we are really sane and at our best.

I have a huge pity for those who lose the loves of their life, whether the world has approved or disapproved, for it is a time when life stands suspended and motionless.

I saw a good deal of the third Duke of Sutherland's first wife, who was a favourite of Queen

Victoria's; her last years were unhappy.   There
was some scandal about her husband's affections
for Mrs. Blair, who became his second wife.

The Duchess used to be a good deal in Torquay,
and was a regular attendant at St. Mary's Church,
and was usually dressed in white.   Queen Victoria
never forgave the Duke for not coming back from
America to his wife when she was dying.   She was
very High Church, and the Duke's sympathies did
not lie in that direction, which caused a good deal
of unhappiness.   The Duke was deeply attached to
his second wife, and when he died left her a mil-
lion pounds sterling.   She later spent six months in
Holloway jail for contempt of Court, Sir Francis
Jeune having ordered her to destroy certain letters,
if I remember correctly, which she declined to do.

Colonel Milman was governor of the prison at
the time, and he said he much disliked having first
class misdemeanants under his care, who arrived in
their own carriages and furnished their own apart-
ments from Maples as did the Duchess.   Mr. Yates,
of *The World,* was also there for libel, and Lord
Russell for bigamy, so he had a dose of his pet
aversions.

I have observed that a man who is not happily
married generally lets the world know all about it
and craves sympathy.   A woman more often ex-
cuses what she cannot justify, and keeps silence
over what she cannot cover or forgive.   Poor Mrs.
Carlyle was an illustration; she tried to justify her
husband to his critics.

How little we really know of the minds of even our most intimate friends, though their faces are photographed on our brains, until we read their writing, then we discover we have only known the garments in which they clothed themselves, the rest has been a sealed book. This was brought home to me particularly when I read Flora Annie Steel's first book. When I knew her in India I never dreamed she was a thinker and so deeply interested in the lives of the people of the country, as her books have proved her to be. When she came to see me in town on our return to England and told me she was writing a book, I did not feel deeply interested and said, "How clever of you," or something insipid like that, and when I read the book I realised how very little I had really known her. But even then I should never have guessed she would be a suffragette of the militant brand.

Mrs. Reeves (Helen Mathers) is more like her writing, or I should say that her writing is more like her. She is very bright, clever and amusing, a thorough woman of the world, and enjoys everything which one gathers to a certain extent from her writing.

Lately I have come to the conclusion there are a number of people who cannot spell. I am not very brilliant in that line myself, so must speak circumspectly. In the days of spelling-bees my sister left me hopelessly in the lurch. But I am not quite so bad as some of my friends. An Oxford young man, now in the army, writing to me a short time ago explaining his financial difficulties, said, "And God only nose what I shall do next." After reading that I thought there might be some truth in the statement.

Another young man of my acquaintance who is perhaps not blessed with a superabundance of brains had some papers to fill, in connection with military work. He made such a jumble of it that another document was sent to him saying, will you please simply answer the following questions, "Yes" or "no." Then followed the list. The answers that were in the affirmative he answered thus:

"Yess."

"Yess."

I should have felt sorry for him if he had felt in any way depressed at his lack of orthography, but it troubled him not at all. He was of a happy nature and a great big over-grown-schoolboy sort of man who apparently enjoyed every minute of his life, and such trifles as spelling were not going to upset him. But he will spell no more. He has been swallowed up in this Armageddon, and now if he could only write and say he was well and happy, if every word was misspelt I would never even tell him of it.

The knowledge of etiquette requires even more careful mastering than spelling and takes a lifetime to learn. To begin with, every Court has its own etiquette, and the arranging of who is to sit next who, and which has to take in which, when you have a few foreign royalties mixed up with English ones, and a sprinkling of native princes and their wives to arrange in proper precedence, is apt to lead to serious attacks of neuralgia.

An American millionaire's wife, who was renting a beautiful villa on the shores of the tideless Mediterranean, settled the question of precedence rather neatly at one of her parties. She was not very well versed in the ways of society, and sent all the ladies in to dinner according to their ages. There were four baronets' wives amongst others. Two of the husbands were Nova Scotia baronets, while the other two held titles from the time of King James. None of these good people were able to enjoy their dinner or be agreeable under such circumstances.

It is hard to remember everybody's little prejudices; not to talk of beer when dining with brewers, to adapt one's speech so as not to hurt the susceptibilities of those we employ and so on.

For instance, it is an insult to ask a man or a maid at a servants' party if their programme is full, especially if it happens to be before supper. They hasten to tell you that they have had nothing but lemonade and a sandwich.

The wife of a well-known peer had been giving a servants' ball, and the following day when attending to household matters came across the kitchen-maid and said to her:

"I hope, Margaret, that you enjoyed yourself last night?"

"No, my lady, I was very much upset."

"I am sorry to hear that. What was the cause?"

"His lordship asked me to dance, and I was engaged to Mr. Jones (the valet)."

"Oh well, I hope you enjoyed your supper."

"Yes, my lady, thank you. I had salmon, turkey, tipsy cake and wine."

"That's right; you had a good stomach full!"

"I know what you mean my lady, but I (*in injured tones*) never heard it called that before!"

It is difficult to please some people.

Mr. Evelyn Burnaby, brother of my old friend, Colonel Fred Burnaby, was once staying with Lady William Graham, and was asked to take Mrs. White Melville in to dinner. He found she had little in common with her distinguished and popular husband. Nevertheless, after trying a variety of subjects they got on famously. After dinner Lady William asked him how he had got on with Mrs. White Melville, as many people found her difficult to talk to, saying, "What had you in common?" "Flatulence," he replied briefly, "and I prescribed peppermint!"

Mr. Burnaby agrees with White Melville in that we shall meet again the animals who have been our faithful companions here.

I was at a large garden party just before the war broke out. The host is a dear old man of over three score years and ten, and very short-sighted. He was shaking hands with us all as we entered and trying to say something kind to everyone. When it came to my turn to be greeted he said in a cheerful voice, "Oh how do you do, so pleased to see you, and *how* are all the little ones." This somewhat upset my friends behind me, who knew my little one was six feet three inches, but I was not going to upset the dear old man, so passed on, replying, "They are wonderfully well considering they are teething."

I was abused later by the friends, who were coming on just behind me, as they said I had so upset their equanimity by my nonsense that they had laughed in our host's face, he, of course, having no idea of the joke.

I was once asked by an old friend, who had seen fit to marry his housekeeper, and who wished to introduce her to society by giving a ball if I would "See him through." I said with pleasure, but would have nothing to do with the sending out of the invitations. He must take that responsibility upon his own shoulders. I would do my best with the rest. That party will remain in my memory to the end of my days. My difficulties began when I was asked to supervise his wife's dress for the occasion. He had presented her with some beautiful diamonds, all of which she was going to wear. So far so good, but she said she must wear her gold chain round her neck as well, with the locket surrounded by her mother's hair. I had to give in, her disappointment was so great at being deprived of it. Then, in addition to this ornament, amongst her diamonds she insisted on wearing in the middle of her ample bosom a brooch resembling the top of a sardine tin.

Neither the host nor hostess had the least idea of catering for a number, and were horrified at my extravagance. Now I always rather pride myself on my powers in this direction, having been doing it more or less all my life. I knew I had allowed enough, but not more than was wise. My feelings can better be imagined than described when in the middle of the evening the host came and told me in agitated voice that the champagne had come to an end, and that there was quite a shortage of provisions. I could not believe what I was told, for I had viewed the supper-table before I went to dress, and it was laden with good things.

I hastily dispatched urgent messages to the nearest hotel to bring more champagne, and then went to make enquiries into the matter. I did not quite understand the butler's manner and was coming to the conclusion he had something to do with the shortage, when I saw one of his understudies bursting with laughter trying to hide himself behind a door. I then became firm, and it appeared that while I was resting before the great event, exhausted by the many arguments I had to have over the arrangements, the lady of the house, shocked at what she considered my extravagance, had moved various dishes, as well as a number of bottles of champagne, and hidden them; she had been hard at work at it for about an hour.

I felt really angry.

CHAPTER XVII

General Macbean and His Royal Playmates—A Sporting Essex Baronet and a Neighbouring Peer—A Difference of Opinion—Uninvited Wedding Guests—Shopping Under Difficulties—Mr. Graham Gilmour—Some of His Prophecies—How they were Fulfilled—In Trouble with the Aero Club—A Clergyman's Curious Attitude—A Fatal Accident—Trophy-laden Officers—Women Chauffeurines—Their Work, Food, and Some Experiences—A Changed World—H.H. Prince Alexis Dolgorouki and His Bride—A Dolgorouki for the Russian Throne—Prince Charlie at Braemar Castle.

THE present General Forbes Macbean, late 92nd Gordon Highlanders, was a playmate of mine when a child. We used to save up our money and send beautiful valentines to one another.

The General's father had, likewise, been in the 92nd and commanded it, but latterly he spent a great deal of time at Darmstadt with his family, Princess Alice being kind to and fond of them all. Thus it came about that my old friend, the present General, used to spend some of his holidays in Germany, his playmates being the Royal children.

A short time ago I wanted a photograph of the ex-Tsarina when she was a child, and asked General Macbean if he would lend me one of his. He replied, "They have all found their way into the waste-paper basket long ago!" I suppose that represents the feeling of us all just now, and I think this war is making us all rather irritable.

A certain well-known sporting baronet who speaks his mind straight, hits straight, and plays the game fairly and squarely, has been feeling annoyed for some time with a peer owning land in the same country. He considers that his neighbour shirked his duty during the South African War and is doing the same now. He therefore explained his views to the peer by letter, stating plainly he considered him "untruthful and a shirker." No notice was taken of this letter, so the peer was asked if he was going to take any notice of the insult. The answer was, "No." He was then asked if he would give satisfaction to the baronet. Again he declined. It so happened that in the middle of these delicate proceedings the peer married, not long ago, and the baronet sent him a wedding present of a white feather done up in cotton-wool and on his visiting-card wrote, "To Lord . . . liar, shirker and coward, a disgrace to the House of Lords and to Knighthood."

Still no notice was taken.

Since then another letter has been dispatched explaining still more fully the baronet's feelings, winding up with, "You appear to have commenced life as a cry baby, and now you have arrived at man's estate you do not seem to have improved. Show this letter to your brother officers if you dare, you lying cur." Rather plain speaking! I wonder what will happen!

Writing of weddings reminds me that my French dressmaker some years ago told me she attended most of the big weddings and receptions in London. I said I supposed her customers sent her invitations, and how kind and thoughtful of them. She replied, "Oh, no, they do not often do that, but I like to go and see the dresses. I just give my card and walk in. It only wants a little assurance, nobody ever makes a fuss." On the contrary I gathered that gentlemen were very kind to her, gave her champagne and good things to eat as well as showing her the presents, in fact she had a good time generally. Perhaps being a smart bright little woman had something to do with this. She spoke broken English very prettily.

That anybody should be able to walk into our houses in that way without the least difficulty explained certain happenings that had puzzled me. My dressmaker was a superior body and quite above suspicion in the way of honesty, but if one person can do things of that kind without question, others can, and no doubt that is what happened at Sir John Ardagh's wedding when some of the presents disappeared. It is rather wonderful people are as honest as they usually are considering what opportunities they have.

I remember an experience of my own once at Gorringes in Buckingham Palace Road during the summer sale. I had come up from Brighton for the day, and was trying to buy a soft washing hat for my baby before catching the return train. I could find nobody to attend to me so wandered about, opened drawers, turned over the things until I came upon what I wanted. I then held it out to first one and then another saying I wished to buy it, would they be good enough to make out a bill tell me the cost or do something in the matter, but, no, they all pushed past me saying "Serving!" Growing weary of rebuff upstairs, I wandered down with the hat on my arm suspended by its strings. Here I met a shopwalker and tried to explain the case, but was told he was too busy to attend to me.

Finally in despair I walked out of the shop into Victoria Station and by train to Brighton with the hat in my hand entirely innocent of any paper or wrappings. Next day I sent the ticket, covered with shop hieroglyphics, from off the hat, by post, to Gorringe explaining what had happened. I received a polite reply and the bill which was settled by return, and all was well. If I could walk away with a hat swinging on my arm what could other people have done if so inclined?

One Christmas much the same sort of thing occurred at Harrods. The attendants were overtaxed by the crush of people, and weary, I could get no one to attend to me, so picked up the book I wanted in that department, also a basket of pears from the fruit stall and walked away with both held protestingly in my hands, keeping a roving eye on the lookout to catch any unhunted assistant.

I had arrived at the door when I caught the eye of a "walker" whom I had known for many years. I explained the circumstances to him, he kindly galloped off, had the things done up, and returned in a surprisingly short time, saying, "That is all right, thank you, madam." Had I not come across my old friend I should have had to repeat my Gorringe experience.

All these things happened before the war. Of course, now we put up with inconvenience in every form without a murmur, though the inefficiency of some of the people who have been pressed into the service of even the most superior emporiums, is highly trying. I find the best chance is to do one's business through the post.

The present time air-raids and bombing recalls to my mind a prophecy of poor Mr. Graham Gilmour, the man whose name will go down to posterity as the first to fly an aeroplane over London, and who met his death on February 17th, 1912, as nearly as I can remember. He had been to a dance in our house shortly before the accident and when saying "Good-bye" with the usual pretty things about having had a good time, I told him he must be sure and come to my next dance. With a grip of my hand and a cheery laugh he said, "Thank you, I should love it, but I shall be smashed up long before then."

All too swiftly his prophecy came true. Other prophecies of his, related and explained to me in 1912, have come true. At that time flying was

Mr. Graham Gilmour

still looked upon more or less by the Government as "flying in the face of Providence" and met with scanty encouragement. Mr. Gilmour told me he so earnestly wished he could impress upon the authorities the great importance of aviation as recognised by the French and Germans. He had been laughed at when he explained he knew as a matter of fact that the Germans had already made their plans, prepared for the moment when hostilities should commence.

Mr. Graham Gilmour told me almost word for word what had been arranged and would happen, exactly as it has done, the number of Zeppelins it had been arranged to send over from Germany at a time, their engine and horse power, and bomb carrying facilities. He predicted they would have to be abandoned in favour of more suitable machines, and many other details I had better not mention. He also told me the three centres that they would chiefly, and firstly, aim at. Every word has proved true. The three centres he mentioned have now been brought to the notice of the authorities though rather late in the day.

He was an enthusiastic admirer of Sir George White, the first baronet, of Bristol, who established the earliest manufactory of aeroplanes in England, and introduced the Bristol biplanes and monoplanes in 1910, encouraged only by patriotism and business acumen, being thwarted often in his endeavours to be "fore-armed."

Mr. Gilmour worked for some time as pilot instructor in Sir George White's Bristol Company, and told me he regarded Sir George as the most patriotic and best business man of the day.

I was one day talking to my friend about the risks he ran when flying; he said he was perfectly aware that he carried his life in his hands every time he went up, but death was not a thing he dreaded, and he hoped when his time came nobody would wear black, he would like all who cared for him to wear red, purple and yellow or some cheerful colours. I noticed whenever he mounted his machine a sort of nervousness in his movements, and yet that does not truly describe what I mean. It was more the look and movements of the highly strung. A sort of, "I am wound up and ready to meet my fate" attitude.

He had expressed a wish that when the smash came he felt so certain was coming, that the machine he was using at the time should be copied in model on his tombstone with a brief notice saying how he met his death.

This was being arranged when I received a letter telling me the clergyman of the parish objected to anything of the kind in *his* churchyard. It seems incredible, small wonder the clergy have lost their hold on the people.

One of the heads of the aviation department, no, I don't mean that, I mean one of the really learned men in the practice and science of flying, who from A to Z knew the art of building and piloting all the chief machines of the day, recently told me he

considered Mr. Douglas Graham Gilmour's efforts
had materially and prominently raised British aviation to its present position; adding, "His name must
ever figure in the early front ranks.   As a pilot he
was invaluable and in the educational work Gilmour played a part second to none, his services have
been of inestimable value in the advance of the
great cause."

I have heard Mr. Gilmour's flying criticised on
the score of undue recklessness.   Certainly a han-
kering after the sensational was one of his characteristics, but it never to my knowledge merged into
the foolhardy.   It was exactly this spectacular element in his piloting that was the compelling attraction to the people.

He was born at Dartford in 1885, and educated
at Clifton.   At an early age he became interested
in the automobile industry, gaining a name for himself as a driver of racing cars and motor-cycles.
In January, 1910, he went to Pau, where he joined
the Bleriot school, gained his pilot's certificate number seventy-five, issued by the Aero Club of France,
with exceptional facility on April 19th of that year.

On his return to England his first flight was
nearly his last, for the tail of his Anzani-engined
Bleriot when flying at Brooklands grazed a telegraph wire which brought the machine headlong
to earth.

Happily he escaped almost uninjured.   He gave
me a piece of the wrecked machine and showed me

the map that was strapped on to his knees when the accident befell him.

Several successful and some sensational flights were brought off after this. It was after he had joined the Bristol Company and was flying one of their machines that he skimmed the Regatta Course at Henley, which led to an enquiry by the Royal Aero Club and to the suspension of his certificate for a month. An unfortunate controversy followed which need not be raked up again.

Death came to him when trying a machine. He left Brooklands at 11:30 that fateful Saturday morning saying he would be back in an hour, which looked as if he did not mean to go far, yet he had reached Richmond and the river when his machine was seen to be descending into the Old Deer Park. Rapidly the descent became excessively steep and ended in a vertical dive.

The monoplane struck the ground full on its nose and turned completely over.

What caused the accident is still a mystery; I am by no means sure in my own mind that he did not turn faint, he had complained once or twice of having felt queer when at certain altitudes. Others think he was caught in an eddy resulting in one wing giving way, but no one really knows. The accident robbed the country of one of its most brilliant and promising pilots. He loved his profession and was always cheery. Many mourned him sincerely.

Had he lived to see his German and aviation

prophecies come true, he would without doubt have been holding now some post of importance. He was very practical, a fatalist, and possessed that most valuable asset, a mathematical mind. He thoroughly appreciated the value of the "pilot's" work. It is the pilot, and the pilot alone who has brought home to the great public the possibilities of aviation and given some insight into its immeasurable future. In fact the general public opinion to-day, so far as aviation is concerned, is far in advance of what we are pleased to call official opinion, as exemplified in high government places.

"Those whom the Gods love die young," is an old proverb that has come back to my mind very many times during the last few years.

Some may think this applies only to innocent little children who leave us before the world has stained their garments. I lean to a different rendering, may it not be those whose hearts are young; there are some who never grow old no matter the years that have passed over their heads.

What a sight it is now to see the boat trains come in, such a mixture of tears and laughter, "By-your-leave please," chatter and fuss.

The number of trophy-laden warriors amuse me, carrying scalps, I was going to say, but I mean helmets, weapons and German et ceteras.

A big six-foot-three relation of mine, coming home from the front a while ago, who disliked carrying about dead men's paraphernalia, was congratulating himself on not being burdened as some of his brother officers were with all these things, and wondering if the joy of them was worth the worry they were causing their bearers, my relation having brought home with him nothing but one historic button and ruined health.

When he arrived at Victoria Station he stepped out feeling very pleased with himself at not having to wrestle with helmets, rifles, gas-helmets and heaven knows what besides, when a man rushed up to him threw an armful or two of his trophies at him saying, "Hold this a minute for me like a good chap," and disappeared to greet relations and hunt up luggage.

Here was drama, here was tragedy, the very thing he had avoided thrust upon him, nothing was going to persuade him to walk about laden with the things, he could not well "chuck them down" which was his inclination, he waited awhile but not then seeing the rightful owner, he charged up to another man who unfortunately for him had empty arms and thrust them all on him saying, "Hold them a minute will you like a good chap," and hastily decamped, hoping the things might in time be claimed and the second victim relieved.

I have a number of friends, widows, wives and bachelor-women, out at the front driving cars and ambulances. The Marquise de Belleroche writing a short time ago gave an amusing though pitiful account of some of her work. She is a bonny, slight, small woman who used to drive her own cars over here before the war, and is quite an experienced aeronaut. She said, for herself she did not mind wading about in seas of mud that came up with the wind like waves on the seashore, but was sorry for the wounded she was driving when for hours she was held up lying on her back in the mud under the car trying to repair the damage caused during its passage through a shell-hole big enough to bury the lot of them.

There is a good deal of excitement attached to it all. Another friend writes to me saying she has been driving a full-blown General full speed somewhere, another day a heavy ambulance waggon laden with men to be most carefully driven to save them pain.

The bachelor-women of to-day are having a good time, being useful, occupied, and experiencing probably fewer of the pin-pricks so disconcerting to most of us.

It is a very true old saying that we cannot walk with the procession and look out of the window. It has fallen to my lot lately to look out of the window, and I see an entirely new world, an upsidedown and topsy-turveydom world, in consequence of the war. I do not think some of the tremendous consequences are fully realised yet. The very foundations of the old social fabric are being shaken. No one who has been in a position to watch what is going on can fail to see that there has been a great social upheaval.

Restraint and discretion have been thrown to the winds in the face of the tremendous sacrifices demanded of us daily and hourly. Yet it is not surprising when people who love one another are constantly being parted with the unspoken though ever-present knowledge that the chances are ten to one they will ever meet again.

It would be strange if the great stresses of the war had not affected the structure of convention which seemed so solid but is in truth so fragile. We must recognise everything is changed and the world will never be the same again. We say to ourselves to-day is ours, who knows what the morrow will bring—— *We will live to-day*——

As I look back at the faces I remember in July, 1914, and again at the same faces to-day, I realise what this war has done to all of us, the strain of fighting under unparalleled conditions, the strain of waiting, the pain of parting, all marked indelibly on every face and every brow. Even those who have no near relatives at the front have aged years with the horrors of it all.

To women the world is especially changed: the opportunity they have been waiting for has arrived and they are showing their metal. The men who gibed at the women saying they would not stick to their work and generally underrated their capabilities and powers of endurance must now have come to the conclusion they overrated their own intelligence.

We women have wandered long in an artificial world of pretence, where national affairs were always left to the men. Many of us have been busy

certainly with the little things that matter so much
and for which we receive no credit and little thanks,
but at last it is recognised that we are not all dolls,
we have come into our own, and mean to keep it;
the opportunity has presented itself and been em-
braced.

Look, for instance, at the real hard work our
women are doing as "chauffeurines," as the French
people call them; many gentlewoman have left luxurious homes to go out and do their bit, driving
big heavy ambulances (without wind-screens, for
they are not allowed), changing as many as four or
five heavy tires in a day single handed, keeping
their car in proper working order and ready for
the daily inspection. In return for all this work,
driving night as well as day when needed, they
receive a private's pay and rations, having to provide their own kit with the exception of the leather
greatcoat.

Our pre-war day chauffeurs, who had several
pounds a week in wages and a washer to clean their
car for them, and who lived on the fat of the land,
would have given up their situations if they had
been called upon to do such work.

One of my friends, who is an attractive person,
was a short time ago driving an ambulance full of
men suffering from shell-shock. The orderly who
was in charge addressed her through the window
that divides the driver from her passengers asking
her if she would try and keep her head as far away

from the window as possible as "the men are very lovish, and I cannot answer for them!"

Nobody seems surprised at anything now. Think, oh think of waitresses in the Athenæum Club! And then the omnibus conductresses who, I am told, help to balance themselves while collecting fares by seizing the hair of the nearest man who politely says, in answer to her laughing apologies. "Oh, don't mention it pray," or "Granted." Even, "Do it again, I like it."

When moving about the world now it is necessary to take one's bearings afresh.

One of my she-male relatives has been nursing at the Russian front under shell fire and having a most exciting time. She was much impressed with the patience of the wounded and dying. When the orderlies began to prepare them for their graves before they are dead, they acquiesce uncomplainingly—anxious to save trouble and time.

The Russian situation fills me with breathless expectation and wonderment. I say to myself is this evolution or revolution? In a measure I am glad H. H. Prince Alexis Dolgorouki did not live to see his beloved country in its present ferment, and yet he always longed for its freedom and would have been profoundly interested in her efforts. The Dolgoroukis are a Russian family of considerable aristocratic and political fame, having been on the throne years before the Romanoffs were heard of. The present General Korniloff's programme to-day is to place one of them on the throne again. I be-

H. H. Prince Alexis Dolgorouki

lieve the member of the family they have in their minds is Prince Pierre Dolgorouki of the Moscow branch. They own large properties and coal mines in the Government of Ekaterinoslav, though naturally they do not get much from them at present, or from their estates in the Crimea.

Prince Alexis's eldest brother generally represented the Tsar at big functions, such as King Edward's coronation, the Queen of Spain's marriage, the christening of the Queen of Rumania's child and so forth. My friend, Prince Alexis, was the third son of the Prince Dolgorouki, who was Secretary of State and Privy Seal to the Emperor Alexander II of Russia. One of the family, a Prince Dolgorouki, I forget which, was Governor-General of Moscow for twenty odd years. He died at the age of eighty, having served under three Tsars. He was a veritable martinet, his word being law. All respected, though many feared him.

They were a very handsome family. Sir H. Rumbolt in his memories speaks of them as the handsomest family he ever saw.

Prince Alexis certainly shared the good looks of his two elder brothers and sister. He was tall, being over six feet; a very fascinating man, witty and amusing, wrote poetry, played the piano, one of those gifted people unable to stick to anything long. The daughter of his eldest brother married Prince Dietrichstein, a cousin of Queen Victoria, but unfortunately an Austrian.

The Cross of St. George was awarded to Prince

Alexis during the Russo-Turkish war. Knowing English well, he acted as interpreter for Archibald Forbes, and Mr. Villiers sent a sketch of him mounted on his grey Arab to the *Graphic*. When the Prince married an English woman Mr. Villiers sent the original sketch to Princess Alexis as a wedding present.

When first the Dolgoroukis went to Braemar Castle, where they spent most of the autumns, they found interesting documents relating to the time when a Dolgorouki delivered important papers to Prince Charles.

Prince Alexis married in 1898 Miss Fleetwood Wilson, only child and great heiress of Mr. Fleetwood Wilson of Wappenham Manor, Northamptonshire. I knew her for some years before she married.

My first introduction to her father came about in rather a curious manner. We had let our house in Park Lane to the late Sir Mountstuart Grant Duff and his wife while we rented for a few weeks a house in Sloane Street. One day when I came in I was informed some game had come for me. I asked who had sent it and was told there was no label on it, but a hare and a brace of partridges had been delivered by somebody's coachman. I thought no more about it, having come to the conclusion some of my people had sent it. A couple of days later I was informed that a gentleman had called to ask if some game had been left by mistake. I wondered if perchance it was the game that had no

H. H. Princess Alexis Dolgorouki

label, so sent word to ask the enquirer to come in and see me.   It was Mr. Fleetwood Wilson, rather ruffled and angry.   Fortunately the game was still untouched, and I had it brought up.   He said when he sent it there was a label attached, addressed, if my memory serves me rightly, to the Hon. Mrs. Adderly, and there was a hare and two brace of partridges.   Poor man, he was much perplexed. The game had certainly been left at the wrong house, was not the amount he sent out, and had lost its label.   Either his coachman, whom he had employed for many years and valued, had been telling him tally-diddles, or I was doing so.   He could not believe it was the coachman and did not like to think I was the culprit.

As I grew a little firm, he said, "Do you mean, madam, that my coachman has been telling me lies?"

I replied, "It seems painfully like it!"

He grunted to himself, wished me good day and departed.   By this time I was feeling a little ruffled also, but could not help laughing.   It was so funny, the angry old man standing one side of the game pointing at it, while I sat the other declining any responsibility or culpability in the matter.   Not very long after this I met him at a dinner-party. He asked to be introduced and we made friends.

The Dolgoroukis were not rich latterly, and I have always understood they had spent freely on their country.

I am glad that in the new Russian flag the double

eagle is to remain, as that was Russian before the Romanoffs. The Dolgoroukis have it on their coat of arms.

The Alexis Dolgoroukis gave delightful parties, both being sociably inclined and most hospitable. Princess Alexis spends a good deal of her time abroad now, but before the war entertained throughout the year at Braemar Castle, 46 Upper Grosvenor Street and their villa on the shores of the Mediterranean and in Russia.

It is not easy to know Russians very well, be they men or women; while all are friendly and many delightful, few are intimate.

After they married the Dolgoroukis built a large house at Taplow amongst the trees that once belonged to Windsor Great Park. They made the place very beautiful and called it Nashdoun, which is Russian for "our home."

The Prince lies in the peaceful little churchyard of Hitchin far from all the turmoil of his native land.

It was a great gratification to Prince Alexis and her husband that our English Royalties were so kindly and appreciative to the foreigner in their land.

I have felt very sorry for Fanny, Princess Alexis. She was so devoted to her husband, and having no children feels very desolate.

Great wealth is very agreeable and oils the wheels of life, but alas, cannot buy or keep happiness for us.

CHAPTER XVIII

SUDDENLY I find I have arrived at my
eighteenth chapter, with many happy memories unrelated, but I must draw rein or perhaps my publisher will look at me as an angry
swallow does a bat, and my readers will grow weary.
I should like to have written a little about Lady
Lloyd, wife of General Sir Francis Lloyd, at present commanding the London district, who has done
such strenuous work since the war began. When
first I knew Lady Lloyd she was pretty Mrs.
"Frankie" Lloyd, a bright, human, and charming
companion. She was then in Egypt seeing her
husband off to the front, and very brave she was.
On her return to England, when they were in Rut-
land Gate, I used to dine and play duets with her

on some of the nights her husband was on duty in St. James's Palace.

Amongst others crowding my memory are Lord D'Abernon, the Rev. —— Moyle (I forget his Christian name), Madame de Falbe, a whole crowd at the Devonshire House ball in 1897, Lord and Lady Dormer (the twelfth baron and his young wife, who was Miss Bald of Monsie Castle, Perth), the Samuel Bakers, Lady Carden of Templemore, and heaps more, but I must write of them another day, only briefly mentioning those whom at the moment my memory refuses to leave alone.

First and foremost, Lord D'Abernon, who was Sir Edgar Vincent when first I met him, younger brother of Sir Howard Vincent, and certainly the cleverest of a clever family. He was raised to the peerage in 1914.

It was quite remarkable the number of important posts he held while yet a young man. When Financial Adviser to the Egyptian Government he was only twenty-five or twenty-six. He was exceedingly good looking and knew it, exceedingly clever and knew it; perhaps a trifle spoilt, but that was the fault of the women. They are responsible for making men strut and preen themselves. As is usual with great brains, he was a bit of egotist, which is only natural. So few companions can be found with the same commodity with whom to exchange thought.

He began life in the Coldstream Guards, where it was hardly to be expected he would remain long.

To an active clever brain such a life would be impossible, as there would not be found many brains with which to exchange thoughts. It was, therefore, not surprising that, after a few years, he resigned and became private secretary to Lord E. Fitzmaurice when Commissioner for East Roumelia.

When in Egypt we saw little of Sir Edgar, he was always hard at work. Lord Cromer thought highly of his ability and integrity. I have not space to recount all the important appointments he has held, but remember that from 1899 to 1906 he was member for Exeter, and is at the present time Trustee of the National Gallery, also since 1915 Controller of the Central Board of the Liquor Traffic.

Lord D'Abernon married the beautiful Lady Helen Duncombe, Lady Feversham's daughter. I am sorry there is no heir to inherit the brains and good looks of this couple. Amongst their homes they have a delightful villa at Venice named Plazzo Guistiniani.

Another who haunts my memory at this moment is the late George Wilkinson, a relative of mine, whose powerful sermons and squeaky, whiny voice, attracted crowds to his church, St. Peter's, Eaton Square. He was an earnest, good man, and popular, retaining a great hold over his parishioners. He only had to ask for anything he wanted for it to roll in. His offertories in church amounted to about four thousand a year, but it is well to remember his congregation was a rich one.

Mr. Wilkinson was really High Church, but when he felt it was policy, knew when and how to put on the brake. Nevertheless, he had the courage of his convictions, for when "commanded" to dine with Royalties one Friday, he begged to be excused as it was a fast day. He never dined out on Fridays.

I have often wondered how it was Mr. Wilkinson escaped being called Anthony; nearly all the north country family of Wilkinson rejoice in that Christian name.

Another parson haunting my memory is the Rev. —— Moyle (I forget his Christian name), but in my childhood he made a great impression on my mind.

He was vicar of a church in Yorkshire. A big, red-faced, red-haired man, reminding me of the photographs I had seen of Macaulay. He was the exact antithesis of George Wilkinson, but an equally powerful preacher. I have seen him move his congregation to tears by his eloquence, while shedding a few himself. My father was a great admirer of his rhetoric.

He had been preaching in our village church the Sunday before we received the news that he had been removed into safe keeping by officers of the law, being unable to account for £1000 he had received for special church purposes from Sir Charles Lowther, and because certain monies in his charge belonging to a girl to whom he was guardian were not satisfactorily accounted for. There were also a few other little shortcomings. He was sentenced to five years' penal servitude, and the last I heard of him he was not well and had been removed into the prison hospital, where he insisted in eating all his poultices!

The Duchess of Devonshire's famous fancy ball in 1897 must not pass unnoticed. It was such a great occasion. All the hairdressers of any repute and prestige had been engaged weeks before to dress heads after certain pictures and representing certain characters.

My hairdresser, Litchenfeldt, of Great Castle Street, began hairdressing and arranging at 6 a. m. on the day of the ball and finished at 10.30 p. m., with one half-hour for refreshment.

There are people who have not recovered from the effects of that ball yet, so heavily had they plunged in jewellery to outdo some of their friends. Not so very long ago an acquaintance of mine was paying off a long jeweller's bill in driblets of £10 at a time. A few wiser folk hired priceless jewels, insuring them heavily for the brief period they were required. One friend of mine who could not hire enough to make the blaze she required sent a special messenger to Paris who came back with a load and the owner of them to see all was right. He stayed until after the ball, and carried them away with him as well as a cheque of four figures for the loan.

The clever and fascinating Madame de Falbe, who gave such celebrated parties at Luton Hoo, had a keen sense of humour and much enjoyed a joke. At one of her big balls the house was overcrowded with guests staying there for the occasion. Amongst them was Mr. Bernal Osborne, at one time member for Tipperary. Owing to the shortage of room, Madame de Falbe, knowing his proverbial good nature, asked him if he would mind his bedroom being used as a ladies' cloak-room for a few hours on the night of the ball. He willingly assented.

Towards the small hours of the morning, when the rooms were beginning to empty, Mr. Osborne thought it would be safe to retire to his room and go to bed. He put the thought into practice and was just entering into his first beauty sleep when he was aroused by an old lady and her daughter groping about for their wraps. He heard the dowager saying, "I can't find my comforter, dears!" The occupier of the bed hearing this, sat up saying, "If anybody wants a comforter here I am!"

Tableau!

Madame de Falbe delighted in this story.

Since writing my last volume of memories, I have been told by a friend in high authority at the War Office that I must have misunderstood what Lord Kitchener said to me respecting the Mediterranean command. I stated he had refused it, and had gone on a tour round the world until such time as a suitable appointment presented itself. That certainly was the impression he left in my mind. The War Office version of this incident is somewhat different. I am told that when the Duke of Connaught resigned the Mediterranean command Lord Kitchener

was approaching the end of his tenure as Commander-in-Chief in India.   He was offered the post
resigned by the Duke of Connaught and refused it.

Then King Edward asked him to take it and at
the same time to begin his new billet by inspecting
the armies of Japan, Austria and New Zealand,
during which probationary period he was to receive
£10 a day "all found," as the servants say.

My informant continues:

"He then accepted the post and went off from
India to Manchuria and Japan, coming back via
Australia, New Zealand, and, I think, Amer-
ica. . . .

"When Lord Kitchener arrived in England the
vice-royalty was just coming vacant, and he made
up his mind to run all he knew for that great post.
In doing so he felt he was heavily handicapped by
having accepted a new post, so he put it that King
Edward had asked him to take the billet, but that
now the King no longer wished to keep him to his
acceptance, and that he was therefore free to chuck
it.   This he did resolutely, and stuck to it.

"The Cabinet tried hard to make him change his
mind and, when they saw it was useless, they offered
the Mediterranean post to Sir Ian Hamilton, who
demurred considerably about accepting it, expressing it as his opinion that it was a barren honour,
carrying no real responsibility or work, and that
he did not care to accept the post unless new duties
were added which would give more scope for his
energies.   Accordingly the Inspector-Generalship

of Over-Seas Forces was tacked on to the Mediterranean command, and when the reports Sir Ian wrote, many of which have been acted on in Canada, West Indies, Panama Canal, Australia, Malay States, Ceylon and China are put together, it will be realised the work was no longer a sinecure."

No longer, I presume, a post requiring only that some beautiful person should sit at Malta and talk platitudes with a great show of diplomatic reserve.

The same authority goes on to say that he does not agree with me that Lord Kitchener regretted not returning to Egypt when, in 1914, he was asked to stay and help us out of our trouble with Germany. On the contrary, he was straining every nerve to get to the War Office instead of returning to Egypt.

This is the official view of the situation. Mine was gathered from what Lord Kitchener told me, or at any rate wished me to understand. No doubt the official perspective differed from Lord Kitchener's, which may account for little discrepancies.

Amongst the congratulations and kind letters I received from those who knew me and others who wrote through my publisher, the one I valued most was from Sir Ian Hamilton, saying he thought I had drawn a most faithful likeness of the life and character of his old friend and comrade, Sir Charles Douglas. This pleased me coming from one who knew Sir Charles so well, as he was the character I had found it the most difficult to portray faithfully, doing justice to his great abilities while recognising his disabilities.

I still feel I have hardly done justice to his great devotion to duty, which he carried almost to ludicrous lengths. The following may perhaps give a little idea of how all-embracing his duties were according to his own rendering. In the long ago days of Sitapur about 1878, when we were all together in that little station, Mr. Douglas, then adjutant of the 92nd Gordon Highlanders, had a heart to heart talk with young Mr. Hamilton, telling him he was permitting me to take up too much of his thoughts, they belonged to the 92nd Gordon Highlanders (in very big capital letters), and it was his, the adjutant's, duty to see that the regiment got the lion's share of every subaltern's attention.

This was rather rough on Mr. Hamilton, but I think he comforted himself with the reflection that he was face to face rather with a social rival than with a military superior.

However, the little storm in the Sitapur tea-cup blew over quite happily, for when the adjutant went on his two months' leave to the hills, he selected Mr. Hamilton to act for him as adjutant and even allowed him to ride on parades his famous and hideous charger "Rhinoceros," so called because of the bump on his Roman nose.

Looking back over those old times when the adjutant considered it his duty to drill and read lectures to Mr. Hamilton on the advantages of parades versus flirtations, it has struck me as most curious that these two officers who, after their early days, hardly met for thirty years, and who had nothing in common except perhaps an ancient affection or admiration for myself, with the most different temperaments conceivable, should have arrived together at the top of the military tree, and should be considered by the bigwigs in authority as alike as two peas in a pod, and interchangeable, Sir Charles Douglas, relieving Sir Ian Hamilton in the southern command, and Sir Ian taking his place as Adjutant-General to the Forces. But I was a little behind the scenes and knew some of the reasons for the game of "General Post."

It may not strike anyone as strange who did not know the character and temperament of the two men as well as I did. To me it has always seemed extraordinary.

It is at all times difficult to write biographies, or even brief sketches of those we have loved or cared for who have been part of our lives, especially when they have at all times been unfailingly good and kind to oneself. Even in the very brief sketches I have tried to give of my friends and acquaintances, I have found it difficult not to look too closely at the pictures. I have had to stand them a little way off to grasp the surroundings and exact colouring. Many are no longer with us, and death so dominates the rest, making the past so hard to deal with faithfully and justly.

I have searched at times, with frenzy, though happily, amongst my memories for what I would like to chronicle, trying above all things not to blaze forth the things that have been kept hidden or the things that have been entrusted to our honourable keeping, when those who trusted us are no longer masters of the situation, no longer able to defend themselves or explain the whys and wherefores, and I should not like any I have mentioned to say with Zechariah, "I was wounded in the house of my friend," for that is what hurts.

The written and spoken word sometimes has a way of getting up and hitting us as it did with poor Ruskin, the tragedy of whose life lay in the fact that the girl he loved rejected him because he could not conscientiously accept her doctrines, which he himself had preached and taught her.

I hope before another book of mine is launched upon the world the peace we all long for may be with us, and yet I dread the day when with bands playing, bonfires burning, church bells ringing, our men come marching home, for it will be a day of agony to many whose dear ones are not amongst the victorious legions.

I think sometimes the part we mothers of men have played in this war has not been fully recognised. It is harder to sit and *wait* than it is to go and fight, and harder still to say "Thy will be done" when "our all" has been done to death. With agony we mothers brought into the world the men we are now asked to give up with a twofold agony and no word of complaint comes from us as, with a drear smile that tries to be cheerful, we bid them "God speed," though we know that death will probably claim them and thousands more. We must be forgiven if we sometimes say to ourselves "What shall it profit us if we gain the whole world and lose our only son?"

The reason and the only reason why we have not gone under during this war has been because of the mothers' sons' big hearts and bravery. Organisation has not done it, discipline has not done it nor wealth of material and money, but the splendid hereditary instinct, the love of home and the mother that makes it, that is what is winning us this war. Hundreds and thousands have gone away cheerily, even gaily, knowing well they were only going to fill a gap for a short time, and then others will take their place, and no word goes forth of what was in those dead men's hearts.

Few men know what home means to them until some tragedy brings it to their hearts, and even then they cannot always find the right label for their feelings, but if they could it would be HOME and MOTHER.

There is so much that is absolutely inexplicable about the situation, both at home and abroad, especially to those who occasionally catch glimpses behind the scenes. We miss our war correspondents who told us what was taking place, now we have to learn it from the foreign newspapers.

But as we grow older and more resigned:

"The soul's dark cottage, battered and decayed,
  Lets in new light, through chinks that time has made."

THE END

INDEX

Adams, v. c., Rev. J. W., 43, 134
Alexandra, Queen Mother—
  her consideration for others, 166
  her interest in "Persimmon," 163
  names brother of "Persimmon," 163
  portrait with dogs painted by Lacretelle, 164
  at Sandringham, 164
  her sense of humour, 163
Anglesey, fifth Marquess of, 27
Archer, Fred, jockey, 262, 277

Bachelor, Capt., 144
Baird, Mr. Abingdon, 8-10, 13
Baird, Mr. Douglas, 8
Balfour, Rt. Hon. A. J., 115, 201, 202
Bancroft, Mrs., 10
Bath, Marquess of, 279
Bathe, Sir Hugh Gerald de, 13
Beaconsfield, Earl, 271, 272, 283, 284
Beaumont, Commander, 98, 99, 100
Belleroche, Marquise de, 330
Benzon, Mr., 25, 26
Bernhardt, Mme. Sarah, 11
Bessborough, Lady, 4
Bismarck, Prince, 208-210
Bolckow, Mr., 171-176
Bolckow, Mrs., 174
Bowles, Mr. T. Gibson, 300
Braddon, Miss, 104
Brampton, Lord, 259, 260, 275-278
Breadalbane, Lord, 297, 298
Brewer, Mr. Charles, 259, 260
Brown, John, 169-171
Brown-Potter, Mrs., 3
Brownrigg, Gen., 241

Burn, Capt. Charles, 202
Burnaby, Rev. E., 271-273, 279, 280, 317
Burne, Sir Owen, 223-229.
Burnham, Lord, 102, 103
Byng, Gen. the Hon. Sir Julian, 298, 299

Campbell, Lady Colin, 197-199
Cardigan, Lady, 141, 153, 308, 309
Carteret, Mr. de, Governor of Jersey, 7
Cassavetti, Mme., 197
Cathcart, third Earl, 132, 134
Cecil, Lady Sophia, 211-213
Chamberlain, Mr. Austen, 117.
Chamberlain, Mr. Joseph—
  characteristics of, 114, 115
  devotion to his family, 117
  fondness for children, 115
  his quarrels with his friends, 114
  takes part in private theatricals, 106, 107
Chaplin, Lord, 14, 15, 86
Chesham, Lady, 260, 262
Chetwynd, Sir George, 15, 23-27, 259, 264
Chetwynd, Lady, 14-16, 23
Cholmondeley, Mr. Henry, 137
Clarke, Col. Sir Stanley, 46, 47
Cleveland, late Duchess of, 199
Clinton, Miss Ethel, 162, 163
Coleridge, Lord Chief Justice, 23, 103
Connaught, Duke of, 51, 171-175, 272
Cooch Behar, Maharajah of, 203-207
Corbett, James J., pugilist, 9
Costobadie, Rev. Hugh Palliser, 29
Cotton, Fred, 249, 250

351

www.ingramcontent.com/pod-product-compliance
Lightning Source LLC
Chambersburg PA
CBHW020831030726
47496CB00001B/186

* 9 7 8 1 4 3 4 4 0 7 7 2 6 *